A Concept of Dramatic Genre
and the Comedy of a New Type

V. Ulea

A Concept of
Dramatic Genre and the
Comedy of a New Type:
*Chess, Literature,
and Film*

Southern Illinois University Press
Carbondale and Edwardsville

Copyright © 2002 by the Board of Trustees,
Southern Illinois University
All rights reserved
Printed in the United States of America
05 04 03 02   4 3 2 1

Library of Congress Cataloging-in-Publication Data
Ulea, V.
A concept of dramatic genre and the comedy of a new type : chess, literature, and film / V. Ulea.
   p. cm.
  Includes bibliographical references and index.
   1. European drama (Comedy)—History and criticism.
  2. European drama (Tragedy)—History and criticism.
  3. Literary form. I. Title.

PN1922 .U43 2002
808.2—dc21
ISBN 0-8093-2452-0 (cloth : alk. paper)   2002018756

Printed on recycled paper. ♻

The paper used in this publication
meets the minimum requirements of
American National Standard for
Information Sciences—
Permanence of Paper for
Printed Library Materials,
ANSI Z39.48-1992. ∞

To Aron Katsenelinboigen,
my teacher and friend,
a scholar whose innovative thought
contributes to so many different fields of study,
including economics, politics, biology,
aesthetics, and religion.
To a man whose great mind
is combined with a great heart
in honor of his seventy-fifth birthday.

[W]hat makes the comic world hang together as a world?
—Caryl Emerson, "Bakhtin's Carnival Idea"

Any theory of comedy must be judged by its consistency to itself and its faithfulness to the data it explains. But in the final analysis, it must also be judged by its fruitfulness, that is, by its ability to untangle old problems and to lead to new insights.
—Paul H. Grawe,
Comedy in Space, Time, and the Imagination

Contents

Preface xi
Acknowledgments xv

Part One. *Dramatic Genre as a General Systems Phenomenon*

1. Dramatic Genre: *A New Classification* 3
2. The Dramatic as an Independent Category: *Chess, Economics, and Literature* 28

Part Two. *Dramedy, Drama, and Comedy:* A New Classification

3. Protagonists of the Same Strata and Status in Different Types of Dramatic Genre 51
4. Literary Works of the Same and Analogous Topics 71
5. A Miraculous Turn: *Fate, Chance, and Predisposition in Comedy, Dramedy, and Drama* 91

Part Three. *The Comedy of a New Type:* The Integration of the Part and the Whole

6. Chekhov and Balzac as the Pioneers of the CNT 111
7. Quasi-Dramatic Effects in the CNT 133
8. Myth and Symbol in the CNT: *The Space of Action and the Implied Space* 151

    Conclusion 164

    Appendixes

1. Variety of Basic Types 171
2. Mixed Types and Branches 173
3. Text, Context, Subtext, and the Literary Work 175

    Notes 177
    Works Cited 187
    Index 193

Preface

This book is an attempt to approach dramatic genre from the point of view of the degree of richness and strength of a character's potential. My main goal is to establish a methodology for analyzing the potential from a multidimensional perspective, using systems thinking. The whole concept is an alternative to the Aristotelian plot-based (externally motivated) approach, and it is applied to an analysis of western and eastern European authors and also to contemporary American film.

This research touches on important questions linked to strategic thinking, decision making, and chaos and order; these are the basic notions forming the category of dramatic genre as approached from a nonorthodox perspective.

The book consists of three parts. Part one is mostly theoretical, proposing a new definition of the dramatic as a category linked to the general systems phenomenon and offering a new classification of dramatic genre. In my classification, dramatic genre is divided into types (pure and mixed) and their variants and into branches (pure and mixed) and their variants. Basic types are defined by the characters' potential, differing in degree of strength and richness, and are the following: comedy (limited and weak potential), dramedy (rich and powerful potential), and drama (average/above average and strong potential). Basic branches are defined by types of outcome (successful, unsuccessful, and ambiguous) and by types of potential. All definitions of dramatic genre, including its types and branches, are given from a multidimensional perspective.

In part two, I perform a textual analysis of some works based on this new classification. Comedies, tragedies, and dramas of the same or of similar topics undergo thorough analysis to reveal what makes them belong to opposite types of dramatic genre. In the process, I reconsider the traditional definitions of dramatic genre of some works in accordance with the new understanding of the notion of the dramatic as linked exclusively to the degree of richness and strength of characters' potential. This part of the book also approaches the question of fate and chance, with regard to tragedy and comedy, from the point of view of the predispositioning theory. The goal of this analysis is to reveal what lies behind these notions and what methods of systems operation represent the category of fate and chance.

Part three is occupied with the analysis of the comedy of a new type (CNT). This was first represented in works of Chekhov and Balzac; although these works were not funny, they were called comedies by their authors. In this part, the emphasis is on the integration of the part and the whole in approaching the protagonist's potential. I introduce the term *quasi-strong potential* in order to reveal the illusory strength of protagonists of the CNT and to show the technique of its analysis and synthesis.

It is not my goal to perform textual analysis on every known work in this book—such a demand would be equal to plugging all existing notions into a formula to show how it would work in each particular case. It would not even be possible to mention all works worthy of critics' attention; moreover, mere mentions would not be enough. There will always be disagreement concerning the importance of works included in and excluded from the analysis. I therefore decided to focus only on works that, in my opinion, are the most revealing examples of the given theoretical assertions. The technique of this analysis can be applied to any work that failed to be examined in this book.

I would like to formulate my basic statements right at the beginning in order to orient the reader in the ocean of assertions and speculations formulating my concept.

This book is, first of all, an attempt to find a structure of dramatic genre, understanding by the dramatic a general core inherent in any type of literature, including prose and poetry, without regard to the question of their theatrical performance. Since any type of literary work can be perceived or subtitled as comic, tragic, dramatic, and the like, I distinguish between dramaturgy, whose specifics are linked to designing a work for theatrical performances, and dramatic genre, which is a constituent part of any literary work, including dramaturgy.

My basic assertion is that the dramatic is invariant to one's emotional perception; it is independent from tears and laughter, contrary to what the Aristotelian school states with regard to the comic. The essential core of the dramatic is a potential that may evoke diverse emotional reactions from spectators. The notion of the dramatic therefore belongs to the general systems phenomenon and must be approached from the point of view of measurement of the degree of richness and strength of a potential of the artistic universe represented in a literary work.

Preface xiii

I began my research with the notion of the comic, traditionally considered synonymous with the laughable, and attempted to approach the concept as independent from the laughable and laughter. The necessity to do so was dictated by my own desire to penetrate the enigmatic nature of Chekhov's comedy that in criticism has never been accepted as such. As a result of my inquiries into the structure of the comic, a more general question arose concerning the concept of dramatic genre comprising the comic and comedy along with its other types. This explains why, in discussing my concept of dramatic genre, I first and foremost refer to the comic and comedy as the most difficult and puzzling part of dramatic genre. I would venture to say that the treatment of the comic and comedy is the litmus test of credibility of any theory of dramatic genre, because if the theory sheds light on the other side of the "moon" (comedy), it will definitely work for the visible "landscape."

Though the proportion of laughter seems to be greater in comedy than in tragedy or drama, and the happy ending or survival is a prerogative of *traditional comedy*,[1] these characteristics cannot be considered sufficient in defining comedy and the comic. It is not laughter or survival that makes a literary work belong to the comedic genre but rather *the weak, limited potential of its protagonists*.[2] Such potential is the touchstone of the comic and comedy, their permanent basic characteristic, the heart and axis around which the comedic world spins.

Thus, my main argument is that dramatic genre deals with the potential of the artistic universe, which can be measured based on the methodology elaborated for indeterministic systems, taking into account the peculiarity of the artistic system when compared to other systems.

As is mentioned above, I distinguish between three types of potential that correspond to three types of dramatic genre—dramedy, drama, and comedy. (The term *dramedy* will be explained later). It is implied here that the degree of the inner strength of the potential—its dual parameter—is in accord with the degree of its richness—its initial parameter. The dual parameter may not always be correlated with the initial parameter, however, which means that the outer strength of the entity—its position in the system—may differ from its inner strength, which is linked to its inner development. A disagreement between the inner and outer evaluations would cause the appearance of some new varieties of dramatic types and branches whose structure will be discussed in the next part of this book.

The development of dramatic genre and appearance of its new types, such as Chekhov's and Balzac's comedy of a new type, sharpens the question of the theory of comedy, in particular, and of dramatic genre, in general. The inability to outline some specific features inherent in comedy of all types, including traditional comedy and the CNT, causes constant confusion of the dramatic nature of these works, which are sometimes called dramas, sometimes tragedies, and sometimes tragicomedies. Regardless of numerous valuable observations made by Aristotelian and neo-Aristotelian schools, the main question concerning the basic structure determining dramatic genre still remains unanswered. It becomes clear that innovations explicitly and deliberately introduced by the two masters of the CNT cannot be explained by traditional, mostly empirical, observations on the comic as linked primarily to the laughable.

In discussing the comic, I refer to a concept independent of the notions of humor, joking, and laughter that have been previously investigated in criticism. The comic embodies the core of comedy; in my research, I separate the notions of the comic from all other assumptions about both amiable and mocking laughter. As will be illustrated, both laughter and lamentation can be present in any type of dramatic genre. Therefore, they must not be confused with core literary categories: the dramatic, the comic, and the tragic. These categories are based exclusively *on the degree of strength and richness of the potential.*

Although some ideas concerning laughter and weeping will be discussed in subsequent chapters, these psychologies are not the focus of the present research. The emphasis of this book is on the structure, function, and processing of the potential of the artistic work and on methods of its measurement.

In summary, I do not aim to deny the Aristotelian and neo-Aristotelian paradigm; however, I consider it insufficient in defining the comic and, accordingly, the tragic and the dramatic. In order to investigate this same notion, I propose not a subbranch of Aristotelian logic but a new theory that implies a complete separation of the comic from the laughable, in particular, and the dramatic from any emotional perception, in general. This notion represents a different epistemological methodology and requires measurement of potential. Therefore, in this work, I attempt to synthesize elements of existing literary methodologies that deal with character and to present a new methodology used for measurement of potential.

Acknowledgments

This book would never have appeared were I not familiar with Aron Katsenelinboigen's predispositioning theory, which one day changed my life completely. No, it was not about some vague, abstract theoretical notions, which add little if anything to the understanding of vital questions. Anyone who has pondered over the meaning of life, over questions of God, morality, fate, and chance, anyone who has had the privilege to talk to this man, take his class, and read his books, has experienced the same feeling of having discovered a lifelong path leading to the core of being.

We have known each other for almost ten years and for my family and me these have been the best years of development and creativity. So, this book is dedicated to Aron Katsenelinboigen in various ways, since during these years of our friendship he appeared in different hypostases, generously sharing not only his theoretical ideas but also his wisdom, humanity, and warmth—all integral parts of his philosophy.

Writing a book is a joy for the author and a pain in the neck for everyone else. I would like to thank all those friends who, after all, did not become enemies. Their patience and assistance supported my illusory impression of life as something easy and wonderful.

This is the second time I feel truly rewarded by the opportunity to discuss my work with Caryl Emerson, who is well known for her innovative way of thinking and sensitivity to nonorthodox approaches to literary analysis. Her responsiveness and immediate feedback combined with a rare ability to see the kernel of the problem makes her irreplaceable in discussing theoretical questions. I was deeply touched by her willingness to contribute to the page-by-page reading of the final draft of this book and to help me improve it.

I do not know how to thank enough Daria A. Kirjanov, my dear friend, a scholar whose own contributions to Chekhov's poetics open up new perspectives and inspire new interpretations. The time that she generously spent on the first draft of this book, thoroughly analyzing all its aspects and making extremely important comments on its structure and way of representation of some of its topics, made it possible for me to make some essential revisions. Her patience and willingness to discuss the turning points of this book, her complete dedication to scholarly research, as well as her enviable human quality supported me tremendously on my way to completion of this book.

I am also extremely grateful to Steven Tötösy de Zepetnek, a scholar whose great contributions to comparative literature and culture and studies in systems and literature cannot be overestimated. His *CLCWeb: Comparative Literature and Culture: A WWWeb Journal* (published by Purdue University Press at *http://clcwebjournal.lib.purdue.edu/*), which unites serious scholars in literary theory, has become a great source of innovative modern theoretical research. The style and methodology of my book were essentially improved owing to Tötösy's keen remarks and valuable suggestions, which he made after reading the first and the final drafts of the manuscript. A part of the early version of this book has been published as an article, "The Comic in Literature as a General Systems Phenomenon," at *http://clcwebjournal.lib.purdue.edu/clcweb99-1/zubarev99.html*.

I also would like to thank my very dear friend John Holman, whose willingness to discuss everything with me—from the intricacies of style to the notion of my terms—is inexhaustible.

I would like to express my special thanks to Gary Saul Morson, whose pioneering introduction of Katsenelinboigen's predispositioning theory to literary analysis created a new era in literary scholarship. At this point, I consider myself a follower of Morson's strategy.

I also would like to express my highest appreciation to Paul H. Grawe, whom I contacted immediately after reading his book. His interest and support, as well as our further discussions, provided me with some ideas concerning the improvement of basic statements of this book.

My very warm thanks to Olga Hasty, my teacher and friend, with whom I discussed my ideas at their early stages. Her questions and remarks concerning the method of my analysis with regard to Chekhov's plays encouraged my further thinking.

I also would like to express my appreciation to Elizabeth Beaujour, whose keen remarks and provocative questions encouraged my further elaboration of methodology of analysis of characters' potential; namely, the integration of conditional and unconditional valuations of the character.

My attempts to apply my theoretical vision of comedy to the directing of Chekhov's plays have come to be appreciated by Carol Rocamora, a translator and director of Chekhov's plays and founder of the Philadelphia Festival Theater for New Plays at the Annenberg Center. Some of my ideas concerning the innovations of Chekhov's comedy have been applied by Rocamora in her staging of *The Seagull*. In this book I use Rocamora's translations of Chekhov's plays, which I like very much.

I would like to thank from the bottom of my heart my dear friends James D. Tisdall and Cindy Alexander and also my former students Siri A. Buurma, Maria Rapoport, Yana Pershersky, Alina Umansky, and Elisabeth Dubin who helped me with the editing of the first draft of this book.

I also would like to express my gratitude to my talented editor, Stella Peña-Sy, a professional and my former student who once expressed interest in my new concept and supported my class "Mystery and Mastery of Chekhov's Comedy," which I teach at the University of Pennsylvania. I would also like to express my gratitude to Angela Burton, my other editor, whose patience and professionalism assisted in producing the final version of the book.

I cannot forget the generosity of Mark Averbukh who provided me with books I desperately needed for my research.

There are still other people whose benevolence and understanding facilitated in various ways this difficult period of time. Among them I include Dasha Shushkovsky, Gail Felton, and, of course, my mother, to whom I promised to dedicate a book of poetry after all.

No words suffice to thank my husband for listening to that constant click-clack of the keyboard in the silence of our house. If this book were not dedicated to Aron Katsenelinboigen, I would definitely dedicate it to him.

Part One
Dramatic Genre as a General Systems Phenomenon

In this part of the book, I address some important methodological omissions, as a result of which dramatic genre remains an unelaborated category. I then consider the dramatic as a general systems phenomenon represented through a multidimensional perspective. In addition, I address the subjectivity of the evaluative process for indeterministic systems, including chess, economics, and literature. The last question will refer to a discussion of the degree of strength of potential, based on the ideas of survival and development in different fields of study.

Dramatic Genre: I
A New Classification

Contemporary scholars admit that the notion of the dramatic goes far beyond theatrical performances and is an integral part of any literary work. In this chapter, I discuss a new classification of dramatic genre that is based on the degree of strength and richness of characters' potential and the evaluations of the degrees. The difference between the potential of artistic and nonartistic systems lies first and foremost in the use of artistic devices, which further sophisticates the whole process of evaluating the artistic work's potential.

Thus, *the dramatic* in the present research is considered *synonymous with the potential of the artistic system.* Later I will discuss all the peculiarities of the artistic potential. For now, I would just like to mention that the introduction of artistic devices generates some new structures not observed in other systems (such as the *implied space* and the *mytholiterary continuum*) that essentially enrich one's understanding of the potential and the methods of its analysis.

The reasons for separation of the notion of the dramatic from the emotional perceptions expressed often through laughter or tears will be discussed in detail in the next chapter after the basic concept is presented. It seems that a clarification of a general idea in the beginning would facilitate the discussion of various details emerging after the main paradigm is described.

In my classification, dramatic genre is divided into types and branches; both types and branches are pure and mixed. There are three basic types and with a total of eighteen varieties.

Pure Types and Branches of Dramatic Genre

Basic types of dramatic genre. The pure types are the following:

- Dramedy—A type of dramatic genre that represents main protagonists with powerful and rich potential. Dramedy exploits the potential that is pregnant with great possibilities

- Drama—A type of dramatic genre that represents main protagonists with average or above average and strong potential
- Comedy—A type of dramatic genre that portrays main characters endowed with limited and powerless potential

The basic types of dramatic genre are formed exclusively by the degree of richness and the degree of strength of characters' potential, which attests both to their inner ability to develop and to their external influence on society.

Variety of basic types. The inner and the outer strength of the potential measured subjectively by the interpreter may not always coincide, however, and such an incongruity of intrinsic and extrinsic valuations forms a *variety* of basic dramatic types (see appendix 1).

A character of weak potential whose outer significance is very small is the subject of either funny comedy or farce, such as in *The Cherry Orchard* or *The Merry Wives of Windsor.* If the outer significance of a character with weak potential is strong, then the work can be either idyllic (idyll is treated in the modern sense) or satirical comedy. It seems that a literary type, the "little man," appeared as an appeal to increase the outer significance of characters with weak potential, thereby ascribing a considerable outer weight to that "humiliated" type. If such a type is meant to play a significant role in society, it may be interpreted, depending on the bias (positive or negative) of one's evaluation, as either utopia (comic utopia), satire (satirical comedy), or satirical utopia (mixed varieties). Utopia is usually based on poor potential that is represented in a highly favorable light. It draws a simplistic picture of the world, whose illusory harmony vanishes as soon as development is concerned. Such is Gary Ross's *Pleasantville* (1998), a satirical utopia set in the 1950s, and Yevgeny Zamyatin's *We* (1920), a Communist utopia of the programmed society that ended in fiasco. In both works, human feelings and desires—the "driving forces" of human development—are in disagreement with the primitive models of living that have been imposed on human beings. Their manifestation serves to reveal the weak potential of the "paradises on Earth," which do not allow humans to develop. Another example of satirical comedy is Mikhail Bulgakov's *The Heart of a Dog* (1925) with the character Sharikov—a street dog who is converted into a revolutionary and becomes the most influential figure in his society. Here the huge discrepancy between Sharikov's inner ability to develop and his outer power, combined with a highly negative evaluation by the writer, makes it belong to satirical comedy.

By the same token, if a character with strong potential is considered insignificant and is evaluated negatively, one may talk about satirical drama. Alexander Griboyedov's *Woe from Wit* (1833) is one such drama, representing its main protagonist, Chatsky, a character of above average potential, in a highly unfavorable light. Regardless of his intellect, or rather because of his intellect, Chatsky does not fit his limited, grotesque environment. His profound monologues in front of the laughing "elite" only emphasize his insignificance in that primitive, pragmatic world, which eventually rejects Chatsky as a foreign body.

Such incongruity between the inner and the outer generation yet another literary type known as the "superfluous man," who appears as a result of society's underestimation of his strong potential. By "underestimation," I mean a lack of extrinsic conditions in society that would allow this undeniably clever, intelligent type to develop and influence the progress of his society. Certainly, his inner strength is not strong enough to overcome all of the obstacles in the way of his development, since irrespective of his intelligence, good education, and many other positive features, he is still incapable of engaging in effective action. This type cannot belong to the powerful type of dramedy, but he is absolutely not a powerless comic type. Alexander Pushkin's *Eugene Onegin* (1833), Ivan Turgenev's *The Diary of a Superfluous Man* (1850), and Ivan Goncharov's *Oblomov* (1859) reveal different sides of this new character type that appeared in nineteenth-century Russian literature.

Branches of dramatic genre. The next step is to determine the branches of dramatic genre. Branches are formed by types of endings and types of potential; for instance, the limited potential combined with successful, unsuccessful, and ambiguous endings respectively generate cheerful, sad, and open comedy. The strong potential combined with different types of endings is assigned for cheerful, sad, and open drama. Accordingly, the combination of powerful potential with types of endings creates three branches of dramedy whose structure will be discussed below. In accordance with the matrix (see table 1), the following pure main branches are formed:

- Succedy: Powerful potential and successful outcome
- Tragedy—Powerful potential and unsuccessful outcome
- Open dramedy—Powerful potential and ambiguous ending
- Happy drama—Normal potential and successful outcome
- Unhappy drama—Normal potential and unsuccessful outcome
- Open drama—Normal potential and ambiguous outcome
- Happy comedy—Limited potential and happy ending
- Unhappy comedy—Limited potential and unhappy ending
- Open comedy—Limited potential and ambiguous ending

The matrix reveals that tragedy is not a type but a branch of dramatic genre. It represents potentially powerful protagonists predisposed to a lethal outcome. The degree of strength of the tragic hero's potential is not sufficient

	Outcome		
Potential	Successful	Unsuccessful	Ambiguous
Strong	Succedy	Tragedy	Open dramedy
Average	Happy drama	Unhappy drama	Open drama
Weak	Happy comedy	Unhappy comedy (black comedy)	Open comedy

Table 1. Branches of Dramatic Genre

to preserve him or her from catastrophe, yet the potential of the tragic character is rich and powerful enough to make him develop and influence his society. For instance, in *Romeo and Juliet,* the deaths of the protagonists change the society in essence by virtue of their unconditional view of love. In a world strictly divided into friends and enemies (a conditional valuation), Juliet's famous monologue "What's in a name?" sounds like a hymn to love as an unconditional feeling, which elevates the couple to the level of the sublime. Conversely, in *The Seagull* (1896), the death of the main protagonist, Treplev, has no influence on his world—it cannot change the way all other protagonists live and think.

The tragic hero has the explosive potential of a star that after its blast may generate a new galaxy. The tragic outcome is not predetermined, however, but only predisposed by features forming the tragic hero's potential, and a decrease of the explosiveness may generate another type of rich and powerful potential that is predisposed to success. Owing to the character's intellectual, physical, and emotional power, this new type may turn disadvantages into advantages and achieve his or her goal successfully. Wit, sensitivity, and a strong analytical mind combined with a rich imagination may prevent a tragic outcome and turn a dangerous predisposition into a successful outcome. This branch of dramedy—dealing with characters of rich and powerful potential that succeed in achieving their goals—I propose to call *succedy* (the term *succedy* is derived from "success"). *A Midsummer Night's Dream,* whose main protagonists at some point resemble Romeo and Juliet, belongs to this type of dramedy. A detailed analysis of their success appear in part two

In addition to the definite outcome, some works leave readers/spectators in obscurity, giving them the opportunity to guess about the outcome and the protagonists' future. Heinrich von Kleist's *Amphitryon* (1807) belongs to this type, in which there is ambiguity not only in his characters' futures but in their present states as well. I will provide a discussion of this play in chapter 2.

Like types, branches can also include outer evaluations of the potential, which generates their varieties. There is no need to discuss all possible combinations creating the varieties of branches, for their number is considerably large, and knowing the principle of their formation, one may easily draw an additional table of new names. For instance, the combination of an unhappy outcome, weak potential, and the important outer position of main characters evaluated positively creates a sad idyllic comedy. This list of characteristics can be continued.

Mixed Types and Branches

Approaching a group of characters: system and aggregate. Types and branches can be mixed and can also be combined with external values (see appendix 2 for details). The combination of characters' potential can be observed both on macro- and microlevels. By macrolevel, I mean a group of characters representing society; the microlevel, accordingly, consists of a single character. In turn, each level is additionally divided into intermediate levels. On the intermediate macrolevel, for example, one may observe a variety of potentials; groups of characters can be formed by individuals with potentials of different strength and significance and thus create a heterogeneous environment. At the same time, on the macrolevel, a group is represented as a unity that is characterized by a single degree of strength of its potential.

Many interesting experiments have been done in modern film concerning this distinction. For instance, *Jakob the Liar* by Peter Kassovitz (1999) represents a gallery of characters whose intellectual and physical strengths vary from limited to very strong. Some characters, such as Misha (Liev Schreiber), are typically comic, while others, such as the main protagonist, Jakob (Robin Williams), or the doctor (Armin Mueller-Stahl), reveal a strong and sometimes powerful potential. All types are united in small circles or groups, forming an intermediate macrolevel on which the Jewish group represents the whole spectrum of potentials, from ridiculously limited to ample. Such a mixture of potentials of different degrees of strength and richness made me wonder about a general value of the potential on the macrolevel. In the beginning, when I approached the potential of the group from the point of view of the average, I assumed that the whole group is represented as having strong, but not powerful, potential, inherent in comedy-drama.

As I considered the group as a whole, however, I came to the conclusion that the wholeness is represented as extremely rich and powerful because of the way the characters interact. Indeed, no matter how different these Jewish characters are, how naive, pragmatic, cynical, or idealistic each singular character appears to be, as a whole they represent a nation with rich and powerful potential—a nation that is artistic, imaginative, active, and strong. Therefore, the bloody outcome that is metaphorically shown as a musical—

the echo of the "radio concert" performed by Jakob for his little girl, through whose eyes the last bloody scene is shown—becomes a real tragedy, a monstrous performance of extermination designed with the red on the white.

To approach the problem of evaluation of the whole from the point of view of the general systems phenomenon, one must distinguish between the evaluation of an aggregate and that of a system when approaching a unity. First of all, both are different representations of the whole: an aggregate is a group of objects; the introduction of relationships between the objects forms a system. Such a differentiation is crucial in evaluating a group of objects because it affects the result. For instance, if a group consists of objects of average potential, the aggregate is considered to be of average potential. On the other hand, the analysis of the relationships between the objects and their interaction during the process of development may present quite a different picture, and as a system, such a group can be evaluated as either strong or weak.[1]

Such an approach is extremely helpful in the evaluation of characters in a group, taking into account peculiarities inherent in social system. In the example of *Jakob the Liar*, the characters' different strong sides (artistry, imagination, sensitivity, boldness, tenderness, and so on) interact in such a way that they increase the group's living forces and willingness to struggle for the future. In the meantime, in terrible conditions, they continue to develop, revealing their intellect, creativity, and sense of humor. They sharpen their physical and mental abilities through diaries, letters, and other forms of activity, supporting each other and leaving a stamp in the memory of generations.

Approaching a single character: changes in the potential. The same task of approaching various characteristics must be solved when referring to a single character (microlevel). The interpreter may approach the character's various features as either an aggregate or a system. In the latter, the question of how to integrate the part and the whole becomes vital. This immediately raises the question of the quasi-strong potential and the methods of its measurement.[2] On the microlevel, moreover, the dynamic changes of a protagonist's potential are often observed, and if the work is structured around one or two main characters (not a group of characters), the question of its genre definition arises.

There are a number of works dedicated to the problem of the protagonist's potential changing from one degree of strength to another. For instance, Jerry Fletcher (portrayed by Mel Gibson) in Richard Donner's film *Conspiracy Theory* (1997) undergoes the rare switch from an extremely limited and weak potential to an extremely rich and powerful one. This protagonist, who was once sharp and brilliant, becomes the victim of political games and is injected with experimental drugs against his will. As a result, he almost loses his intellectual ability, making him look mentally retarded in the eyes of others and causing everybody to treat him as mentally disabled. However, the remains of his potential strength allow him to overcome his present state and regain his former power. In the end, the spectator meets Jerry Fletcher in his entire splendor.

From the local point of view, this character, whose potential strength is unknown to the spectator, represents a switch from weak to powerful potential; but from the global point of view, his potential was just temporarily reduced, leaving his might untouched and making it possible for his potential to regenerate. Thus, one can say that his potential was only partially damaged; this is also the case with the protagonists of *A Midsummer Night's Dream*, who, under the influence of witchcraft, temporarily lose their ability to see clearly. From the global point of view, both plays belong to type DCD (dramedy-comedy-drama);[3] if the initial degree of strength of protagonists' potential is not taken into account, then one can talk about type C (comedy) for *Conspiracy Theory*.

The new classification: concerning a confusion of types and branches in criticism. The new classification assists in differentiating between some types and branches of dramatic genre that were traditionally taken for one another. This concerns not only such branches as happy comedy and succedy but also subbranches, such as funny comedy and funny drama. These two subbranches have traditionally been considered comedy because of the high degree of the laughable exploited in both. The fact that laughter may occur either as a result of a protagonist's wit or as a reaction to his or her foolishness is not taken into account. One can easily distinguish, however, between sharp-witted protagonists evoking one's laughter through their great sense of humor and simpletons having no clue of what is going on.

Charlie Chaplin's hero is not comic, though he is extremely funny. His outer clumsiness only emphasizes his inner richness. For instance, Chaplin's character in *Modern Times* appears in the beginning as a man easily manipulated by the monstrous mechanism of civilization. Even in the beginning, however, one can notice peculiar features that distinguish him from the crowd. At first, his inability to adjust to the rhythm of the modern city and his clumsiness, which causes his constant accidents and incidents with the management, seem to be a sign of the very low intellectual power of this poor thing. Unlike his colleagues, who successfully meet the requirements, he is a foreign body in this programmed environment. It soon becomes clear, however, why this personage cannot adapt to his industrial pragmatic society—his virtuoso performance in the café reveals a highly artistic nature that cannot be subjugated to the routine imposed on it by robotics. There are numerous scenes that suggest the wit and resourcefulness of Chaplin's hero. He often wins because of his nonstandard way of thinking; for instance, he reasonably assumes that it is better to stay in prison for stealing food than to die from hunger on the streets, and so he decides to go to a restaurant to order some food. After feeding himself, he calls the police.

While the policeman makes a phone call to report the incident, Chaplin's hero does a very unexpected thing—he gives a friendly smile to an unsuspecting salesperson and takes a cigarette and postcards from the counter. Such an unexpected turn (which is against common logic in actuality) is a challenge to stereotypic thinking, in accordance with which one who is caught by the police is expected to obey the law. No one would think the opposite—that the man has nothing to lose, so why not have a good cigar in addition to a great dinner? The crime is not large, and the punishment will be the same anyway.

Unlike Chaplin's hero, Jim Carrey's comical characters are incarnations of foolishness and emptiness. Carrey's hero is typically a comic character with a very limited potential. Everything that happens to him, all his misfortunes, are the result of his foolishness and local-mindedness. Chaplin's and Carrey's characters belong to different types of dramatic genre; the former is a character of drama, and the latter is a typically comic fool. (In the present book, I discuss only Carrey's comical characters.)

Funny drama has become very popular at present. It exploits characters of average or above average potential, representing them in laughable situations that do not, however, affect the degree of richness and strength of the potential. Such funny dramas as *My Best Friend's Wedding* by P. J. Hogan (1997) and *Grumpy Old Men* by Donald Petrie (1993) are called comedies, but according to my classification here, they are not. In *My Best Friend's Wedding*, all the funny episodes showing the failures of Jules Potter (Julia Roberts), as well as her attempts to interfere with her friend's marriage, are certainly laughable, but they have nothing to do with the comic. Julia Roberts plays an intelligent young woman, elegant and sensitive, whose desire to love has an indisputably rich dramatic nature. Analogously, the plots of *Grumpy Old Men* and its sequel, *Grumpier Old Men*, are woven from laughable scenes enacted by characters of mostly dramatic potential. Only a few characters can be considered purely comical, such as Grandpa (Burgess Meredith) and Mama (Ann Guilbert). All the leading characters possess strong dramatic potential, however, and the relationships within the group also suggest strong potential. Even such a seemingly funny couple (the bride is taller than the groom) as Jacob (Kevin Pollak) and Melanie (Daryl Hannah), by virtue of the protagonists' inner harmony, cannot be perceived as comic. The funny appearance of this couple only highlights the richness inherent in their relationship.

Among television shows, the popular sitcom *Married with Children* is a classic example of a purely funny comedy. Starting from the main protagonist, Al Bundy (Ed O'Neill), all the characters in the show represent genuinely comic potential. They deliberately demonstrate their pragmatism, local thinking, and very poor ability to develop. The characters' limitations are nevertheless represented in a positive light, creating a cheerful comedy, not farce or satire.

It is not only funny drama, however, that is often confused with comedy. One of the biggest mysteries of dramatic genre is tragicomedy, whose definition has been always vague and contradictory. Mar vin T. Herrick writes.

> In the early Renaissance . . . tragicomoedia was a term that defied satisfactory explanation. Among ancient authorities, Plautus alone had used the term, and no one was quite sure what he meant by it or how to classify his own tragicomedy of Amphitryon, which presented gods (Jupiter and Mercury) disguised as mortals and involved in domestic intrigue, i.e., traditionally tragic personages involved in traditionally comic affairs. (1)

As one can see, tragicomedy is traditionally approached from the point of view of the social status of its protagonists in combination with the degree of the laughable. Critics often mistakenly take protagonists' status for their potential, without taking into a consideration the fact that there are numerous cases in which social status is in disagreement with protagonists' potential strength. This is valid for both modern and ancient comedy, in which gods, kings, and heroes appear as characters of very limited and weak potential. This only confirms that without inquiring into the structure of the character's potential one will fail to understand the differences between characters of the same stratum and status in opposing genres.

According to Giambatista Guarini, tragicomedy combines "noble characters, not noble actions, a story which is credible but not historically true, heightened yet tempered effects, delight not sorrow, the danger not the death . . . [with] . . . laughter which is not dissolute, modest pleasures, a feigned crisis, an unexpected happy ending and—above all—the comic plotting" (qtd. in Hirst 4). However, as my analysis reveals, all features mentioned by Guarini can be combined with different potentials; they may be structured as succecomedy, as tragicomedy, or as dramecomedy.

Aristotelian Approach to Characters in Drama

Behaviorism versus potential. The new classification combines the modern theory of predispositioning with the traditional observations on comedy and tragedy (taking into account their structural elements, such as types of outcomes). The new classification absorbs previous achievements and develops them in accordance with modern thinking. Aristotle's great contribution to the theory of genre was the systematization of its manifold features. His thorough analysis of the structure, function, and genesis of tragedy, comedy, and epic poetry drew one's attention to artistic devices inherent in different literary genres. He discussed the quantitative structuring of tragedy, and he established rules for the portrayal of tragic personages and for the formation of epic poetry. All this was an excellent guide for authors and historians.

At the same time, the Aristotelian school paid no attention to the character's potential. Aristotle stated in *Poetics* that the principal element of the dramatic work was the plot, which he considered the main "moving principle."

> Tragedy is essentially an imitation not of persons but of action and life, of happiness and misery. All human happiness or misery takes the form of action; the end for which we live is a certain kind of activity, not a quality. Character gives us qualities, but it is in our actions—what we do—that we are happy or the reverse. (*Basic Works* 1461; 1450a, 16–20)

The Aristotelian philosophy resembles behaviorism, which has never inquired into the individual's inner structure, genetic code, or system of emotions; therefore, an observation on a person's behavior is the only possible way to speculate about his or her character. In the Aristotelian concept, the plot reveals the character through action, focusing on behavior rather than potential and predisposition.

Needless to say, behavior can sometimes be in disagreement with the one who performs it. It may, moreover, hide the personality of the individual and greatly deceive the observer. The development of genetics made it possible to research physiological structures that had never been discovered before. The Aristotelian tendency to consider character as a secondary concern suggests the absence of such analytical tools, which enable one to inquire into protagonists' potential. This absence has caused constant confusion and misrepresentation of the types of dramatic genre. Writers and critics have often used external features in defining the dramatic genre of a literary work; for instance, Dante's surprising decision to call his *Divine Comedy* a comedy was based simply on the happy ending of the story. In my classification this work belongs to succedy.

"Poetics" and "Physics": concerning the paradigm of thinking in Aristotle's theory of tragedy. Aristotle's neglect of the character's potential echoes his deterministic philosophy of development of the physical world. As Katsenelinboigen notes, physicists work with systems whose changes require millions of years. In this sense, one can speak of physical objects' slow-going process of change. Such physical laws as the law of gravity have made scientists believe that the universe is ruled by a set of firm, basic, unchangeable laws. The model of physics has remained a powerful one.

Unlike physical systems, however, social and biological systems are subject to rapid change; therefore, attempts to apply the methodology elaborated in physics have limited success. Only some individual parts of the system can

Dramatic Genre 13

be successfully linked via programmed relationships, while the system as a whole represents a more sophisticated way of uniting all its elements.

In Aristotle's theory of tragedy, characters are equal to fixed physical objects ruled by laws; they are subjugated to plot development, which unfolds in compliance with these laws. In accordance with Aristotelian theory, the object cannot change the law, in the same manner, the character is unable to change the plot. In his treatise *Physics*, Aristotle discussed the intelligible reality in which everything in the world of nature was thought to be causally dependent. This theory of causality holds that all events are determined by previously existing causes, and human behavior is precluded by them. The statement that "whatever is moved, is moved by something" appeared first in *Physics* and was elaborated by Aristotle in his *Metaphysics:* "There must, then, be such a principle, whose very essence is actuality. Further, then, these substances must be without matter; for they must be eternal, if *anything* is eternal. Therefore they must be actuality" (*Basic Works* 878; 1071b, 19–22).

Two ideas are important for our current discussion: (1) the object is moved by the external cause; and (2) there is a universal principle of movement that exists independently as an eternal cause. In other words, the object develops owing to the movements of other objects, which, in turn, are moved by the eternal principle. As Aristotle sees it, the object as such has no inner resources for its movement and development. This philosophy has shifted to the realm of art. In speaking about the cause, Aristotle notes in *Physics:*

> We must explain then (1) that Nature belongs to the class of causes which act for the sake of something; (2) about the necessary and its place in physical problems, for all writers ascribe things to this cause. . . . Now intelligent action is for the sake of an end; therefore the nature of things also is so. . . . Each step then in the series is for the sake of the next; and generally art partly completes what nature cannot bring to a finish, and partly imitates her. If, therefore, artificial products are for the sake of an end, so clearly also are natural products. (*Basic Works* 249–50; 198b, 10–15; 199a, 10–15)

Hence, according to Aristotle, "the end" is "the truth" that exists before the beginning and predetermines the structure of events. In *Poetics*, a parallel to the concept of causality is apparent. "Tragedy, however, is an imitation not only of a complete action, but also of incidents arousing pity and fear. . . . Even matters of chance seem most marvelous if there is an appearance of design as it were in them . . ." (*Basic Works* 1465; 1452a, 1–7).

In Aristotle's concept, the plot is seen as a principle that is intended to "move" characters. Consequently, characters, whose internal mechanisms of development are not taken into account, are equal to objects whose movement depends on external causes (such as peripeteia and discovery). The echo of this philosophy can be found in Nietzsche's destructive principle, and Schopenhauer's principle of ruling characters and universe. In addition, the correction of moral imbalances becomes a central idea in Hegel's concept of tragedy; according to Hegel, tragic heroes serve as a means of reconciling conflicting moral statements—another echo of the Aristotelian paradigm of the "principle." Even some modern and substantive research on tragedy is captivated by the concept of the "ruling principle" that determines protagonists' lives. George Steiner, in *The Death of Tragedy*, speaks of a type of tragedy that depicts the tragic hero struggling with inevitability. He calls this type of tragedy "the true tragedy" (xii). Steiner writes:

> Outside and within man is *l'autre*, the "otherness" of the world. Call it what you will: a hidden or malevolent God, blind fate, the solicitations of hell, or the brute fury of our animal blood. It mocks us and destroys us. In certain rare instances, it leads us after destruction to some incomprehensible repose. (9)

It seems that the view of a character as a puppetlike figure whose inner potential and predisposition are completely insignificant impoverishes the notion of the tragic character, his or her resourcefulness, and the inner factor that is the true cause of the character's failure. As the analysis reveals, it is first and foremost the character's predisposition that leads him or her to a certain outcome. Even in seemingly deterministic cases, such as in *Oedipus the King*, the protagonist's action is a matter of his wild temper in combination with his *conditional thinking*.[4]

It would therefore be a simplification to assume that a complete determination by the supernatural was the subject of the greatest classical tragedies. Besides, Greek tragedy gave birth not to singularity, not to one "genuine" kind but to a spectrum of tragedies. Steiner's interpretation of development as a convergent process is therefore a matter of his own bias. The process of development can be interpreted as either convergent or divergent, though in actuality, the creation of diversity is the way in which nature generates new forms more effectively. Various types of tragedies are branches of the same tree, whose roots cannot be determined by a single characteristic pertaining to the fatalistic role of gods, especially because the question of outer influences on the system is much more sophisticated than that.

Northrop Frye's "Anatomy of Criticism" in the light of predispositioning theory. Now that the general concept of dramatic genre has been presented, let us discuss in detail the ways of measuring protagonists' potential, using a multidimensional approach and a chess model.[5] As I mentioned before, from the functional point of view the degree of strength of the protagonist's potential is related to his or her ability to develop and to influence the development of the outer world. This is the main difference between my approach to dramatic genre and that given by Northrop Frye in his *Anatomy of Criticism: Four Essays*.

Frye outlines five types of the hero's power of action: (1) "superior in *kind* both to other men and to environment" (a divine being); (2) "superior in *degree* to other men and to environment" (the hero of romance); (3) "superior in degree to other men but not to his natural environment" (a leader); (4) "superior neither to other men nor to his environment" ("one of us"); and (5) "inferior of power and intelligence to ourselves" (33–34).

As follows from this description, Frye establishes the degree of one's power based on one's interactions with *other people*. However, any system with either limited or rich potential has its hierarchy. Aristophanes' *Frogs*, for instance, represents a system that includes gods, poets, and simple people who act in accordance with their current status; namely, poets write poems, gods command, and simple people obey. But the question is to what extent the superior characters are responsible for the development of their universe.

As further analysis will show, gods and leaders in comedy are formal figures unable to change their system, while in drama and dramedy they influence the development of their universe and, besides, are able to develop themselves. Thus, the existence of a hierarchy does not shed light on the nature of protagonists' basic differences, which requires a different approach. Frye's outline draws one's attention to the degree of protagonists' superiority, and on this point, our positions coincide. Superiority itself is considered sufficient, however, and the fact that it can be a mere formality is not taken into consideration. This causes contradictions in Frye's classification; for instance, Frye states that the low mimetic mode based on the type called "one of us" is typical for comedies. Naturally, the question arises, how does one classify gods and heroes of comedies who are definitely not "some of us"? As Elmer Blistein notices:

> Jupiter's presence has strikingly different results in the different versions. Jupiter's presence in Plautus leads inevitably and reverently to the birth of a divine hero; his presence in Molière succeeds in raising bedroom farce to the level of high comedy and leads to the birth of a semi-divine hero; his presence in Dryden creates, along with a potential sweeper of the Augean stables, a farcical triangle of an arrogant cuckolder, a shrewish strumpet, and a pompous cuckold. (99)

Understanding the insufficiency of the parameters introduced in his outline, Frye switches from an analysis of the character's social status to an analysis of plot structure. Frye's further speculations about comic and tragic structures are based on the traditional idea of successful/unsuccessful endings in tragedy and comedy.

> Also there is a general distinction between fictions in which the hero becomes isolated from his society, and fictions in which he is incorporated into it. This distinction is expressed by the words "tragic" and "comic" when they refer to aspects of plot in general and not simply to forms of drama. (35)

The idea of the isolated protagonist corresponds with an unsuccessful ending, while the incorporation of the character into society is analogous to a happy ending. Frye writes, "The theme of the comic is the integration of society, which usually takes the form of incorporating a central character into it" (43). However, the introduction of this parameter of "integration" into society generates new contradictions within Frye's classification. Suppose that the idea of integration is combined with the high mimetic mode, defined by Frye as the possession of great passions and powers of expression and belonging to epic and tragedy. What type of genre should we discuss in that case? For instance, the main protagonists of *A Midsummer Night's Dream* all possess characteristics inherent in mode three: they are characters of great passions, expressing themselves in a way that elevates them to a higher level than that of the common environment; they are subject to social criticism; at the same time, they are incorporated into society. Frye's classification only sharpens some questions for which the answer requires a different, non-Aristotelian approach that would be linked to the analysis of protagonists' potential, not to the plot structuring or hierarchy.

The character's potential: aspects of analysis. The analysis of the character's potential is important for understanding the essence of dramatic genre. As further analysis will show, some comedies and tragedies exploit the same topics and represent protagonists with seemingly analogous behavior. Without referring to the character's potential, it would be impossible to detect the main difference between the similar characters represented in different dramatic genres, especially when it concerns the CNT.

In analyzing the protagonist's potential, I will refer to the following aspects:

- The character's physical and intellectual abilities, including cleverness
- The type of the character's vision, namely, local/global, comprehensive/disjointed
- The character's use of certain methods (reflexive and selective), styles (positional and combinational), and ways of connectivity of elements (programming, predispositioning, and randomness)[6]

- The character's ability to set a goal, to choose a direction, and to elaborate a strategy
- The character's presence/absence of will and inner energy required for achieving a goal
- The character's experience
- The character's knowledge
- The character's values
- The character' genesis

Positional and Combinational Thinking in Literature

Positional and combinational styles in chess and literature. The question of a character's use of certain styles and methods in his or her decision making requires a special discussion, for it becomes crucial in understanding a character's psychology and the degree of his or her limitations. Applying Katsenelinboigen's terminology, which is borrowed from the game of chess, one may say that, in general, characters are divided into the two following types of players: positional and combinational.

In defining the combinational style in chess, Katsenelinboigen writes:

> The combinational style features a clearly formulated limited objective, namely the capture of material (the main constituent element of a chess position). The objective is implemented via a well defined and in some cases in a unique sequence of moves aimed at reaching the set goal. As a rule, this sequence leaves no options for the opponent. Finding a combinational objective allows the player to focus all his energies on efficient execution, that is, the player's analysis may be limited to the pieces directly partaking in the combination. This approach is the crux of the combination and the combinational style of play. (*Concept of Indeterminism* 57)

In the combinational style, the player is not concerned with the creation of a predisposition for his future development since he is completely seized with the goal, which is a material objective. In the process, everything not linked to the capturing of the material objective is not considered by this type of player, and the question of what kind of predisposition will be created *after* the goal has been achieved is not of his concern. Unlike the combinational player, the positional player is occupied, first and foremost, with the elaboration of the position that will allow him to develop in the unknown future. In playing the positional style, the player must evaluate relational and material parameters as independent variables. Katsenelinboigen writes:

> (1) First and foremost, the weight function includes not only material parameters as independent (the controlling) variables, but also positional

> (relational) parameters. (2) The valuation of material and positional parameters comprising the weight function are, to a certain extent, unconditional; that is, they are independent of the specific conditions, but do take into account the rules of the game and statistics. (*Concept of Indeterminism* 50)

The positional style gives the player the opportunity to develop a position until it becomes pregnant with a combination. However, the combination is not the final goal of the positional player—it helps him to achieve the desirable, keeping in mind a predisposition for the future development. The Pyrrhic victory is the best example of one's inability to think positionally. Katsenelinboigen writes:

> As the game progressed and defense became more sophisticated the combinational style of play declined. . . . The positional style of chess does not eliminate the combinational one with its attempt to see the entire program of action in advance. The positional style merely prepares the transformation to a combination when the latter becomes feasible. (*Selected Topics* 21)

According to Katsenelinboigen, the positional and combinational styles in chess signify two different approaches to overcoming obscurity. One approach represents the system from its end and is based on the creation of a program that links the initial step with the final goal. In so doing, the combinational player makes unconditional valuations of material parameters when it concerns the result, but he does not take into account positional parameters as independent variables.[7] For instance, when the combinational chess player compares his sacrifices with the winning material, he applies unconditional values; at the same time, he does not pay attention to the position, for he is completely concerned with obtaining a concrete material. The combinational style can be interpreted as a degenerated case of the positional style, for in actuality the combination is only a part of the position, whether or not it is acknowledged by the player.

In open-ended systems, such as life and literature, the neglect of a position may cause serious failure, if not disaster, because the winner may in the next minute become a loser. Napoleon's defeat in Russia is a perfect example of this—the moment of Napoleon's celebration at the capture of Moscow was the beginning of his end.

In life, the focus on a position with a combination ingrained becomes a requirement, since life is an endless process of change. As has been shown with regard to survival and development, the same task of forming a perpetual continuity is inherent in a literary work; therefore, the outcome in a literary work is not the point of destination but rather a point of departure for the interpreters. Decisions made by characters shed light not only on the question of their momentary success or failure, but they also reveal their predisposition for future development. Types of goals, evaluations, methods, and styles tell us a great deal about a character's view of the world and psychology, including how to handle his emotions and hidden urges.

The next two parts of this book are dedicated to a detailed analysis of the predisposition of characters, including types of decision making. Here, I just want to mention that characters with limited, poor potential are generally distinguished by very primitive decision making; as a rule, they base their decisions on reactive methods, and even if they use selective methods, they apply local, conditional valuations. Such characters cannot understand the meaning of unconditional values. All of their decisions are based on simple programs and primitive combinations without any concern for the future. In more sophisticated cases, there might be an odd combination of opposing characteristics, such as a combination of global goals with local valuations, which may confuse the interpreter. But, as I show in future chapters, even if characters with limited potential set global goals, they are not able to elaborate strategies to achieve them. Moreover, if such characters are ambitious and aggressive enough, they may even destroy themselves, being trapped by their local mindsets.

Literature is full of such examples, which, unfortunately, have not always been analyzed deeply and thoroughly. Such is Balzac's Goriot, who in criticism receives mostly positive and sympathetic evaluations. The new terminology linked to the character's decision making in particular and to his potential in general, however, allows one to penetrate into deep levels of his psychology and discuss it in analytical terms.

Positional style in works of O. Henry. It is not only a character but also the artist who can be judged based on the types of methods he or she applies to an artistic work.[8] The combinational style is a prerogative of mysteries, such as Sir Arthur Conan Doyle's famous novels, in which most of the details and descriptions are tied directly into the mystery that will be solved in the end. As soon as the reader knows the end, he or she can successfully link it to the beginning in order to see what kind of details were missed in the first place. On the other hand, O. Henry creates a predisposition while writing his stories, and all of the details he introduces require predispositioning as a method of analysis. Even after knowing the ending, therefore, the reader is still puzzled with the unexpected outcome and can hardly suggest a successive link between the beginning and the end, since the linkages are semiefficient.

A reader of O. Henry should know how to evaluate a predisposition of characters, how to establish weights, and how to approach material and relational parameters as independent variables; in other words, O. Henry's reader must be a master of positional thinking. The pathos of O. Henry's works is directed towards uniqueness rather than statistics; there is always a hidden opposition in his works between a narrow-minded observer who evaluates everything probabilistically and a keen reader who notices some small, "inessential" details and ascribes significant weights to them.[9] For instance, when reading a description of Old Behrman in "The Last Leaf," one can only shrug one's shoulders in bewilderment—how can such a worthless creature do such a heroic thing?

> Old Behrman was a painter who lived on the ground floor beneath them. He was past sixty and had a Michelangelo's Moses beard curling down from the head of a satyr along the body of an imp. Behrman was a failure in art. Forty years he had wielded the brush without getting near enough to touch the hem of his Mistress' robe. He had been always about to paint a masterpiece, but had never yet begun it. For several years he had painted nothing except now and then a daub in the line of commerce or advertising. He earned a little by serving as a model to those young artists in the colony who could not pay the price of a professional. He drank gin to excess, and still talked of his coming masterpiece. For the rest he was a fierce little old man, who scoffed terribly at softness in anyone, and who regarded himself as especial mastiff-in-waiting to protect the two young artists in the studio above. (1417)

It is not clear what type Mr. Behrman is—a drinker; an ambitious man incapable of realizing his intent; a mediocre artist who does nothing; or an angry little creature that, besides, is cynical when it concerns compassion and sympathy. This is what the common reader may see on the surface, and this is what will provide puzzlement in the end, after the reader finds out that Old Behrman does keep his word concerning the masterpiece—he paints an ivy leaf on the wall to save the life of a young artist who was waiting in her bed to die with the last leaf. But is there anything in the description of Behrman that would suggest a different predisposition of his character in the beginning? In order to answer this question, let us refer to Katsenelinboigen's explanation of conditions in which an analysis of a predisposition is the only way to approach the entity:

> A much more challenging problem arises when there are no statistics, stochastic programming or sequential analysis to generate probabilities, considering especially that sequential analysis starts with some a priori probability distribution and may take an incredible amount of time or resources to produce an optimal solution. Additionally, there may be

unique situations that by definition preclude any reliance on frequency of events whatsoever. In this case, rather than observe a highly uncertain behavior of individual objects, we look at the behavior of the total ensemble formed by these objects, since the latter, generally speaking, are more amenable to statistical patterns; in other words, we reduce a unique situation to some previously known one by stripping the former of its specific unique features. This, however, is a pretty risky procedure since the specific features of a unique event could be quite significant, and eliminating them might result in a drastically distorted estimate of the likelihood of the situation occurring. (*Concept of Indeterminism* 27–28)

The situation described by Katsenelinboigen is the subject matter of O. Henry's stories. A reader who approaches O. Henry's characters from the point of view of a standard situation reduces their specific quality to that which is previously known and thus strips them of the important features that make them unique. Knowing of this standard thinking, O. Henry plays a game with the unsophisticated reader who is going to soon face an unexpected outcome.

But how exactly does he create a description of his characters? What is that which suggests a unique type, not some mediocre creature? In order to answer these questions, one must thoroughly inquire into the way O. Henry combines various material and positional parameters, which may seem weird and even inappropriate to more traditional readers. To me, the very first line describing Old Behrman is indicative—a combination of Michelangelo's Moses, a satyr, and an imp makes this figure quite exotic. Behrman's portrait is the first sign that this character is woven from controversies, which cannot be integrated in a whole in a complete and consistent way.

The probabilistic approach in the evaluation of this character would be, therefore, "to pick only the essentials from among the initial parameters, together with their valuations. These valuations are fully determined in a way that they completely and consistently integrate all the elements of the system." (Katsenelinboigen, *Concept of Indeterminism* 29) This explains why the majority of readers omit those details that would not otherwise allow them to consistently integrate all the characteristics; by such characteristics I mean a description of Behrman as a drinker and loafer combined with negative evaluations. But as soon as we see his uniqueness and understand that such an approach would be inaccurate from the point of view of the future, we should refer to predispositioning as a method:

> The new methods assume a deeper dissection of the system into its constituent elements and an integral evaluation of its various states

> through a linear polynomial. But how are the states to be structured or which parameters are to be selected, so that the weighted sum of them would approximate a holistic assessment of a given state? This is an age-old problem, conveyed in a maxim that "the total is greater than the sum of its parts." To solve this problem, we need a special weight (evaluative) function.
>
> With these functions, we assume the existence of incomplete, though varyingly incomplete, valuations of individual essentials. By *essentials* I mean elements that constitute the skeleton of a state. The relations between the essentials I will call *positional parameter*.... (Katsenelinboigen, *Concept of Indeterminism* 29)

Using this approach, one should examine not only what O. Henry's character says or does but how he says it and how he does it and then give it a weight. For instance, Behrman's excessive drinking and impassioned speeches reveal a highly emotional nature that he tries to hide from people. The remark that he "scoffed terribly at softness in anyone" only highlights to what extent this character is vulnerable. His guardianship of two young artists further implies that he is a caring person with moral values. Besides, his desire to create a masterpiece and mention of Michelangelo and Moses may suggest that his ideals are global and sublime, but as a nervous kind, he finds his inspiration by scandalizing the public.

Thus, we have a set of all parameters, both material and relational, that are controversial. The next step is to establish weights and to integrate the parameters into a whole. In so doing, each interpreter will make subjective evaluations. To me, the fact that Behrman is a drinker is less important than the fact that he is a caring, imaginative person; and the fact that he is moral and idealistic deep inside is more important than the fact that he is cynical in public. Also, his "à la Michelangelo Moses" beard is a sign that Behrman creates his appearance deliberately, basing his decision on his set values, and this is his attempt to "correct" or slightly "improve" on nature. Above all, his dream about the creation of a single, but genuinely perfect work—the acme of his life—reveals him to be a strong believer in the truth within himself, a believer who may go to the extreme when it concerns his belief. I value this last detail as extremely significant.

After dissecting this structure into its material and relational parameters and giving them weights, I synthesize them in a new wholeness in order to gain a holistic view of the character. In my interpretation, Behrman appears to be a sensitive, idealistic man, who is yet ambitious and irascible, and is highly predisposed to extreme behavior and fanaticism. Such a kind is typical of heroes and fighters for truth.

Approaching the potential of the artistic work. The methods of approaching the potential of a system were first introduced and elaborated in Katsenelinboigen's work on indeterministic systems.[10] Let us analyze the role of the excerpt below from a multidimensional perspective in order to see how the potential of the world described in Gogol's *Dead Souls* can be measured based on this single digression.

> On entering the room Chichikov had for a moment to screw up his eyes, for the glare of the candles, the lamps, and the ladies' dresses was terrific. It was all flooded with light. Black coats flitted about, one by one or in groups, here and there, like flies flitting about a sparkling sugar-loaf on a hot July day when the old housekeeper breaks and splits it up into glistening lumps before the open window; the children all look on, gathered round her, watching with interest her rough hands lifting the hammer while airy squadrons of flies, floating on the breeze, fly in boldly as though the house belonged to them and, taking advantage of the old woman's dim sight and the sunshine that dazzles her eyes, cover the dainty morsels, here in scattered groups, and there in dense crowds. Sated by the wealth of summer which spreads dainties for them at every step, they fly in, not for food but to display themselves, to parade up and down over the heap of sugar, to rub their hind legs or their front legs one against the other, or to scratch themselves under their wings, or stretching out both front legs to brush their heads with them, to turn and fly out again and to fly in once more in new persistent squadrons. (Garnett 20–21)

The description of the party at which Chichikov arrives greatly contributes to the structure of the novel's implied space.[11] Unlike the space of action (such as Verona in *Romeo and Juliet,* or Sorin's estate in *The Seagull*) which is determined by the artist, the implied space is created by the interpreter through various metaphors. Using different styles and methods, the interpreter establishes efficient and semiefficient linkages between artistic and nonartistic structures; as a result, new objects appear to form an implied space.[12] Both the implied space and the space of action have a degree of abstraction; for the space of action, it would be a more general view of its particular mechanisms of development, while for the implied space, it would be an abstract representation of its concrete structures and their interactions.[13]

I think it is necessary to emphasize that I differentiate between the implied space and the subtext in the following way. In criticism, the subtext often includes everything that is implied in a literary text; to me, however, the subtext concerns only the interpreter's *conclusion* of the text;[14] the creation of *a new space* belongs to the implied space formed through various artistic devices, such as allegory, symbols, and metaphors. On the level of the implied space, an interpreter generates new entities that appear as a result of his or her own valuations of the material and relational parameters defined in the space of action.

Thus, the implied space is generated by new entities (destiny, Arcadia, and the like) that are not present in the space of action; they are "products" of the interpreter's evaluation of material and relational parameters in the space of action. As a result of such evaluations, new intertextual associations are established, requiring integration into a whole. In addition to allusions to mythology, there can be allusions to any other source, both artistic and nonartistic, including the interpreter's own newly created structures elevated to the level of myth.[15] The creation of myth is a prerogative of the implied space that serves to build a scale of unconditionality upon which structures of the space of action will be weighed.[16]

Each writer has his or her own technique of creating semiefficient linkages between the space of action and the implied space; therefore, there cannot be a general rule of "switching" from one level of abstraction to another. As will be shown below, however, there is a methodology of establishing the transitional steps from one space to another, which can be described as a search for a "bridge" between the spaces and a further investigation of where it leads.

In the excerpt above, the flies become a "bridge" that connects the space of action to the implied space. In the former, the flies appear as a metaphor of "black coats"—small groups of officials gathering here and there and promenading along the ballroom. As the metaphor extends, however, the flies acquire the features of fantastic creatures—flies-officials—that in turn generate the appearance of new beings. First of all, this concerns a mentioning of a "sparkling sugar-loaf" about which the flies are flitting. With the introduction of this new object (the sugar loaf) that has no analogy in the first part of the comparison, the development of the implied space begins.

Indeed, although the flies have "prototypes" in the space of action—the officials—the sugar-loaf appears to be an object pertaining only to a symbolic sphere with a broad field of meanings (which should be supported and developed by a subsequent analysis of other symbols). One possible interpretation could be that the sugar-loaf symbolizes success and delight, which the flies-officials are eager to suck from life. This symbol of sweetness and beauty is followed by that of the old housekeeper, who also lacks correspondence with the space of action. Moreover, the figure of the housekeeper seems to be gigantic in comparison to that of the flies, signifying a change in the proportions of the world of living beings, to which flies-officials belong. This change, first, influences the scene in the space of action, making the reader wonder about who would be such a "giant" for the officials; second, it elevates the implied space to a new level of generalization, which one should discuss by approaching the housekeeper's character from a multidimensional perspective.

From the structural point of view, the position of the housekeeper suggests that this character is responsible for order in the house and is the manager of that space. Her function of breaking and splitting the sugar-loaf, as well as the way in which she endows everyone with some portions of success and delight, generates an association with a goddess of fate. However, the housekeeper's power is restricted by the sun, which dazzles the old lady, and thus does not allow her to determine completely the course of life in the house.

Aside from the flies and the housekeeper, there are also children "watching [the housekeeper] with interest" and the way she manages their space. Like the housekeeper, the children have no prototypes in the space of action—they are just notions, symbols generated in the semi-implied space. Their proportions in comparison to both the flies-officials and the housekeeper suggest their intermediate position in the house. Filled with the idea of youth and curiosity, the symbolism of children is associated with new forces appearing in the universe. With these entities, a new relational parameter is introduced: the opposition between the old lady and the children can be interpreted as the opposition between the established and the rising.

The house itself conveys some essential symbolism enriching the structure of the implied space. The room in which the housekeeper operates is described as having "the open window"—a symbol of the world as an open-ended system. Two things are emphasized with regard to the window: it lets the flies "fly out and in," and it gives an idea of the world beyond the house. The world outside of the house is represented as extremely rich and beautiful, so that the house with the sugar-loaf is not the only place for the flies' delight (the summer "spreads dainties for them at every step"). This essentially reduces the authority of the housekeeper and her supreme position as the ruler of the world. The flies do not depend on her as a distributor of goods; they "fly in, not for food but to display themselves, to parade up and down over the heap of sugar." This is a parade of their independence and freedom from pragmatic needs in the open-ended system that generously produces a diversity of forms.

After the implied space is discussed, all the new notions are elevated to the more abstract level of generalization. On that level, one can talk about the universe as an open-ended system that constantly generates new driving forces and extends the diversity of forms. That universe is represented as a semibalanced system that avoids destructive extremes (complete order and complete disorder).[17] But what does all this add to the understanding of the space of action?

I believe that the implied space here assists in answering, in general terms, the question of why Chichikov did not succeed in achieving his pragmatic goals. Chichikov's vision of the world as a system that can be completely programmed is in disagreement with the actual way the universe develops; life rejects any attempts to determine it, and it dazzles the programmer in the way that the sun dazzles the old housekeeper, limiting her in her (futile) attempts to manage the house in a complete and consistent way. Such an analysis suggests that the potential of Chichikov's world is very limited and poor unlike the potential of the surrounding universe. Chichikov's environment, therefore, is a comical environment unable to develop.

Such a global approach to the concept of the artistic work is possible only when all of its layers are analyzed and synthesized. After attaining a global vision, one can see better the role of various details, descriptions and the like.[18] This methodology allows an effective penetration of the system's structure, including that of the artistic system with its sophisticated net of material and relational parameters. Chapter 8 provides a more detailed discourse on the integration of artistic and nonartistic elements and the role of implied space in measuring of the potential of the artistic work.

Summary

The structure of dramatic genre comprises types (pure and mixed) and branches (pure and mixed). Types are formed with characters' potential—poor, average/above average, rich—and their inner valuations, which are correlated with the degree of strength of the potential. Branches appear as a result of a combination of types of potential and types of outcomes. In accordance with this, three pure main types are discussed: dramedy, drama, and comedy. The branches are the following: tragedy, succedy, open dramedy, happy/unhappy/open drama, and happy/unhappy/open comedy. The addition of other characteristics, such as outer valuations or the degree of the laughable/funny, serves to introduce additional variations of types and branches, including subtypes and subbranches.

The creative process is distinguished by different stages; each stage consists of particular styles (positional and combinational), methods (reflexive and selective), and ways of connectivity (programming, predispositioning, and randomness). In the process of creation, the artist combines all of these.

The combinational style is concerned with the creation of combinations that would allow one to obtain a material through setting a concrete goal and elaborating a program. The positional style is focused on the creation of a predisposition for future development, with combination as its stage.

The introduction of the concept of styles—positional and combinational—is an essential step forward in approaching both a literary work and literary characters, whose decision making reveals much about their limitations and abilities to develop. Characters in the literary work are distinguished by their decision making. Primitive characters use reactive methods based on conditional and local values and banal combinations. Characters who think positionally are concerned with future development, and their combinations are the results of a thoroughly elaborated position that holds a predisposition for the future.

The Dramatic as an Independent Category: *Chess, Economics, and Literature*

This chapter contains a discussion of the core of dramatic genre—a potential—and the degree of its richness and strength; this will naturally lead to a discussion of the comic, the most complicated issue of dramatic genre. Since the question of the comic in literary criticism is approached from three basic points of view—the role of laughter, the idea of survival, and the happy ending—the discussion of the comic as the core of comedy is structured around these three points.

Dramatic Genre as an Unelaborated Category

A definition of an unelaborated category. A category is generally considered unelaborated when, first, it has no elaborated degree (i.e., when it operates only with extremes), and second, when it is reduced to another category.[1] When reading general, modern definitions of dramatic genre, represented in such respected sources as *Merriam-Webster's Encyclopedia of Literature,* one notices some important omissions concerning intermediate stages; the theory operates on two extremes—comedy that is based on the light and tragedy that is based on the serious. Comedy-drama is also defined as a combination of these two extremes, seriousness and lightness, without establishing the degree and magnitude of each:

> Comedy . . . The genre of dramatic literature that deals with the light or the amusing, or with the serious and profound in a light, familiar, or satirical manner.
> Comedy-drama . . . Serious drama with comedy interspersed.
> Tragedy . . . A drama of a serious and dignified character that typically describes the development of a conflict between the protagonist and a superior force . . . and reaches a sorrowful or disastrous conclusion. (260)

The degree of seriousness, which is different in different works, is not discussed in the statement above, creating a major problem in defining a genre of literary works whose degree of seriousness creates a spectrum. Not only is there no degree assigned to the initial parameter (seriousness), but there is no explicit discussion of the dual parameter (its evaluation).

Katsenelinboigen's system of measuring an entity: initial and dual parameters. As Katsenelinboigen states, entities consist of initial and dual parameters necessary for explicitly measuring the power of their impact on a system's development.

> In analyzing any entity we distinguish both, as the initial objects (parameters), that is, elements, as the initial relations (parameters) between these elements.... The initial parameters necessarily include those that make up the anatomy and the physiology of the system. We shall refer to them as *essentials*. The initial parameters may also contain the *relations* between elements; the concept of relations requires separate treatment. The initial parameters (the essentials and the relations) can have *dual* parameters that act as a kind of a motive force of the system. Let us call the dual parameters *attractors* or *repulsors*. (*Concept of Indeterminism* 21–22)

In physics, such attractors are forces; in economics, they are prices; in a social system, one talks about moral values. As a rule, psychologists consider emotions equal to valuations, ignoring the fact that emotions are formed by initial and dual parameters and, at this point, are coupled and not single characteristics. For instance, in analyzing an emotion such as fear, Katsenelinboigen reveals that fear is not an evaluation of a situation but an initial component of the emotion whose magnitude is represented in linguistic variables (such as a "great fear" or a "little fear"). The dual parameter of fear is the valuation of its degree and magnitude, without which it would not be possible to make a decision; that is, to be able to choose between different, sometimes even conflicting, feelings. For instance, my beloved cat, Lily, is torn between two great emotions when approaching our vacuum cleaner—those of fear and curiosity. The magnitude of her fear can be measured by her hair, which stands on end as she circles the monster. Compared to her great desire, however, the fear is less powerful since it is eventually "pinned down" by her curiosity, which makes her approach the devil and even touch it quickly. This means that the significance (dual parameter) of her fear (initial parameter) succumbs to the better significance of her curiosity, whose degree may be equal to fear.

Just as any other emotion, fear appears after an evaluation of the danger has been made, and fear in turn goes through the process of evaluation that establishes its degree and magnitude, including its dual parameter. In some cases, emotions like fear may appear as reflexes, and such an instantaneous, instinctive feeling arising (for instance, from an object falling or rolling toward the observer) is responsible for one's confusion of emotions with evaluations. On the level of reflexes, emotions are fused with the objects that cause them. This makes it possible to teach people general rules of behavior. The evaluation of the falling object in the construction area or the stranger approaching the child must be unconditionally negative. In cases other than reflexes, one should discuss a chain of initial and dual parameters, which can be described as the following:

1. The appearance of an object (initial parameter)
2. Its evaluation (dual parameter)
3. Appearance of certain emotions *as a result of such an evaluation* (initial parameter)
4. Their evaluation (dual parameter)

Here, the appearance of emotion is a result of one's subjective evaluation of an entity. This link may not necessarily be programmed, contrary to what some scholars assume, especially those who attempt to derive laughter or weeping from a situation. A detailed discussion of this subject will be provided later.

Introduction of degree and magnitude to initial and dual parameters. The establishment of the degree and magnitude of both initial and dual parameters of the entity provides us with the ability to measure it properly. Only in unelaborated systems is the degree not established explicitly, with the magnitude existing in binary terms.[2] The explicit introduction of degree and magnitude to the initial and dual parameters of the entity is crucial for literary criticism, especially when it regards an old question such as the role of laughter in comedy. Concerning laughter and the laughable, it seems that the degree of its initial parameter is not taken into account by some scholars discussing major problems concerning dramatic genre, namely, comedy, one of its types. Like many other scholars, Paul H. Grawe notices this omission with regard to comedy:

> Just as bad, once we have made the basic mistake of equating comedy and laughter, we also fail to notice that many of the greatest comedies, Shakespeare's best comedies, for example, are often much less funny than obviously second-rate, cliché-ridden, hack comedy and some of the greatest comedies contain very little that is laughable. (5)

Like Grawe, I differentiate between the comedy of trivial action and the comedy of witty, intelligent characters of works termed "comedies" (by either their authors or their critics) with a subsequent degree of the laughable in them. However, I do not consider this second type to be comedy; I call it succedy.

Subsumption of the notion of the comic by the laughable. The notion of the comic in literary criticism is reduced to the laughable/funny. According to the *Encyclopedia of Aesthetics*, "Since the Greeks, laughter has been the characteristically comic response, and throughout history, theories of laughter have shaped theories of comedy" (Kelly 1: 402). Grawe, on the other hand, writes: "Because the most fundamental questions are brought the true meaning of laughter as the essential element of the comic, the field can resemble a very contentious contest over a highly specialized topic" (9). However, this nonorthodox statement is not supported in criticism simply because it requires a reconsideration of the category of the comic, which is traditionally connected to laughter.

To Aristotle and his school, the laughable is what makes comedy, comedy, and the most recent attempts to define the comic have all addressed the question of what can become an appropriate subject of laughter and for what reason. Stemming from the notion of the laughable and the harmless nature of defect or ugliness, the Aristotelian idea of the comic equates comedy with an imitation of the lives of a lower type of character. In this context, Richard Janko's translation highlights the role of laughter as an integral part of the Aristotelian concept of comedy:

> Comedy is a representation of an action that is laughable and lacking in magnitude, complete, [in embellished speech,] with each of its parts [used] separately in the [various] elements [of the play] represented by people acting and [not] by narration; accomplishing by means of pleasure and laughter the catharsis of such emotions. It has laughter as its mother. (*Poetics I* 49)

There is obviously no comedy without laughter for Aristotle, and this is certainly true for traditional comedy, which exploits laughter to a great extent. For all their diversity and their inquiries into different aspects, all subsequent concepts—including the most recent—agree on the laughable nature of the comic. As Elder Olson states, "[T]he comic includes only the ridiculous, the ludicrous, the things which are taken as such by analogy, the witty and the humorous" (23). A. M. Bowie represents this traditional Aristotelian paradigm of thinking that is linked to the idea of harmless distortions: "One might say, therefore, that comedy holds up a miraculous mirror to the audience, which does not simply reflect, but refracts and distorts in a kaleidoscopic manner" (15).

The traditional understanding of the comic, as a structure rooted in the laughable/ridiculous, remains prevalent in modern criticism. The constant attempt to link the comic and the laughable, including jokes, humor, ridicule, and so on, is explained by the fact that very often in comedy the notion of the characters' potential and the laughable conflate into one, complicating the outlining of the comic as an independent structure. Though critics admit that comic theory is the least-elaborated field in the theory of drama, the Aristotelian paradigm remains favored. Richard Keller Simon writes, "Comic theory has received relatively little critical attention, far less than theories about more serious subjects" (12–13). According to Grawe, "Comedy has been misdefined for two millennia and, on the basis of that misdefinition, comedy has been relegated to an almost Cinderella-like position compared to her sister, tragedy" (9). Many empirical descriptions of comedy have been based on combinations of insufficient external characteristics relating to its genesis and plotting.[3] Aelius Donatus's review of comedies may serve as a good example of such empirical descriptions:

> The writings of all comedies are taken from four things, namely, name, place, deed, and outcome. Those taken from name are like *Phormio, Hecyra, Curculio, Epidicus*. From place, like *Andria, Leucadia, Brunducina*. From deed, like *Eunuchus, Asinaria, Captivi*. . . . There are three forms of comedy. One is *comoedia palliata*, in which Greek costume is worn; some call this *tabernaria*. In *comoedia togata*, called so according to the type of the characters, the costume of togas is desired. *Comoedia Attelana* is composed of witticisms and jokes, which in themselves have an old elegance. (29)

Marvin T. Herrick notes:

> He [Donatus] also listed a variety of Roman dramatic forms, such as *praetextata, togata, attellana, rhyntonica, tabernaria, mimus*, without describing any of them in detail. Perhaps he deliberately avoided any explanation because he was not sure himself of what they were. . . . Acron offered a comment on the Ars Poetica 288 that led only to confusion. Acron stated: "There are kinds of comedy: *stataria, motoria, praetextata, tabernaria, togata, palliata*." (2)

It is obvious that new features appearing in comedies and tragedies required an analytic framework to avoid overwhelming theoreticians with the multitude of their specific aspects. Naturally, such entropy cannot be regulated without a global, comprehensive vision of the phenomenon of the dramatic genre. Empirical observations expanding wildly may quickly turn into a jungle.

Dramatic Genre and General Systems Theory

Reasons for considering the potential as the core of dramatic genre. Since the main definition of dramatic genre is based on the idea of seriousness and lightness (see *Merriam-Webster's Encyclopedia of Literature*), my question is, how does one measure the degree of seriousness? The diversity of literary works creates a wide range of novels, stories, dramas, and poems, which reveal different degrees of seriousness to be measured. The question concerning the degree of seriousness of the artistic work is linked directly to the measurement of the degree of power of any system. To take something seriously means to admit to its significant influence on one's development. At this point, one should refer to a measurement of the potential—the only way the degree of strength and richness of the entity can be defined. Thus, the degree of seriousness of a literary work is linked to the degree of strength and richness of its protagonists' potential, making the dramatic a phenomenon.

The need for finding isomorphism for types of dramatic genre. The theory of dramatic genre (based on the assumption that it is synonymous with dramaturgy) has been primarily occupied with the differences between tragedy and comedy, rarely searching for the isomorphic structure of all types of dramatic genre. The importance of the establishing of isomorphisms for different systems, however, was very well understood by proponents of general systems theory.[4]

The founder of general systems theory, Ludwig von Bertalanffy, writes:

> Thus, there exist models, principles, and laws that apply to generalized systems or their subclasses, irrespective of their particular kind, the nature of their component elements, and the relations or "forces" between them. It seems legitimate to ask for a theory, not of systems of a more or less special kind, but of universal principles applying to systems in general. . . . A consequence of the existence of general system properties is the appearance of structural similarities or isomorphisms in different fields. There are correspondences in the principles that govern the behavior of entities that are, intrinsically, widely different. (32–33)

Concerning dramatic genre, the fact that it becomes an integral part of any artistic work allows one to talk about isomorphisms of different dramatic types—a core that would contribute to the definition of the category. The next step should be directed towards establishing the degree and magnitude of the initial and dual parameters structuring the category, thus enabling a classification of the various types and branches that appear as a result of the measurement of the system's constituent parts.

Approaching the potential from a multidimensional perspective. Katsenelinboigen defines the notion of the potential from a multidimensional perspective. From this perspective, the potential of the system can be described in the following way: *Functionally,* the potential is linked to the system's ability to develop. From the *structural* point of view, the potential of the system consists of the following characteristics:

- Orientation (types of goals)
- Energy
- Will
- Cleverness (an independent parameter that is responsible for the integration of various characteristics)
- Physical and intellectual might
- Knowledge
- Experience
- State (material parameters and their coordinates)
- Position (in addition to material parameters—also includes relational ones)
- Values[5]

All these features can be transformed and applied to systems, even those that are not human systems.

Processing reveals styles, ways of connectivity among the system's elements, and methods for the system's transformation. The operative methods include reactive, or reflexive (taken from the Katsenelinboigen's typology), and selective. The ways of connectivity among the system's parameters—programming, predispositioning, and randomness—are represented from the point of view of their completeness and consistency. Programming is the formation of complete and consistent linkages between all the stages of the systems' development. Predispositioning is the formation of semiefficient linkages between the stages of the system's development. Randomness is the formation of inconsistent linkages between the stages of the system's development. The styles of system development are numerous, but in the present work we will focus on only two—positional and combinational.

As a rule, the development of a system is described as either depending on a chance occurrence or determined by the law as another extreme of a complete imbalance. Darwinism emphasizes the exclusive role of chance occurrences in the system, giving top priority to randomness as its method. This paradigm of thinking influences scholarly works, including literary criticism. For instance, Olson states that "in nature the ridiculous always occurs by *chance*" (19). This speculation is very questionable and leads to the more general problem of the role of chance occurrences in systems with different predispositions.[6] Later, we will discuss this problem in detail with regard to chance and fate in tragedy and comedy.

Conversely, creationism states that the system develops comprehensively; that is, that programming is the only method that participates in the development of the system. As Katsenelinboigen notices, both schools neglect the fact that the process of the system's development includes all methods, which may vary on different stages, depending on the system's goals and conditions. Thus, for literary analysis the understanding of methods that structure the decision-making process is crucial since it encompasses a wide field of artistic creation—from the general design of the work to the depiction of decision making by particular characters.

The *operator's* perspective represents the operator's set of values, which influence his or her decision making.

The *genetic* approach is concerned with the way the potential of the system was formed.

The potential of a system is revealed in complete measure when all the perspectives are taken into account. Needless to say, for those who seek simplifications and intend to approach a system from a single perspective, such a methodology may seem redundant. For those who understand the importance of such an approach, however, this method of thinking prevails. As an example of the consequences of simplifying methods of thinking, Katsenelinboigen often refers to Marxists. He states that Marxist theorists attempt to attribute everything to the economy, neglecting the great importance of all other independent factors (most significantly, human relationships). Such a theory is derived from extreme situations, when a lack of material objects is linked directly to people's deaths. It is true that starvation and epidemics appear from time to time in societies with a low standard of living, but as their economy changes, all other factors reveal their independent status.

Systems methodology is also a productive way of analyzing literary structure.[7] The multidimensional approach can be applied to both a particular literary work and to its individual characters.[8] In his book *Comparative Literature: Theory, Method, Application* (1998), Steven Tötösy de Zepetnek emphasizes the important role of a systems approach to literature, arguing that systems theory assists in better integrating the various artistic and nonartistic elements in a literary text.[9] Concerning the dramatic genre, the notion of the comic and comedy cannot simply be derived from the happy ending or the seriousness of the topic or the hierarchy inherent in society. All factors must be considered as independent characteristics, thereby acknowledging the multifaceted nature of this category, which is apparent when approached from the point of view of its structure, function, processing, genesis, and the role of the operator.

Subjectivity of the Evaluative Process

Subjectivity of the evaluative category: chess and literature. According to Katsenelinboigen's predispositioning theory, objectivity of intrinsic evaluations appears only as a result of complete and consistent linkages among all parts of the system. Extrinsic evaluations of programmed and nonprogrammed systems, however, could be just as objective as subjective, depending on various factors whose discussion goes beyond the scope of the present topic.

As mentioned above, another common temptation for critics dealing with laughter is to determine conditions in which the appearance of laughter can be linked with the initial conditions in a complete and consistent way. Such an attempt is a result of a lack of understanding of the nature of the evaluative category, which for indeterministic systems is based on subjectivity.

This pioneering approach to the evaluative process is the subject of Katsenelinboigen's work on indeterministic systems. The roots of one's subjective evaluation lie in the fact that the executor cannot be separated from the evaluator, who evaluates the system in accordance with his or her own particular ability to develop it. This can be observed in chess, in which the same position is evaluated differently by different chess players, or in literature with regard to hermeneutics. Katsenelinboigen writes:

> The subjective element arises not because the set of positional parameters and their valuations are formed based on a player's intuition. Rather, the choice of relevant parameters depends on the actual executor of the position, that is, the particular strengths and weaknesses of a given player. The role of the executor becomes vital because the actual realization of the position is not known beforehand, so future moves will have to be made based on the contingent situation at hand. (*Indeterministic Economics* 70)

In talking about subjective and objective valuations of the positional variables, Katsenelinboigen explains why subjectivity of the managerial decision is inevitable:

> The original subjective evaluation of the situation by the decision-maker is critical in the creative strategic management. Subjectivity of the managerial decisions is inevitable due to the intrinsically indeterministic nature of the strategic management, meaning that the subjectivity arises not just because of the lack of scientific foundation in business management. The effective approach to the strategic decision-making, as demonstrated in the game of chess, presupposes that each player has a unique, individual vision of his strategic position. To make it more systematic, one should not substitute the player's intuition with some objective laws that relate essential and positional parameters, but rather complement the intuition with the statistical analysis. (*Concept of Indeterminism* 164)

When approaching a literary work that is an indeterministic system, one interprets its structure based on one's ability to explore it. In each particular case, the interpreter endows each artistic element with a weight, then integrates them all into a whole in accordance with his or her vision and skills to wield the manifold artistic elements; this process cannot be unified. One may agree or disagree with the weights ascribed to certain parameters or with the way they are integrated into a whole. However, one must understand that no interpretation can be called "wrong" unless it is based on facts that contradict the information provided in the text or it reveals a gap between the logic of the analysis and the examples chosen by the critic. By "information" I mean characters' names, their positions, origins, preferences, and the like. For instance, if in my research on myth in Chekhov's plays I propose an association between Shamraev, the manager of Sorin's estate, and Poseidon, I must base my speculations on details provided in the text; namely, the name of the protagonist, his position as the manager of the estate, his love for horses, and the like. This would assist me in finding an isomorphism between both characters, no matter how "contrived" it may seem to other scholars who would integrate all these details differently. A detailed discussion of this method of analysis will be the subject of subsequent chapters. I should stress now that only material parameters and their valuations can be objectivized and made uniform, but relational ones are mostly subjective and individual. Katsenelinboigen writes:

> The evaluation of predisposition raises some difficult issues regarding the implementation (follow up or continuity) of this assessment using uniform and objective methods. My thesis in a nutshell is the following: while the set of essentials and their valuations (particularly semi-conditional valuations) can be *objectified* and made *uniform*, the set of positional parameters and their valuations is largely *individualized* and *subjective*.
>
> In constructive terms, the difference between individualized and uniform assessment comes to the fore when we try to isolate the operator (one assessing the position) from the one who has to follow up on it (execute it). When assessment is individualized, the one doing the assessment is inexorably linked to the one doing the implementation. By contrast, uniform methods of assessing a position allow anybody (with some qualifications) to attain the same result. This issue will again come up when we look at subjectivity versus objectivity.
>
> Individualized as well as uniform methods of assessing a position can be duplicated to a degree (ultimately, even *formalized*). Subjectivity and objectivity reflect the degree of reproducibility of the result. Subjective assessment implies that the operator (one assessing the position) has no explicit clear-cut knowledge of his method and so it cannot be duplicated by anyone else (often times, including the operator himself). Subjectivity with regard to positional parameters is informed by the fact that these parameters are formulated and assessed by the players themselves who are

often times unable to formalize their thought processes. (*Concept of Indeterminism* 34–35)

Attempts to derive laughter from a situation in a complete and consistent way. The neglect of subjectivity causes confusion in approaching some basic problems in literary criticism, including the concept of laughter, which is traditionally associated with a search for an algorithm. Hegel, for instance, attempts to trace laughter to the contrast between the object and the method of its representation.[10] Freud attributes laughter to a subconscious reduction of tension; Schopenhauer does the same based on the idea of incongruity.[11]

As one can see, the common approach is to attempt to derive laughter from the initial parameter—whether it is incongruity or tensions or any other condition—assuming that *anyone* would react in the same way to the same situations. Descartes therefore affirms that laughter is a manifestation of joy mixed with either surprise or hatred or both. Thomas Hobbes links laughter with glory, saying that "[s]udden Glory, is the passion which maketh those Grimaces called Laughter" (43).

The establishment of a programming linkage between the initial conditions (a situation) and the final outcome (a laughing reaction) is still unrealistic, as tempting as it may be. As experience shows, laughter cannot be derived directly from certain situations. In reality, anything can arouse either laughter or tears—these manifestations are symmetrical, for they can be applied to similar feelings. There are people who cry after receiving exciting news and people who scream and laugh in analogous situations; there are people who are in tears after overcoming an infirmity, and there are people who start laughing for the same reason; there are people who are so relieved after having good sex that they laugh, while there are also people whose sexual relief is celebrated by tears. Even sorrow can be manifested as either laughter or weeping. In her discussion of two Bakhtinian paradoxes regarding the comic and the laughable, Caryl Emerson points out that "Bakhtin never systematically discussed the relations . . . between laughter and tragedy, or between comedy and ethical duty" (9).

Joy, rage, anger, love, relief, tension, and the like, represent a wide range of emotions whose evaluation may be manifested in laughter, as well as in tears.[12] Even physical pain and some unpleasant feelings, such as excessive tickling, can be accompanied by laughter.[13] It would therefore be a mistake to link the notion of the comic with laughter, for laughter could be manifested from many evaluations, including those linked with lethal outcomes. As a leading theoretician of the neo-Aristotelian school, Olson notices, "[W]eeping, for instance, can betoken extreme joy as well as extreme grief, as we all know, or can find out by watching the next Miss Universe when she wins the contest; and laughter presents the same ambiguity" (11). Irrespective of his understanding of the indeterministic nature of human reactions, however, even Olson did not escape the temptation to find a successive linkage between the initial condition and the final reaction to it.

In his *Theory of Comedy* (1968), Olson, following Spinoza, reasonably assumes that laughter is not an emotion but an expression of another emotion *katastasis*. Analyzing the emotion conducive to laughter, Olson writes:

> Indeed, we are now in a position to define that emotion: it is a relaxation, or, as Aristotle would say, a *katastasis*. . . . We can see now why this is a pleasant emotion, for concern of any kind induces tension; the relaxation of concern involves, as Aristotle would say, the settling of the soul into its natural or normal condition, which is always pleasant. Because it is pleasant, its anticipation is also pleasant; which is the reason why people are pleased when a favorite comedian is announced, and why one listens to a joke with pleasure, even before the point is reached; and the fulfillment of the anticipation is pleasant as well. (16–17)

In defining *katastasis* as the initial condition for laughter, Olson first discusses a proper degree of relaxation that would allow one to settle "the soul into its natural or normal condition, which is always pleasant" (16). At this point, he explicitly discusses the degree of the initial parameter—relaxation—and implies a positive evaluation of it. He does not, however, discuss the degree and magnitude of the dual parameter, assuming that the so-called normal condition is evaluated positively and with the same degree of strength by everyone (a unification of the evaluative process). His initial statement that a certain degree of relaxation evokes pleasant emotions in anyone is therefore questionable since relaxation can also be evaluated negatively by certain types, especially the artistic one, for which the "normal condition" may signify mere routine and boredom. The degree and magnitude of such a negative evaluation may tremendously influence one's behavior in such a way that one might even seek strong stimulants, such as drugs or alcohol, to change that condition. Olson's first generalization is therefore fit only for a certain group of people, but if the group consists mostly of the artistic type, it may not work at all.

The next statement of Olson's theory is built upon his previous conclusions about the proper degree of relaxation and this, he assumes, "is the reason why people are pleased when a favorite comedian is announced, and why one listens to a joke with pleasure, even before the point is reached; and the fulfillment of the anticipation is pleasant as well" (17). Once again, the chain of assertions is built upon the assumption that everything that follows relaxation—the comedian and the jokes—will be evaluated positively by everyone and will thus generate pleasure again and again. But what if the "favorite comedian" suddenly bothers a spectator for some subjective reason, even though the spectator is relaxing? To discuss this would mean to admit that the comic is something else, and that it may or may not be correlated with laughter or pleasure; because regardless of these reactions, the spectator is still able to distinguish between a comedian and a tragedian even if the former performs deaths and the latter laughs hysterically.

After the chain of assertions is almost completed, Olson proceeds to the last part of his proof. He insists that a combination of the following will lead one to laughter: the excessive pleasure of a spectator, a favorite comedian, and some sudden turn in a comedian's jokes. He writes, "any excess of this emotion, particularly when sudden, will lead us . . . to laughter; because the sudden is always the unexpected and because emotions which are unexpected will always be excessive" (17). Yet again, even if fulfilled, all these conditions cannot prevent the appearance of quite different reactions, such as indignation, which may occur in case the joke is indecent and is evaluated as highly negative by the spectator. In general, however, Olson's formula may work for a certain group of spectators and, at this point, has everything to do with a calculation of the probability of the comedian's success. It may have the pragmatic application of assisting directors and producers in creating a favorable atmosphere, which would further the spectators' laughing reaction. At the same time, these observations have nothing to do with the notion of the comic and comedy, which cannot be derived from the spectators' emotional state.

Laughter and weeping appear as subjective reactions to certain evaluations, and their occurrences cannot be programmed. Katsenelinboigen distinguishes between subjective and individual values in the sense that the latter can be objectivized, but the former always remains a part of the unique that cannot be formalized. For example, one can analyze a customer's particular preferences for food and make a special menu and recipes so that anyone could prepare them. One can then say that the customer's individual values are objectivized. However, one may not be able to calculate which day the customer would ask for a certain combination of foods or ingredients because this would necessitate a consideration of a great number of initial and dual parameters and their various degrees—a subjective choice that is impossible to predetermine.

The same can be said of laughter and tears, which, as shown above, can be calculated based on statistics in only some particular, simple cases. Unification does not work for the majority of other cases, however, for the linkage between one's evaluation of the entity and one's reaction to it is subjective—it is based on the observer's subjective choice of self-expression. Olson states that

> the human body tends to cathart any excessive emotion by certain physical outlets, such as laughter and weeping. Since these outlets are few, and the emotions many, an ambiguity ensues which parallels that of verbal ambiguity when a single word may represent many distinct, and sometimes even contrary things. (11)

It seems to me, however, that the ambiguity arises not as a result of the "few outlets" but as a result of the *subjective expression* of the evaluation of emotions; the expression may change even within the same observer in analogous situations regardless of the number of "outlets."

It seems that both laughter and weeping belong to a multifunctional category, but scholars typically attempt to discover a single function of laughter that can shed light on this phenomenon. George Meredith, for instance, focuses on the corrective purpose of laughter. Konrad Lorenz associates laughter with group behavior among animals; he analyzed specific situations in which aggression was thwarted and a laughlike phenomenon appeared among herds. Alexander Bain's concept represents the violent nature of laughter, which stems from one's attempt to discomfort or suppress his rival. Analogously, Henri Bergson outlines the destructive function of laughter: "[L]aughter is, above all, a corrective. Being intended to humiliate, it must make a painful impression on the person against whom it is directed" (187). All of these observations on the functions of laughter certainly complement each other and enrich our understanding of this phenomenon that cannot be limited to a single function. They once again confirm that the correlation between the evaluation and its manifestation cannot be unified.

Objective methods of evoking laughter and their subjective evaluation. Characters may evoke either sympathy or indifference, and this cannot be completely controlled by the author, since he or she does not determine one's perception of the protagonists. The author may, however, elaborate devices to partially influence the audience's emotional state and thus assist the reader/spectator in adjusting to the author's valuations. From the viewpoint of genre recognition, certain artistic devices serve to control the degree of one's emotional involvement. In the traditional comedy,[14] for instance, the author finds a way to alienate the audience from the protagonist in order to decrease the degree of emotional involvement. Some of the devices can be formalized while others are the property of their creators.

All artistic devices used in comedy fulfill the same function: humor, jokes, word play, and other similar devices are intended to serve as "separating" means that keep the observer alienated from the observed. In extreme cases, this alienation may elicit cruelty and heartlessness on the part of the reader/spectator. At the same time, all these devices may evoke pity and sorrow in a particular reader/spectator, suggesting that the application of artistic devices does not assist in creating uniformity in the audience's reactions. Different interpretations of the same characters then result. The reaction to humor, jokes, funny incidents, and the like, depends on the individual. The artist may intend to create a very laughable situation, but the reader can be left totally indifferent or bored. Not every reader/spectator would enjoy distortions of the comic character, even though pure—comical—comedy implies "harmless" distortions intended to prevent the common spectator from feeling for the protagonists.[15]

In choosing one or another type of dramatic genre for his or her work, the artist attempts to moderate the intensity of the audience's emotional involvement. This means that even if one feels for the comic character, it would not be the deep emotional stress typical of a reaction to tragedy. Different nouns are used to describe the differing degrees of one's emotional involvement: thus, the word *pity* is used to emphasize a feeling typical of the strong toward the weak; the word *compassion* conveys the idea of a confluence of values inherent in the observer and the observed. (Such a merger is based on the idea of equality between the observer and the observed.) Conversely, some readers/spectators may feel deeply for the comic character but remain indifferent to the tragic hero's misfortunes. With regard to the comedy of a new type, the audience's involvement can oscillate between very strong (as in drama or tragedy) and light (as in traditional comedy). The reasons for this variation in reactions will be discussed below.

The further development of comedic genres and the appearance of unfunny comedies, including Balzac's *Human Comedy*, emphasized that comedy could exist with less laughable content, thus proving that the laughable (in all its varieties, including the ridiculous and the funny) and the comic are not synonymous. Nor should they be derived from one another.

Survival and Development with Regard to Dramatic Genre

The outcome and a predisposition to development. One more aspect must be discussed: the influence of traditional and new paradigms of thinking on literary criticism. In criticism, the category of survival becomes a basis for defining the dramatic genre of a literary work. Grawe writes, "Comedy as seen from a formal perspective is the representation of life patterned to demonstrate or to assert a faith in human survival, often including or emphasizing how that survival is possible or under what conditions that survival takes place" (17). Most of today's research on comedy considers survival to be a sufficient defining characteristic of comedy. A fundamental study on survival as a core of comedy was published in an anthology *The Terrain of Comedy* (1982). The understanding of survival proposed by the editor of the anthology, Louise Cowan, however, is based on the idea of local tactics. For instance, talking about *infernal comedy*, Cowan states that here survival is related to the various types of deceit that come into play during the process of maintaining hope. True, for a short term such tactics may preserve one's hope, but they will eventually lead to complete destruction. We need only to recall Stalin's Russia, where hope was based on deceit, in order to appreciate the inevitable tragic outcome of such an approach.

It seems to me that a new millennium requires a more modern approach to the concept of survival, based on new views of economics and general systems theory.

While thinking about comedy, I asked myself two questions: (1) Is the category of survival a sufficient condition for comedy? and (2) Is it really the category that distinguishes comedy from other genres? I reflected on three plays to answer these questions: *Romeo and Juliet*, *Oedipus the King*, and *The Seagull*. The idea of survival is present in all of them. In *Romeo and Juliet*, the society survives through the reconciliation of the families. (Though the question remains, for how long?) In *Oedipus the King*, the protagonist survives along with a part of his environment (again the question remains as to the longevity of such survival). In *The Seagull*, the death of a protagonist is combined with the picture of the world surviving, though the same question of the strength of such survival is in the air.

One may argue that survival in comedy implies a survival of the whole, including every character. But how does this operate in the comedies mentioned above (including Balzac's *Human Comedy*) that end in disaster—death and loss—and that are woven from scenes of world disintegration? This question is puzzling, and the answer requires a nonorthodox methodology. In addition, one may wonder if such a question is valid only for modern times or if it is also relevant to ancient comedy, since dramatic genre is a developing category and may essentially change in time. Surprisingly, the question of survival is vital for some ancient comedies, such as Aristophanes' *Frogs*, in which it becomes the subject and turning point of the play. At the beginning of *Frogs*, Dionysus visits the underworld in order to take back to Earth the best tragic poet, who could help Dionysus's citizens establish order in their city. Dionysus must then choose between two distinguished poets—Aeschylus and Euripides—who are portrayed as complete fools. The idea of survival thus becomes very questionable; a world guided by such obtuse gods and silly poets would hardly survive.

While talking about survival, especially in works with happy endings, one must think of what lies beyond the happy ending; in other words, about a predisposition to long-term survival. In actuality, the artist creates an open end, making the reader/spectator speculate about the future development of the universe. In some cases, therefore, a happy ending may be very questionable in terms of the protagonists' ability to develop in the future. For instance, in *A Midsummer Night's Dream*, Hermia's father, Egeus, does not seem to accept his daughter's choice but is simply obeying Theseus's order. By the end of the play, Theseus announces his will and demands that "couples shall eternally be knit." In remembering Egeus's former resistance to his daughter's love, his unwillingness to reconsider his decision, and his highly emotional and vulnerable nature that does not tolerate others' superiority, one may assume that this character predisposes the system to further conflicts and changes—either positive (most likely) or negative. The same analysis is required to understand whether or not the final reconciliation in *Romeo and Juliet* will lead the society to a new development.

First and foremost, it is not the outcome but the predisposition created at the end of the artistic work that is the artist's focus. The main puzzle for the reader, therefore, is how to judge the outcome that occurs in a specific environment. O. Henry's "The Gift of the Magi" (1906) may serve as the best example of how an author integrates the outcome with a predisposition for further development. In the story, two young people who are deeply in love want to buy Christmas presents to surprise and entertain the other. The only problem is that they are very poor and have too little money to buy what they think would be the best present. In order to make their dreams come true they sacrifice their most valuable things. Alas! Their intentions end in fiasco—their gifts are useless without the original possessions, which were sold in order to buy the presents. Thus, in the end, the lovers appear to be losers and their current position is ridiculous. But is it really so? The story provides rich material for debate and differing opinions; but the author wants to make his statement clear, and the last lines of the story are exactly about the way he sees a predisposition for the future development of the couple.

> The magi, as you know, were wise men—wonderfully wise men—who brought gifts to the Babe in the manger. They invented the art of giving Christmas presents. Being wise, their gifts were no doubt wise ones, possibly bearing the privilege of exchange in case of duplication. And here I have lamely related to you the uneventful chronicle of two foolish children in a flat who most unwisely sacrificed for each other the greatest treasures of their house. But in a last word to the wise of these days let it be said that of all who give gifts these two were the wisest. Of all who give and receive gifts, such as they are wisest. Everywhere they are wisest. They are the magi. (12)

The message is clear: though from the local point of view the protagonists have failed, from the global perspective they have gained. They have gained each other's love and respect by revealing their mutual loyalty and willingness to sacrifice materials in the name of the relationship—the most valuable gift in the world. In the game of chess, this sacrifice of material or relational parameters for the sake of a predisposition is called a positional sacrifice. Katsenelinboigen writes that in the case of a positional sacrifice, both the material and the relational are "forsaken for the sake of improving the positional parameters, that is, the actual compensation for the sacrificed material is by no means apparent" (*Indeterministic Economics* 83).

In creating a predisposition of his characters to future development, the artist plays a sophisticated game with the reader. To perform a proper analysis, one should wield a special methodology that would allow one to inquire into the potential of the universe represented by the artist.

Survival and development as two paradigms of thinking. In general, artistic works show a certain stage of survival of the universe, and the question is how to distinguish between those stages. In approaching the notion of the dramatic genre, I applied Katsenelinboigen's concept of the development of indeterministic systems. Katsenelinboigen outlines two types of survival in talking about socioeconomic systems—short-term survival and long-term survival (*Indeterministic Economics* 33–35). Following Russell Ackoff's typology (45), Katsenelinboigen further distinguishes between three categories—survival, growth, and development—that, though interrelated, are independent. To elaborate these categories, he approaches them from the functional, structural and process-oriented points of view:

> From the functional point of view, survival represents an extreme case with emphasis placed on maintaining a minimum level of vital parameters comprising the system. Growth presupposes an increase (as judged by a preset criterion) in the values of parameters already incorporated into the system. (*Indeterministic Economics* 33–35)

Development is accordingly defined as the creation of changes in both materials and the relationships between them. Katsenelinboigen states that development is responsible for the changeability of the system:

> From the structural point of view, survival is aimed at preserving the existing objects; growth indicates an increase in the number of existing objects; and development implies a variety of objects (with new ones appearing in the course of development) as well as their interrelations.
>
> From the process-oriented point of view, survival is a search for a stationary state; growth must facilitate the creation of a complete and

consistent mechanism of coordinated growth of the sought-for variables; and development implies the creation of a mechanism that supports both the creation and the resolution of incompleteness and inconsistency in the existing mechanism....

... long-term survival is impossible without growth, and long-term growth presupposes development. Proceeding in the backward direction, it is obvious that long-term development as long-term growth require survival.... I am a proponent of the primacy of development with growth and survival allotted a subordinate role. (33–35)

Development and dramatic genre. My approach to dramatic genre is based on distinguishing between development and survival, for it assists me in making a more detailed classification of types of artistic universes represented in literary works. I thus distinguish between these systems: those that do not survive, those that survive without development, and those that are able to develop with survival implied.

One can speak about the survival of the Chekhovian comedic universe. For instance, irrespective of Treplev's suicide, Arkadina will continue to amuse her audience in Kharkov, and Nina will continue in her plans to "rise" in Elets; Uncle Vanya will somehow participate in keeping the estate with Sonya; and the three sisters will continue to dream about Moscow. As analysis reveals, however, there is no hope for development in the plays; the movement of life is just a continuation of the same, a repetition of a cycle that cannot be changed. In creating his characters' predisposition, Chekhov finds a way to reveal their inability to develop. This lack of internal change kills Treplev and makes Trigorin depressed. The same thing happens to Uncle Vanya, who envies the achievements of others and blames all his troubles on them. Even such a seemingly creative protagonist as Astrov causes only destruction in the estate.

The same can be said for Balzacian protagonists, whose lives are devoted to their utilitarian interests and pragmatic needs. No innovative thought can appear in such an environment, and the protagonists ultimately become victims of their way of life and their way of thinking. Their ruination does not, however, change the essential predisposition of the world, as it does in tragedy or drama. The comic hero, whether a villain or a virtuous character, cannot have an impact on the stationary state of his universe. Even the death of the comic character fails to influence the primary balance of his world. Chekhov's comedy is a graphic example of such unchangeable routines that continue despite death *(The Seagull, Three Sisters)*; love *(Uncle Vanya)*; and protagonists' losses *(The Cherry Orchard)*.

Conversely, the worlds of tragedy and drama often represent the idea of societal development through protagonists' failures or deaths. At this point,

Gary Waller's definition of comedy and tragedy—accordingly based on joy and terror—presents a problem (2–3). The tragic hero is not the one who dies but the one whose death has an impact on the world. Tragedy is thus concerned with a loss of a "star of the first magnitude," whose potential is uniquely rich. *Romeo and Juliet* is the best example of how the protagonists are able to stop a society's destructive feud and direct it to its new development. In terms of development, Romeo and Juliet refused to survive without each other because this would stop their mutual development. They preferred to stay together in death and thus became a symbol of true love—a strong impetus for the development of their society.

To conclude, the outcome serves to reveal a predisposition of the entire system to further development. No matter how many characters survive in the end, the question of their ability to develop remains open. There can be different combinations of the outcomes, in which either society, protagonists, or both survive; but in some cases, a small group of survivors are able to develop, while in others the entire group of characters are not able to move further. The story of Noah's Ark can serve as an example of the former and *The Cherry Orchard* of the latter. The world of comedy has a limited potential that enables its survival but not its development.

Though the question of the protagonist's potential, with regard to genre, has not been approached in literary criticism from the point of view of predispositioning theory, one may find some hints; for instance, Aristotle draws one's attention to the fact that comedy is "action . . . lacking in magnitude (*Poetics I* 49)." Aristotle does not analyze the cause of this low magnitude because he considers only actions, not characters. Nevertheless, in terms of predispositioning, actions of low magnitude imply limited potentials for those who are involved in them. Frye states that "Aristotle's words for good and bad are *spuodaios* and *phaulos*, which have a figurative sense of weighty and light" (33). Even so, these notions are not elaborated by Aristotle, and one may wonder if that which Aristotle called "weight" was about one's social status or one's inner ability. Unfortunately, there is no clear answer, because the analysis of protagonists' potential was not a concern of the Aristotelian school.

Bergson, in his essay "Laughter" (1900), contrasts the mechanical and the living and states that the comic consists of something mechanical. He does not develop his observations on the nature of the mechanical, however, and considers it to be in connection with the laughable, affirming that the mechanical generates laughter. In light of the current analysis, it is possible to speculate about the structure of the mechanical as outlined by Bergson. Obviously, an object with a limited potential gives the impression of something mechanical, for it is lacking in an inner ability to develop. The object with a weak potential is predisposed to a certain programmed way of acting;

it is not capable of changing its automatic behavior, which makes it resemble a mechanism.

Therefore, Bergson's statement that "the comic does not exist outside the pall of what is strictly human" (62) is not valid as soon as the focus is shifted from laughter to potential: any system with a weak potential can be perceived as comic by any other system that may or may not be human.

Summary

One should distinguish between dramatic genre and dramaturgy; the latter is a type of literary work intended for theatrical performances.

The notion of the dramatic is linked to the potential of literary characters and their universe, so that when the artist subtitles his work, he or she implies the degree of strength and richness of the potential of the world he created. Therefore, the notion of the comic as linked to the limited potential cannot be reduced to the laughable/funny and vice versa.

The potential makes the dramatic belong to the general systems phenomenon. The potential of the entity must be approached from a multidimensional perspective to present a broader view of its various aspects. The use of artistic devices in structuring the potential of the artistic work makes the process of evaluation more sophisticated, enriching the notion of the potential in general.

It is neither the degree of the laughable nor the type of outcome, including survival, that distinguishes different types of dramatic genre but rather a predisposition to further development created in the work.

Part Two
Dramedy, Drama, and Comedy:
A New Classification

In this part of the book, I perform textual analysis to illustrate some of the theoretical statements made in part one. This part contains a comparative analysis of types and branches of dramatic genre from three basic points of view. First, I approach main characters of the same strata and status as represented in different dramatic types and branches. I analyze kings, gods, lovers, and servants from the point of view of the richness and strength of their potential, which reveals the essential differences in their representations in dramedy, drama, and comedy.

Second, I consider works of the same or of similar topics from the point of view of changes in the magnitude of topics in comedies, dramedies, and dramas. My analysis is based exclusively on the potential of analogous characters—"twins"—without regard to humor, jokes, or other devices traditionally discussed with regard to the "light" type of dramatic genre.

Third, I focus on the old question of fate and chance in comedy and tragedy. My discussion of this problem is based on Katsenelinboigen's predispositioning theory, which concerns stages of the system's development and the role of chance occurrences.

As a result, the dramatic genre of some works is either redefined or clarified in accordance with the degree of richness and strength of their characters' potential.

Protagonists of the Same Strata and Status in Different Types of Dramatic Genre   3

In this chapter, I compare protagonists of the same strata and status with regard to their potential. We go through a gallery of kings, servants, gods, and lovers in order to reveal what makes some extremely limited and others very sophisticated, without regard to their social or divine status or to the amusing situations in which they may find themselves.

Obtuse Gods

Gods as authority: concerning a degree of idolization. In the context of the predispositioning theory, the first question that naturally arises is how characters of supreme status are represented in comedy. Do they lack their great potentiality or do they retain their powerful potential? Traditionally, the appearance of gods in comedy has been explained exclusively from the point of view of genesis as linked to behaviorism. While speaking of gods as comic figures, critics refer to comedic cults, which prescribed certain behavior to gods; but critics do not inquire into the structure that makes it possible to represent gods as comic figures. Kenneth J. Reckford writes:

> When we think about religion and comedy, we are apt to think of holiday license, the way that disgraceful words, gestures, and actions are sanctioned by religious tradition in the theater of Dionysus. But although this *aischrologia* is a basic, much-loved component of Old Comedy, what is still more basic—and what lies behind Dicaepolis' Phalos—is the affirmation of life, the sense of something to celebrate. (48)

But if comedy exploits religious symbols in such an indecent way, it may not be far from cynicism, no matter what justifiable goals it is based on, including "the affirmation of life." Cynicism appears as a result of a derision of values, which are considered global and unconditional and often serve as strategic constraints in the development of the future. If the mockery is in a universe that is based on such values, it becomes a cynical attack—an encroachment on its basic principles of development, which are meant to preserve it from a crash. It is highly unlikely that such a barbaric intention structured Old and New Comedy, whose introduction of the world of "divinities" had nothing to do with nihilism of the moral and sublime but rather had to do with a clarification of what fits in those categories.

To me, the introduction of gods in comedy only sharpens the question of the inner and the outer, the imitation and the original, from the point of view of their potential and predisposition to development. Comedies that exploit god figures send an important message to the audience concerning the appearance that can be deceptive; one must therefore know how to distinguish between intrinsically rich and poor entities, even if they have the same appearance.

Gods and heroes in comedy are not intelligent supreme beings humiliated by local-minded mortals, which would otherwise be a cynical mockery of the sublime. They themselves are incarnations of pragmatism and narrow-mindedness, making it possible to represent them in a state of disgrace without drifting into cynicism. It is true that even the idea of representing divinities in an unfavorable way may seem blasphemous to some readers/spectators, but in this case one should discuss the problem of the authoritative mentality—to what extent one is willing to idolize one's leader even if that leader makes horrible mistakes or is an empty creature. Another extreme of this would be the mockery of a decent person.

The relationships between people and gods in different religions reflect the attitude to leadership inherent in different ethnic groups. For instance, as Katsenelinboigen shows, it is typical for the Torah to represent God as a being to whom one can talk, not to whom one exclusively prays and bows. It is always a dialogue between God and a human being, a conversation, that teaches both sides; and it is not only the person, but God as well, who may change his previous thoughts and reconsider his actions as did happen when Moses persuaded God not to destroy the Jewish people (Numbers 14:11–20).

According to Katsenelinboigen's interpretation of the Torah, despite human beings' limited ability to govern the world, God feels that it is extremely important to establish parity with them, and so he chooses some men with whom he establishes a covenant:

> According to the covenant, God agrees to multiply the people of Abraham, to make him the progenitor of many peoples, and to give him and his descendants all of the land of Canaan forever; a Jew, on the other hand, must obey the testament handed down by God demanding that every Jew be circumcised.[1] (*Selected Topics* 268)

Based on the above, the idea of gods in comedy pertains to a general understanding of limitations inherent in anything, including divinities, and of the danger that may occur as a result of blind subjugation to authority. It is the same idea expressed in the Hans Christian Anderson story "The Emperor and His New Clothes" that urges society to be critical and not to judge by the shell but by the pearl growing inside.

Aristophanes' "Frogs." The first thing that catches one's eye in Aristophanes' *Frogs* is that the author introduces characters of high strata and supreme status as typically comedic personages by virtue of their poor potential. However, even in such an apparently comic work, in which all characters are the same in terms of their potential, there is still a hierarchy in place. An "intellectual" circle of poets and their "judge," Dionysus, is opposed to Heracles, who is an incarnation of brute, physical force. In other words, the degree of strength and richness of the potential oscillates from weak and poor to very weak and poor.

At the beginning of the play, Dionysus visits the underworld in order to bring back to Earth the tragic poet who could best help his citizens establish order in the city. Dionysus has a very important mission; he must choose between Aeschylus and Euripides, two significant poets whom he equally respects and values. As he admits to Pluto, "For one I think wise; the other I love" (108). This judge of poetry, however, whose choice is supposed to influence his citizens' future, is nothing but a narrow-minded, obtuse creature calling himself a "son of a keg." Despite the fact that his intellect has a very low power, Dionysus seems to be a genius in comparison to Heracles, who appears as an incarnation of a supreme physical force and supermasculinity. The latter only intensifies the contrast between the two of them, especially since Dionysus is the incarnation of cowardice; each time he sees danger, he wets his pants:

> *Xanthias:* You're absurd. Won't you stand up quick before some stranger sees you?
> *Dionysus:* But I'm weak.
> Bring a sponge for my heart.
> *Xanthias:* Here, do it yourself—Where? O golden
> gods, is there where you wear your heart?
> *Dionysus:* It was afraid
> and crept down into my lower bowel.
>
> (70)

This pathological coward has no dignity—he demands his servant exchange clothes with him in order that he not be recognized by his enemies:

> *Dionysus:* Come then, since you love boldness and are manly,
> You become me, and take this club

and lion-skin, if you are not faint-hearted.
In turn, I'll be the baggage boy.

(71)

The contrast between Dionysus and Heracles, however, is a comical opposition because Heracles' glamorous appearance is about muscles, not about brains. When Dionysus tells him that the reading of Euripides' *Andromeda* arouses a desire in him, Heracles thinks that Dionysus speaks of an awakening of sexual desires. In order to clarify his statement, Dionysus tries to find an adequate analogy that can be easily understood by the obtuse Heracles, so he compares his feeling to a "desire for pea soup":

> *Dionysus:* In fact while at sea reading Euripides' Andromeda, I was racked by a desire so strong you can't imagine.
> *Heracles:* A desire? How big?
> *Dionysus:* Small as Big Molon!
> *Heracles:* For a woman?
> *Dionysus:* Oh, no!
> *Heracles:* Then a boy?
> *Dionysus:* Not at all.
> *Heracles:* A man then?
> . . .
> *Dionysus:* I can't say,
> But I'll tell you through a riddle.
> Have you ever had a desire for pea soup?
> *Heracles:* Pea soup, my god, a thousand times.
> *Dionysus:* Clear, or shall I speak another way?
> *Heracles:* Not about pea soup. I know it well.

(53)

The emphasis on material parameters, such as pea soup, suggests a high degree of primitivism in characters who are not designed for more sophisticated tasks. Heracles is unable to understand desires other than those linked with carnal pleasures; likewise, Dionysus is incapable of appreciating relational parameters in life and art. Dionysus is shown as an extremely stingy creature—stinginess signifies the neglect of relational parameters and the exclusive focus on material ones. Stingy people are willing to sacrifice their relationships with others in the name of material things because they are too narrow-minded to understand the consequences and to see one step ahead—the fear of losing materials blinds them. The scene in which Dionysus bargains with the corpse, who wants to be paid for carrying Dionysus's heavy luggage, becomes a great satire about such a narrow, pragmatic mind that at one moment wins a penny and loses a fortune at the next:

Dionysus: You there! I mean you, dead man!
You sir? Want to carry a little luggage?
Corpse: How much?
Dionysus: These here.
Corpse: Will you pay two drachma?
Dionysus: No, by Zeus, less.
Corpse: (to his pallbearers) Go on, down the road!
Dionysus: Wait, my friend. Perhaps I can deal.
Corpse: If you won't plunk down two drachma, forget it.
Dionysus: Take one-and-a-half.
Corpse: Hell, I'd rather be alive again.

(58)

Stinginess is often correlated with a lack of artistic imagination, since the artistic imagination deals with sophisticated relational parameters not appreciated by the pragmatic mind. It is therefore no wonder that Dionysus is completely insensitive to metaphoric language and is unable to understand a simple figure of speech:

Charon: Take the oar! If anyone's sailing, hurry up!
What are you *doing*?
Dionysus: Me? Nothing
but sitting on the oar, as you ordered.

(59)

Naturally, the question arises, what kind of judge of poetry could this simpleton be? This does not, however, much concern an environment that is little better than its supreme judge. The two poets, Aeschylus and Euripides, appear as extremely pragmatic, vainglorious creatures whose only concern is to win the struggle for a "throne near Pluto," the god of the underworld. The poets are seized by petty, worldly passions, striving for special treatment and valuing momentary pleasures. They curse as "peddlers," struggling for their ridiculous privileges, so that even Dionysus cannot take it any longer; he tries to discontinue their senseless quarrel, reminding them that such indecent behavior does not befit poets of their stature. All in vain! They do not listen to any admonitions and get carried away. In their struggle for primacy, they come to resemble street vendors who fight for the same spot. They humiliate each other, trying to nullify the other's achievements, but there is nothing witty and thoughtful about their criticism, just simple, primitive profanity. Aeschylus calls Euripides "a creator of freaks," while Euripides claims that Aeschylus is nothing more than a "flowery, crackling braggart."

The way in which they compete reveals their common primitivism and common inability to see their blunders and inaccuracies because they are one and the same kind. If Aeschylus overtakes Euripides in one part of the competition, Euripides has his revenge in another part. In general, they appear to be two extremes—idealism and pragmatism—which are similarly distinguished by banal thinking and limited abilities. Such a binary view of the world as represented by two distinguished poets suggests an extremely poor and weak potential of the entire society, whose acme is so ridiculously trite. It is obvious that neither of them would be able to propose any valuable suggestions concerning the salvation of the citizens. As a matter of fact, both poets reveal a very primitive understanding of politics and economics while trying to present their models of survival, and although Dionysus gives his preference to Aeschylus, neither choice would change the situation in essence.

The story is therefore not about decent, noble characters in amusing situations but about primitive creatures who, owing to their poor potential, reduce philosophical issues to buffoonery. By the same token, the surrounding world is represented as a profane universe: creatures inhabiting it are "swindlers" and "thieves" and "complete ignoramuses" in the "business of art." The ugly potential of the entire universe is represented by the "frogs-swans" accompanying Dionysus on his journey along the river. Frogs-swans are freaks of nature, a strange combination of beauty (swans) and ugliness (frogs), whose existence suggests the degeneration of the world in which even the Muses are fond of the croaking songs of their swampy "Pegasuses."

Mercury and Jupiter in Plautus and Molière. Funny situations cannot be considered without regard to the characters' potential; likewise, chance occurrences cannot be approached without regard to the predisposition in which they appear. In the next two chapters, I discuss both statements in detail, considering works with the same topics, but of different dramatic types, and the role of fate and chance. Here I will make just a brief comparison of different methods of representing gods in literary works, such as Plautus's and Molière's versions of *Amphitryon*.

Unlike Dionysus in *Frogs*, both Mercury and Jupiter in Plautus's play are represented as gods of great intellect. Their intrigues are sophisticated, and it is little wonder that the mortals are incapable of uncovering them. The situations are no less laughable than in *Frogs*, but the degree of richness and strength of the gods' potential is different, making one think about a different type of dramatic genre (see chapter 2).

In Molière's version (1669), the main topic in the prologue concerns the strength of Jupiter who constantly changes his appearance. Mercury assures the Night that despite Jupiter's stooping "down to the level of mankind," he still retains his mighty potential:

Night: But, granted he may stoop from that exalted station
Down to the level of mankind,
Accept all joys that he in human hearts may find,
Join in their trivial conversation,
If only through all this capricious transformation
He'd stick to human nature, then I wouldn't mind.
But seeing Jupiter as beast,
As serpent, bull, or swan, I balk;
That's not attractive in the least,
And I'm not surprised if people sometimes talk.
Mercury: Let carpers carp, they'll do no harm.
In shifting shapes there is a charm
To which their minds can never rise.
In present case and others this god knows what he is doing . . .

(*Amphitryon* 135)

As follows from Mercury's last remark, Jupiter never loses his power and always remains a supreme creature, irrespective of his multiple appearances. Molière's Jupiter and Mercury are gods with strong potential. The degree of strength of their potential is described in criticism in the following way: "This Jupiter is not a god but a *grand seigneur* . . . this Mercury is neither a vaudeville clown nor a stooge nor a divine flunkey, but a worldly wise and slightly world-weary courtier" (Mantinband and Passage, "From Plautus" 130). This suggests that Jupiter and Mercury in Molière's version are gods of drama, not of dramedy or comedy.

Lovers in Comedy, Dramedy, and Drama

"Much Ado about Nothing." As mentioned above, critics do not differentiate between comedy and funny drama because without inquiring into potential, only external characteristics linked to the evocation of laughter are taken into account. This presents quite a superficial view on the nature of characters, which cannot be limited to the single function of generating laughter. The potential of protagonists of funny drama and comedy are different. First of all, this concerns characters' intellectual abilities, which in funny drama are above average. The next difference concerns characters' emotional state, which in funny drama is much richer and presents a developed spectrum of feelings.

Shakespeare's dramatic diapason is uniquely wide—his plays oscillate from comedy to dramedy, encompassing practically all known types of characters' potential. In criticism, all of Shakespeare's plays that do not belong to tragedy are called comedies; in actuality, they represent a wide range of dramatic types and branches, including funny drama and succedy. *Much Ado about Nothing* is traditionally considered a comedy, but judging from the potential of its protagonists, it is a typically funny drama.

As critics notice, the "near-tragic" plot of this play "looks a good deal less threatening and causes no major disruption of the play's predominantly comic tone" (Jensen 68). By the comic tone, they presumably mean jokes scattered generously throughout the play, though the same can be said of *Romeo and Juliet*, in which constant witty squabbles are combined with laughable scenes involving such characters as the nurse and Mercutio and his friends. The statement that the plot "looks a good deal less threatening" for some unclear reasons therefore seems very questionable. This is the typically Aristotelian approach to a situation of taking the point of view of an event as such without regard to the participants. However, the event as such (i.e., the plot) is a schematic description of the sequence of occurrences represented on a very abstract level of structuring, which *cannot* reveal the degree of "threatening" because the potential has not yet been introduced. Only by switching to another level of abstraction, on which various characteristics form the "meat" of the work, can one talk about a predisposition based on characters' potential. As I show in chapter 4, the same plot can generate different predispositions in different works, owing to characters' different potential.

No special analysis is required to see that the protagonists in *Much Ado about Nothing* possess well-developed, rich potential. They are sharp, witty, full of energy, and very inventive; their quips and wisecracks gush forth easily. Each piece of dialogue reveals the protagonists' fresh sense of humor, which has nothing to do with the platitudes and banality typical of characters with a limited potential. This perpetually brilliant exchange of witticisms is an important factor in the attraction between the lovers, Beatrice and Benedick:

> *Beatrice:* I wonder that you will still be talking, Signior Benedick; nobody marks you.
> *Benedick:* What, my dear Lady Disdain! are you yet living?
> *Beatrice:* Is it possible disdain should die while she hath such meet food to feed it as Signior Benedick? Courtesy itself must convert to disdain, if you come in her presence.
> *Benedick:* Then is courtesy a turncoat. But it is certain I am loved of all ladies, only you excepted: and I would I could find in my heart that I had not a hard heart; for, truly, I love none. (1.1.115–27)

Wit and a sense of humor are not the exclusive prerogatives of the high strata in *Much Ado about Nothing*—servants, too, are clever and humorous. The servants enter the verbal duels with their masters equally, suggesting a rich potential of the play's entire universe. The intrigues fabricated by the characters are sophisticated because they involve smart protagonists who are able to evaluate the predisposition of their partners, though the tricks played by the heroes are dictated by either good or bad intentions. So Hero plays a benign game with her shrew cousin, making her proud cousin "overhear" the "news" that Benedick is madly in love with her. Hero hopes that this will change Beatrice's attitude and make her fall in love with Benedick. The same trick is played on Benedick, who is told a "secret" that Beatrice is madly in love with him and is dying to see him. The astute friends find the right tactic to unite the "difficult" couple, so that both scoffers swallow the bait:

> Beatrice. [*coming forward*] What fire is in mine ears?
> Can this be true?
> Stand I condemn'd for pride and scorn so much?
> Contempt, farewell, and maiden pride, adieu!
> No glory lives behind the back of such.
> And, Benedick, love on, I will requite thee,
> Taming my wild heart to thy loving hand.
> If thou dost love, my kindness shall incite thee
> To bind our loves up in a holy band;
> For others say thou dost deserve, and I
> Believe it better than reportingly. *Exit.*
>
> (3.1.108–16)

At the same time, the strength and richness of the protagonists' feelings in *Much Ado about Nothing* are essentially less than those in *Romeo and Juliet*; this is linked to the degree of elaboration of the characters' potential, especially illustrated by the couple Hero and Claudio, the main characters who in some way echo Romeo and Juliet. If Juliet's death signifies the end of Romeo's world, in *Much Ado about Nothing* the news of Hero's death upsets Claudio but does not change his intention to live. One should not forget that unlike Romeo, Claudio becomes a direct cause of his bride's "death," for his suspicions and cruelty debase her deeply.

Nevertheless, this fact makes Claudio only remorseful; he never thinks about joining his beloved in death as did Romeo. Claudio merely vows on Hero's "grave" to remember her forever. At the same time, he is full of other plans, including the marriage to Leonato's strange niece. This latter fact makes the differences between Romeo and Claudio crucial, and the degree of richness of Claudio's love is revealed.

As Leonato states, his niece is a complete reflection of "late" Hero—the two girls are like two peas in a pod. So he asks Claudio to marry his niece and Claudio agrees to do so. This decision reveals that to Claudio, the identical appearance may substitute for the inner uniqueness of his beloved—a fact that suggests a different degree of strength of this lover's potential. Such a move would not be possible for Romeo, for whom any "identical twin" would be no more than an empty imitation of his beloved, whose soul cannot be substituted. Therefore, the potential of the main characters in *Much Ado about Nothing* is average but not rich as it is in dramedy. At the same time, as shown above, it essentially differs from the potential in comedy; combined with a happy ending—both couples are united in the end—and a high degree of the laughable/funny, this play matches the characteristics inherent in funny drama.

"The Taming of the Shrew" and "The Merry Wives of Windsor." The relationship between Beatrice and Benedick echoes that between Petruchio and Katharina in *The Taming of the Shrew*. Indeed, the inner richness of the couple is revealed through their subtle sense of humor and innate wit. Imagination and artistry of the beloved become the ground for the development of their feelings. The characters express themselves in an elegant and passionate way, thus creating a palette of colors embellishing their universe. Each is sensitive to every word and gesture of the other, and like witty actors-improvisers, they clash on the "stage" of their feelings, creating a spectacular performance of two glamorous minds.

Such an emphasis on the wit and intelligence of the lovers is perhaps a Shakespearean model of the "ideal" love—love that has the potential to develop, through the sparkling imagination of the beloved. The "taming" of the shrew is therefore nothing but a chance to reveal the rich potential of the couple and its predisposition to develop in the future, successfully avoiding the everyday routine that kills common love. One who gets doused by the inexhaustible fountain of their humor will remember it as the best verbal show:

> *Katharina:* Mov'd! in good time! Let him that mov'd you hither
> Remove you hence. I knew you at the first
> You were a moveable.
> *Petruchio:* Why, what's a moveable?
> *Katharina:* A join'd-stool.
> *Petruchio:* Thou hast hit it; come sit on me.
> *Katharina:* Asses are made to bear, and so are you.
>
> (2.1.194–99)

It seems that their feelings are not as deep and rich as those in dramedy, in which the degree of one's emotional involvement is greater.[2] However, there is a predisposition for positive change in this couple, and one can easily imagine that the creative alliance will develop in Katharina and Petruchio after marriage, with each finding no substitution for the other and enjoying every moment of their mutual artistry. At this point, I would define this play as a potential dramedy.

The Merry Wives of Windsor relies on "the farce of situational intrigue in which one-dimensional characters are manipulated into cleverly arranged comic complications" (Champion 61). This play comprises characters with apparently limited potential, whose feelings are based on pragmatism; this becomes the starting point for a main character, Fenton, who decides to marry Anne Page because of her wealth. Though he later admits that he is truly falling in love with Anne, Fenton still does not find an original way of expressing his feelings because his intellectual and emotional limitations do not allow him to change. His bride is no better—a few banal phrases about love spilled by Fenton are enough to capture Anne Page's heart and she falls in love:

> *[Fent.]* No, heaven so speed me in my time to come!
> Albeit I will confess thy father's wealth
> Was the first motive that I woo'd thee, Anne;
> Yet wooing thee, I found thee of more value
> Than stamps in gold, or sums in sealed bags;
> And 'tis the very riches of thyself
> That now I aim at.
> *Anne.* Gentle Master Fenton,
> Yet seek my father's love, still seek it, sir.
> If opportunity and humblest suit
> Cannot attain it, why then—hark you hither!
>
> (3.4.12–21)

The superficial, schematic relationship between the protagonists reflects an inner poverty typical of puppetlike, comedic personages. They find it easy to fall in love and easy to hate, easy to do bad things and easy to confess—their weak potential prevents them from feeling deeply and searching for the meaning of life. From the villains to the righteous, they are the same simple creatures unable to develop; their changes are external and do not touch their nature in essence. Sir John Falstaff, a "Flemish drunkard," a "whale with so many tuns of oil in his belly," a "greasy knight," cares only about the satisfaction of his base instincts, which rule his behavior. This oaf experiences no love, nor has he remorse for his amoral actions; but even if he had, it would as the turn of a weather vane.

"*A Midsummer Night's Dream.*" Another of Shakespeare's plays that is traditionally called a comedy, *A Midsummer Night's Dream,* is the opposite of both the profane universe of *Merry Wives of Windsor* and the average/above average society in *Much Ado about Nothing* and *Taming of the Shrew*. As C. L. Barber writes, "[T]his more serious play, his first comic masterpiece, has a crucial place in his development" (11). Based on its protagonists' rich potential, which enables them to develop their feelings and prevent them from catastrophe, *A Midsummer Night's Dream* appears as a wonderful example of succedy. The main characters exhibit an emotional and intellectual richness that allows them to discuss the deepness of their attachments and to make deliberate choices, thus withstanding not only an onslaught from Hermia's father, but also the dangerous consequences of witchcraft.

The play begins on a very dramatic, nearly tragic, note. Two lovers Hermia and Lysander cannot be united in marriage because of the bride's father, who has another husband for his beloved daughter in mind. The conflict between Hermia's deep feelings for her beloved and her filial duty could become the subject of a tragedy. Theseus, Duke of Athens, demands that Hermia should obey her father, who is like a god to her in the family hierarchy:

> *The.* What say you, Hermia? Be advis'd fair maid.
> To you your father should be as a god;
> One that compos'd your beauties; yea, and one
> To whom you are but as a form in wax,
> By him imprinted, and within his power,
> To leave the figure, or disfigure it.
> Demetrius is a worthy gentleman.
>
> (1.1.46–52)

The emphasis on the divine position of the father in the family only increases the danger of Hermia's rebellious refusal to follow the Duke's order. But nothing can threaten Hermia, who deliberately makes her choice and explains it with no hesitation to her cruel judges. Her emphasis is on the uniqueness of her feelings, which cannot be transferred to anyone else. Even death cannot stop her from making her choice; she refuses to accept a proposal from another man and only exclaims with bitterness, "O hell! To choose love by another's eyes!"

> *Her.* I do entreat your Grace to pardon me.
> I know not by what power I am made bold,
> Nor how it may concern my modesty,
> In such a presence here to plead my thoughts;
> But I beseech your Grace that I may know
> The worst that may befall me in this case,
> If I refuse to wed Demetrius.
>
> (1.1.58–64)

Like Hermia, Lysander reveals his deep feelings and willingness to fight for his beloved to the end:

> *Lys.* I am, my lord, as well deriv'd as he,
> As well possess'd; my love is more than his;
> My fortunes every way as fairly rank'd,
> If not with vantage, as Demetrius ;
> And, which is more than all these boasts can be,
> I am beloved of beauteous Hermia:
> Why should not I then prosecute my right?
> Demetrius, I'll avouch it to his head,
> Made love to Nedar's daughter, Helena,
> And won her soul; and she, sweet lady, dotes,
> Devoutly dotes, dotes in idolatry,
> Upon this spotted and inconstant man.
>
> (1.1.99–110)

The depth of the heroes' feelings, along with their high intelligence and strong will, make them characters of rich and powerful potential typical of dramedy. The sudden change of their potential that occurs as a result of the outer influence of the magic transforms them temporarily into limited comical figures; however, as soon as they reacquire their previous strength, they immediately demonstrate their unmistakably rich potential. Therefore, this play belongs to the DCD type. A further discussion on the sudden change of the main protagonists' potential, with regard to their predisposition, is provided in chapter 5.

"Turandot." Despite the fact that Carlo Gozzi states in the preface to *Turandot* (1762) that his play is tragicomedy, from the point of view of characters' potential this play is a clear example of succedy. Gozzi's argumentation is based on the traditional understanding of tragicomedy as a combination of funny episodes and tragic circumstances. The outcome of *Turandot* is not tragic, however, and it remains unclear in terms of the orthodox definition why Gozzi insisted that he created a tragicomedy, not a comedy. Obviously, Gozzi's artistic intuition whispered to him that *Turandot* somehow differed from traditional comedy, but a lack of theoretical vision did not allow him to support his intuitive guess with strong rational arguments.

Like *Amphitryon*, *Turandot* exploits laughable situations, humor and jokes to a great extent; however, all these do not influence the strength of the protagonists' potential. As befits succedy, the story with a dangerous predisposition ends successfully owing to the heroine's great potential. The play begins with the story of Prince Calaf's ordeal: his escape from a cruel king who wanted to kill the prince and his family. From the very beginning, Calaf appears as a noble character of strong will, whose selflessness and love for his parents amaze even his enemies. After suffering losses and misfortunes, Prince Calaf eventually decides to serve in King Altoum's army.

He shares his plan with his teacher Barach, whom Prince Calaf had missed so much and whom he unexpectedly meets in Peking. Surprisingly, Barach's reaction is not what Calaf had expected; the teacher implores his favorite pupil not to go to the king, who has a very bad reputation. He tells Calaf of the king's daughter, gorgeous Turandot, the most beautiful and cruel creature in the world, whose unique beauty lures young men to Peking to gain her love. However, it is not only her unprecedented beauty but also her supreme intellect that makes Turandot unattainable to her admirers. She uses her brilliant mind to make up riddles, which no one has ever been able to solve. Thousands of princes have already paid with their lives in the attempt to solve three of Princess Turandot's riddles.

To emphasize the destructive influence of that beauty, Barach tells the prince that a dangerous charm radiates even from her portrait, so that no one could withstand the temptation to see the beauty. Although the prince laughs at Barach's words, he soon becomes a victim of his carelessness. Seized by curiosity, Calaf takes Turandot's portrait from the ground, where it had been thrown by one of Barach's friends who was executed right after that. Even trampled and covered with dirt, this portrait still possesses a harmful charm that instantly makes anyone obsessed who dares to look at it. And Prince Calaf is also unable to avoid the destiny of his predecessors; in a few moments, he has been caught by the representation on the canvas and is changed completely:

> *Calaf: (who is all the while staring at the picture)* It is useless for you to try to frighten me. What a beautiful, bright face! What lovable eyes! What smiling lips! Oh fortunate on earth is the man who could possess so beautiful a vision of unity and harmony. And that I could possess it *(hesitating a bit, then resolutely)*. Barach, do not reveal my identity. This is my moment to try my fortune. Here is the most beautiful woman who has ever lived, and here also is a powerful empire. (Gozzi 47)

Obviously, such a powerful combination of outer (beautiful appearance) and inner (great intellect) strength elevates Turandot to the level of the strongest creatures. In actual fact, she feels and acts like a goddess; life and death—everything is in her power. Unlike all other competitors, however, Calaf is not inferior to her: if she poses riddles of great complexity, he solves them; if she has a strong effect on people whose lives have been changed because of her, he has the same impact on her, making her finally reconsider her behavior. This puts the protagonists on the same level of potential strength.

One of the most important proofs of Turandot's powerful potential is her ability to drastically change the sign of her potential from destructive to creative, not *after* but *before* the irretrievable could happen—a very rare quality inherent in some genuinely powerful creatures. Turandot's confession in the end reveals a deep emotional turn in her psychology as a destroyer. She is capable of reconsidering and improving herself and of using her aptitude for good.

> *Turandot:* Learn the whole truth, Calaf. I won only because of your own emotions. You disclosed the names to my slave, Adelma; otherwise I would not have known. In your excitement last night you told her the two names, and she told me. The world knows that I am not capable of an injustice, and the world should also know that your faithfulness and your nobility have finally penetrated my heart—and softened it. Now, live and enjoy your victory. Turandot is your wife. (103)

Smart and Foolish Servants

Let us now make a comparative analysis of the potential of servants in different works, taking Carlo Goldoni's and Beaumarchais's plays as examples; namely, Truffaldino from *The Servant of Two Masters* (1745) and Figaro from *The Barber of Seville* (1775). These two characters are of special interest because both succeed in their intrigues, though the nature of their success differs. Therefore, the focus of my analysis will be on the servants as decision makers, which should shed light on the different degrees of strength of their potential.

"The Servant of Two Masters." This play tells the story of a muddle-headed servant, Truffaldino, who constantly overestimates his poor skills and abilities but still succeeds in serving his two masters. Princess Beatrice Rasponi from Turin, whose twin brother Federigo has been killed in a duel by her beloved, Florindo Aretusi, comes to Venice to visit Clarice, the fiancée of her late brother. She dresses in her brother's clothes in order to appear in front of the Bisognosi family in the capacity of Clarice's fiancé. Beatrice pretends to be Federigo because she needs money in order to continue the search for her beloved, who has fled Turin to escape the death penalty. It is good luck that brings Princess Rasponi and Florindo Aretusi to the same hotel in Venice, but it is bad luck that brings Truffaldino to the same place. This empty-headed cheat could cause the deaths of the sweethearts; he misleads them and confirms to each that the person they are looking for is dead. Nevertheless, regardless of the obstacles, which Truffaldino unintentionally creates, the desperate lovers finally embrace each other.

Truffaldino is certainly represented as a comical type with an apparently disjointed vision that does not allow him to see two steps ahead. Whatever his actions, they are not in correlation with the entire situation, so his local moves ruin the global intent. For instance, in order to earn more money, he decides to find one more master and thus increase his salary tremendously. This is how he comes to be a servant of both his mistress Beatrice and her beloved Florindo. Having no clear strategy of how to satisfy both masters at the same time, Truffaldino simply decides to lean on good luck. He assumes that his intuition will assist him in making the right decisions, but—alas! Neither his intuitive behavior nor his rational thinking prevents him from his ridiculous blunders.

Truffaldino behaves as a weather vane; he literally rotates between his masters, instantly changing his direction in accordance with new orders. In so doing, he demonstrates his complete obtuseness. This is a pure case of a lack of intelligence and an inability to perform self-analysis. Careless and sclerotic, Truffaldino, nevertheless, courageously accepts a job offer from Florindo and immediately proceeds with his new duties. He goes to the post office to see if there are any letters for his masters, happy that he may serve the two of them at once and proud of his own cleverness. Meanwhile, he takes three letters and mixes them up in his pocket, having no concern for how he will later distinguish between them, especially because he is illiterate. Only when he meets one of his masters face-to-face does he suddenly realize his mistake.

However, this character is unable to learn from his mistakes. He makes one blunder after another, sometimes coming unscrewed, sometimes getting punished. His intellectual abilities are so poor that he is unable to recognize one of his masters in the picture:

> *Truffaldino: (Searches the pockets of Beatrice's suit and finds a small portrait.)* What a pretty little picture! I seem to know that face. Yes, of course, it's just like my other master. But, no, it couldn't be him. He never wears clothes like that. (Goldoni 43)

This attempt to identify the person in the picture based on clothes, not on facial features, attests to the highest degree of stupidity in a character. Truffaldino, however, has a different opinion of himself. He believes in his cleverness and good taste, and he does not hesitate to serve a table for Beatrice, confidently dictating to the owner of the hotel, Brighella, where to put certain dishes. Although Brighella agrees to serve the way Truffaldino tells him, he nevertheless points to the fact that the sauce and the meat are served improperly—they are too remote from each other. The arrangement of dishes reveals Truffaldino's disjointed way of thinking, since one who cannot see how meat relates to sauce can hardly be expected to make brilliant moves in life. The inability to recognize closely related things suggests that such a type cannot be successful even in making simple local decisions; this is also true with regard to Truffaldino's constant mistakes.

It is not only Truffaldino but also his masters who are lacking in potential; neither Beatrice nor Florindo catches the servant in a lie, even a very primitive one. Such carelessness can be explained by the fact that both masters are extremely vulnerable and are focused mostly on their goal of finding each other, so they have neither the time nor the desire to analyze their servant's tangled lies. Even if in some cases in which they should be able to catch him lying, they are too preoccupied with their unresolved problems to verify everything he says.

"*The Barber of Seville.*" Unlike *A Servant of Two Masters*, *The Barber of Seville* ends happily, owing to the wit and intelligence of its main character, Figaro. In his preface, Beaumarchais discusses the strong potential inherent in his protagonists. He states that they are not traditional simpletons, who have no ability to make smart decisions, but clever, intelligent characters capable of sophisticated choices. Beaumarchais states that the genre of a play depends on its characters, not on its plot development. He claims that the plot of his play could be the subject of either comedy, tragedy, or drama. Though Beaumarchais did not develop his observations into a theoretical statement, he nevertheless emphasized the role of the characters in the creation of types of dramatic genre. Beaumarchais therefore insists that this is a comedy of a different type, despite the fact that he calls *The Barber of Seville* a comedy. In our terms, it corresponds to funny drama, taking into consideration the above average potential of protagonists and the great proportion of laughable scenes.

Figaro appears as a character with a good intellect, wit, and strong abilities to realize his intent. Unlike Truffaldino, who lacks clarity about how to manage things, Figaro is always certain about his tactics and strategy. While Truffaldino is illiterate and unable to read the address on an envelope, Figaro is a creator of comedies, and his works are published and staged. In the beginning, Figaro appears and is working on a new piece. Beaumarchais pays special attention to this scene, for it provides the audience with an understanding of the decision-making ability of the protagonist. In the very beginning, Figaro is represented as a smart and professional dramatist, whose sharp mind is revealed through the way he works on certain poems, trying to avoid banal meanings and vulgar images. He severely criticizes the bad taste and street humor inherent in the contemporary comedy appealing to the masses; he wants to elevate the modern comedy to the level of sophisticated, sparkling comedic art:

> *Figaro:* [...]
> That's not bad. Up to now. What next?
> And dies off too soon...
> Yes, good wine and idleness
> Fight for my heart...
> No, they don't fight, they rule there together, peacefully:
> *Reign* in my heart.
> Can you say "reign"? I don't see why not. When you're writing a comic opera, you can't stop to look at every word. Nowadays, if a thing isn't worth saying, you sing it.
> [...]
> I'd like to end with something beautiful, brilliant, glittering, something with a kick in it. *(He goes down on one knee and writes as he sings.)*
> Reign in my heart.
> If one takes my tenderness,
> The other gives me happiness.
> No, no. That's flat. That's not it. I need a clash, an antithesis:
> If one is my mistress
> The other...
> Yes, perfect:
> The other's my tart.
> Well done, Figaro. *(He writes as he sings.)*
>
> (Beaumarchais 21–23)

In the process of working on his comedy, Figaro criticizes contemporary writers, who do not pay attention to the quality of their comical verses. At the same time, he is very demanding of himself; he is against vulgarity and rhymed nonsense, and he perpetually strives for witty, fresh ideas in his satirical songs. In this sense, he works as an innovator of the comedic genre and his editing reflects his decision making in general. As a matter of fact, when elaborating strategies in life, Figaro is as inventive and masterful as in editing his work. His talent as a writer working on different types of characters assists him in penetrating the psychology of the people surrounding him in life. He thus bases his strategy on people's predisposition, finding a genuine approach to both his friends and his enemies, and as a rule succeeds in his intrigues.

In the preface to *The Barber of Seville*, Beaumarchais notes that the appearance of this intelligent type dictates some new technique of development of his other characters. According to Beaumarchais, Figaro is not the only one who is endowed with a witty mind—Figaro interacts with other intelligent protagonists who cannot be easily manipulated. For instance, Bartholo, the central figure and the target of Figaro's intrigues, is not a man whom one can easily twist around one's little finger. This old and jealous guardian of the charming Rosina is very careful and smart. Extremely perspicacious, Bartholo immediately figures out what his lovely Rosina is up to and what her subterfuges are about.

By making Figaro's opponents strong, Beaumarchais strengthens this character's potential. Figaro must confirm his ability to find original solutions to help his friends achieve the desirable at every minute. For instance, Bazile, a music teacher, proposes a plan to help Bartholo get rid of his rival, Prince Almaviva. Bazile suggests slandering the prince, tarnishing his reputation so that Rosina will not accept his proposal. Upon receiving the news about this treacherous plan, Prince Almaviva gets very upset. Figaro explains to him, however, that rumors may only work if the one who spreads them has authority in the circle to which he appeals. As Figaro states, Bazile has no name and is not accepted in high society; his plan is therefore good only for servants who would discuss rumors in the kitchen.

Unlike Truffaldino, whose behavior is local and reactive, Figaro makes his decisions based on a general concept. His principle is to comprehend the situation in essence, to have some global vision before taking any concrete steps. For instance, in discussing with Almaviva how to approach Rosina, who is watched by numerous guards, Figaro first proposes a general strategy that will later assist him in creating some particular tactics. Such an approach has nothing to do with Truffaldino's spontaneous moves, which can sometimes be successful, but are mostly predisposed to failure. However, Figaro is a character of funny drama, not succedy; his potential is above average but not powerful. He represents a sharp-witted type that does not go beyond daily problems to the sphere of a philosophical view of the world.

Summary

The degree of strength and richness of characters' potential cannot be exhausted by their social status, which only reflects outer valuations of the characters' influence on society. As is shown, however, the inner and the outer may sometimes coincide.

It is not amusing situations and laughable actions that make characters belong to the comedic type but their limited and weak potential that does not allow them to cross the border of commonality and primitive thinking. Any type of character can be involved in funny situations, but these do not necessarily reduce his or her potential to weak and poor. The type of situation has nothing to do with the type of characters' potential.

Gods, kings, heroes, and other supposedly noble and intelligent creatures are not mocked or humiliated in comedy—they just do not appear as such in the first place. The common mistake in approaching such characters in comedy is that interpreters often confuse two things—a common representation of supreme/divine creatures in reality or religion and their appearance in the artistic work. Gods or rulers or poets in comedy must not be compared to their noble "prototypes"; this could otherwise be perceived as cynical mockery. One must analyze the potential of a character as it appears in *the artistic work* (either in film or in literature) in order to see whether or not the view of the artist is cynical. All allusions that may arise with regard to reality or to other texts, both artistic and nonartistic, serve to elevate the analysis to the second stage of measuring characters' potential, which is discussed in detail in part three.

Literary Works of the Same and Analogous Topics 4

This chapter contains an analysis of seemingly "identical twins"—Don Juans, Amphitryons, and other characters sharing the same name and fate and having the same inclinations. The similarities, however, do not preclude the characters' possible inner differences. Comedies, dramedies, and dramas of the same topics are compared and analyzed here from the point of view of their protagonists' potential. In the process, some common definitions of genre are either reconsidered or proved in accordance with the new classification.

Amphitryon: From Comedy to Succedy

Plautus's *"Amphitryon."* As mentioned previously, Plautus was the first to introduce the definition of tragicomedy in his dramatic works. Like many other writers who were concerned with the definition of genre but had no theoretical vision, Plautus tried to approach the genre of his play from the point of view of strata, making his character Mercury define the play in the following way:

> Why do you wrinkle your forehead? Because I said that this would be a tragedy? I am a god, and I'll change it if you wish. I'll make a comedy out of the tragedy and yet leave all the lines the same. . . . I'll make it a mixture, a *tragicomedy*. I don't think it is proper for me to make it entirely a comedy wherein kings and gods appear. What then? Since the servant also has a part, therefore let it be, **as I said, a tragicomedy.** (1)

In his definition of tragicomedy, Plautus considers the protagonist's status paramount and therefore states that the combination of servants and kings creates tragicomedy. But if one agrees upon such a definition, then any comedy that combines different strata, such as Aristophanes' *Frogs*, should be called tragicomedy. One can intuitively feel that Plautus and Aristophanes' plays cannot belong to the same category, however, irrespective of their similar structures (a combination of gods and servants). This feeling has a perfectly rational explanation from the point of view of characters' potential.

Amphitryon is based on the myth of Amphitryon, son of King Alkeus and husband of Alcmena, the woman whose beauty seduces Jupiter during Amphitryon's absence. Assuming the form of Amphitryon, Jupiter penetrates Alcmena's house and spends a night with her. As a result, Alcmena, who is already expecting Amphitryon's son, becomes pregnant once more with Zeus's child. Upon Amphitryon's arrival, she gives birth to both children—Ificles, son of Amphitryon, and Heracles, son of Zeus. In the play, all the misunderstandings and confusions accompanying the protagonists' encounters with their doubles are intended to evoke laughter, for instance, a scene in which Amphitryon's servant, Sosia, meets Mercury, who has taken Sosia's appearance, or when Alcmena shows Amphitryon a goblet he had supposedly presented to her.

When Amphitryon comes home from the war, he suspects that something has gone wrong, but he cannot find an explanation. He eventually realizes that his wife has spent a night with someone else in his absence. Naturally, this makes him furious, and he demands an explanation from her; but against his expectations, his wife blames him for being cruel and jealous and promises to leave him if he does not stop his humiliating interrogations:

> *Amphitryon:* You say I arrived yesterday?
> *Alcmena:* Do you deny that you left today?
> *Amphitryon:* Naturally, I deny it. This is
> the first time that I'm in your presence.
> *Alcmena:* Speaking of "presence," what about
> the goblet they "presented" you with?
> The golden one . . . Will you deny
> you gave it to me this very day?
> *Amphitryon:* I never gave you the cup, or mentioned
> it, though I was going to—
> Hey, who told you about that cup?
> *Alcmena:* You told me yourself, when you
> gave it to me with your own hands.
> *Amphitryon:* Just a minute, please. You know,
> Sosia, something's fishy here.
> How the devil would she have known
> about the goblet I received?
> Sure you didn't see her before
> and tell her all about it, eh?
>
> (75–76)

The whole scene devolves into complete confusion. Amphitryon's perplexity seems to be reasonable, however, and is not the misunderstanding of a simpleton who is unable to see the obvious (a typical situation in comedy). Amphitryon's inability to find out what is really going on in his house has nothing to do with a decrease in his intellectual power—the event itself is unusual, and therefore no rational thinking would have helped to uncover the mystery. Without any doubt, Amphitryon is a character with a strong potential. He is a successful warrior and a victor in a war with the Thebans—very dangerous enemies who have never before been conquered. As Sosia says:

> All our troops have come back safely,
> mission accomplished, enemy slain.
> The mighty battle is all finished,
> and our foes are finished too.
> The city that has caused the death
> of many Thebans good and true,
> by our strength and military
> prowess it has been laid low—
> and mostly by the skill and luck
> of my own master Amphitryon.
>
> (46)

Alcmena also highly appreciates the talent and courage of her husband. "At least there is one thing to praise: / he'll be a hero all his days" (69).

Amphitryon undeniably possesses unusual military talent. During the war, he reveals great intellect and professionalism combined with physical strength. He is able to elaborate a keen strategy to defeat his cunning enemies. He has not, of course, achieved the greatness of his impostor, Jupiter, but he is the best among mortals. Nevertheless, regardless of Amphitryon's great professionalism, his potential strength is not enough to make him a character of dramedy; the nature of his feelings, which are based on jealousy and anger, suggests a limited spectrum of emotions that is mostly one-parametric and directed towards his insulted ego.

It is unclear what he sees in Alcmena—a piece of property or a universe that may enrich and develop him. He acts and talks like a desperate warrior who is losing a battle but not as a sophisticated lover whose soul and mind are both elevated and depressed by the feeling that is no longer mutual. There are no powerful philosophical or psychological generalizations in his monologues that would reveal the richness of his inner state. All he says is related to current events, which essentially lowers the degree of strength and richness of his potential. Taking into account the happy ending and the great proportion of the laughable, one can define this play as happy funny drama.

Molière's and Kleist's "Amphitryon." There is more farce in Molière's *Amphitryon* than in Plautus's play, yet Molière's main characters seem to be less characters of farce than they are of drama/farcical drama, by virtue of their average, but not limited, potential. As critics notice:

> This Amphitryon is not a Theban warrior but a testy young nobleman of secondary, but not inferior, rank, vain, irascible, youthfully rash, aristocratically impatient; but yet upright, understandably and humanly angered and bewildered; this Alcmène is no passive human instrument for a divine will, but a virtuous young wife, tender but not lacking in mettle; this Sosie is not a slave but a gentleman's valet. (Mantinband and Passage, "From Plautus" 130)

Unlike Plautus's scenes with Alcmena and Amphitryon, which arouse the reader's sympathy and compassion, Molière's farcical scenes with the same protagonists evoke only laughter, since no deep feelings are involved. Even Plautus does not achieve in his dialogues the high dramatic effect that Heinrich von Kleist attains in his free translation of Molière. Kleist's *Amphitryon* began as a translation of Molière's version but gradually turned into a new dramatic work whose originality still puzzles critics and directors.

According to critics, "Kleist's *Amphitryon* is a problematic work. It is easy to see why no performance worthy of the name was attempted until 1902 at the Vienna Burgtheater and why its stage history has been a brief chronicle" (Mantinband and Passage, "From Molière" 208). The main problem with staging this play has been that the outcome of Kleist's version is ambiguous; it is unclear if the play ends successfully or not. As critics note, the final scene achieves its tragic climax when Alcmena faints after the truth is revealed:

> Amphitryon in the last line of the text calls to her, and the final syllable of the text is her answering "Ah!" Depending on the inflection of that syllable and its accompanying gesture, an actress can turn this entire work at the very last second into a shattering tragedy or into a conciliatory comedy. (Mantinband and Passage, "From Molière" 207–8)

This puzzles critics and directors of all times. The confusion with regard to Kleist's play was increased by the fact that Kleist's contemporaries did not perceive his characters as comic but yet did not know how to interpret such an ambiguous outcome. So, Kleist's work—based on an unusual combination of characters' powerful potential and an ambiguous ending—only sharpened the question of dramatic genre and made explicit the necessity to switch from empirical observations to theoretical conclusions.

In comparison to two other versions, Kleist's *Amphitryon* demonstrates a deep and rare attachment between the lovers. If Plautus's Amphitryon is seized with fury, Kleist's character suffers from unrequited, deep-rooted love, suggesting a feeling that is richer than the ambitious, insatiable obsession of his double. Analogously, unlike Plautus's Alcmena, who only feels outrage at her husband's suspicions, Kleist's Alcmena is seized with an all-absorbing love for Amphitryon and is willing to die for it. Kleist's protagonists as lovers are certainly endowed with extremely rich potential, this makes them characters of dramedy regardless of the outcome, which may only specify the branch, and turns the play into either tragedy or succedy depending on one's interpretation.

Three Types of Stingy

Molière's Harpagon (*The Miser*, 1669) is one of the most obnoxious characters in literature. Barefaced pragmatism achieves its acme in him, and he becomes a literal incarnation of human degeneration. Harpagon is not a businessman; he collects but does not invest his money. Though this fact sometimes upsets even him, he is unable to change his way of living because parting with his savings is the most painful thing in the world to him. Like Molière's Harpagon, Alexander Pushkin's Baron (*The Covetous Knight*, 1830) is not one who likes to make investments, preferring to keep his wealth in a trunk in his basement, where he goes down to spend time in looking at his riches. At first sight, these two personages seem to be identical twins: their complete disregard for friends and members of their families and their concern with materialistic things make them characters of the same kind. However, being of the same kind does not always mean being on the same level. The comparison of these two freaks of nature may surprise one.

Significantly, a traditional analysis that does not inquire into protagonists' potential would likely emphasize the similarity of these characters, while an analysis of their predisposition would shed light on the different degree of strength of their inner characteristics. Indeed, if protagonists feel the same way, behave analogously, and are concerned with identical problems, what else could be different about them? Is it really important to delve into details if the main structure is clearly outlined?

When it concerns the analysis of a potential, a consideration of all parameters is required because to evaluate a potential one must work with a combination of certain characteristics, not judge it by a single parameter. For instance, stinginess can be inherent in both a character with strong potential and one with weak potential, but in order to receive a holistic impression, it is important to see what other parameters form the potential and to ascribe weights to them.

"The Miser" and "The Covetous Knight." Harpagon appears to be a pragmatic, empty creature who is completely lacking in imagination. A few lines

would be enough to describe this unsophisticated character, whose passions (except for those regarding his savings) are insignificant and superficial, and who easily exchanges his bride for the box of money that his son offers him. Anything unrelated to materials is beyond his comprehension.

Relational parameters are absent from his vocabulary—he does not know what relationships are for and what their use is. He therefore ruins his connections with the world, seeing nothing important in these ephemeral feelings that unite people. In proposing marriage to a beautiful young girl with whom he is infatuated (and who he hopes will reciprocate his feelings), Harpagon still tries to squeeze a dowry from her impoverished mother. Instead of making positional sacrifices to win the young bride's favor, he wants to know what profit he would receive in marrying her. Noticing the mutual interest between his son and the young bride, Harpagon nevertheless makes no attempt to improve his position. On the contrary, by trying to avoid any expense, he shows his worst side and alienates his bride even more.

Pushkin's Baron, on the other hand, has a keen mind and always pays attention to relational parameters. Though his savings play the most important role in his life, his reasons are different. First of all, he is a man of dark and mighty passions, with a powerful imagination and a brilliant intellect. Wealth for him is not a valuable material but a source of inspiration, arousing his imagination and making a poet of him. Each time he descends into his basement, he anticipates an unforgettable spectacle. Alone with himself, he changes from a greedy old man into an artist who overflows with gloomy fantasies:

> Baron: As full of hot impatience as a rake
> Before a meeting with an artful temptress
> Or artless maid caught in his web of lies,
> So did I wait all day for that sweet moment
> When I could visit this my secret cache
> And faithful chests. O blessed say! For I
> Into my sixth, as yet but half-filled chest,
> Can put to-day this gold that I have hoarded—
> The merest handful, true, but treasures grow
> Little by little. I do remember reading
> Of some great prince who bade his men-at-arms
> Each lay of earth a handful at his feet.
> This done, there rose a lofty hill before him,
> And from its crest the prince could gaze upon
> The vale below dotted with snowy tents
> And watch the vessels plough the azure sea.
> Thus I by bringing here my daily tribute,

However scant, have wrought my own great mount
And from its summit can with pride survey
That over which I rule ... All, all I hold
In sway ... Like some dark, brooding demon I
Sit on my hidden throne ... If so I wish,
Majestic palaces will rise before me,
And lively nymphs, a merry, laughing throng,
Come running to my bloom-filled, scented gardens;
The muses will pay homage to my person.
And freedom-loving genius be my slave.

(1: 109)

His treasures open a hidden world of human passions, of struggles between vices and virtues—a world that delights and enthralls him more than anything else. The Baron permeates the darkest corners of his victims' souls, listens to their thoughts, and watches their dreams, using the power of his vicious imagination. The basement becomes his sacred place, protecting him from the outer world of mediocre people, whose ordinary dreams and unimaginative desires make him scream. It is his theater, in which he is both director and spectator; he states that real life starts here, where he can master the entire world.

Not only other people's lives but also the Baron's own destiny and death occurring as a result of his evil deeds become the subject of this wild fantasy. In his mind, he stages scenes in which he plays the role of a villain whose punishment looks as picturesque as his crimes, and he truly enjoys his gloomy part. This character indisputably possesses enough vicious might to influence human fates and govern the hidden world of passions.

In addition, savings have the highest value for the Baron because, as he admits, he has accumulated his wealth through enormous effort; namely, at the cost of his passions, which he has always suppressed. The price of his riches therefore equals the price of his life, and in entering his basement, he imagines the life that he could have had:

> *Baron:* None know how many torturous abstentions,
> Curbed passions and desires, oppressive thoughts,
> Days filled with endless care and sleepless nights
> My treasures cost me!
>
> (1: 112)

The monologue is woven from the strong passions and powerful desires that structure his rich, though destructive, inner life (which is opposed to the mediocre daily life of commoners). Conversely, the Baron's son, Albert, is an incarnation of inner emptiness and vanity; his only concerns are for his outer appearance and the impression he makes at court. This youth blames his father for his pathological stinginess, which humiliates the son in front of both friends and enemies. Albert accuses the Baron of excessive pragmatism, without understanding how ridiculously materialistic his own desires are. In fact, he is ready to sacrifice his own life in the name of his helmet, which was damaged during a fight. In order to exact revenge on the Prince, who dared to damage the only helmet he had, Albert forgets all precautions and continues to fight with his head unprotected.

Analyzing this episode, one may assume that Albert has inherited his father's genes. But this is not so. There is an essential difference between the two of them; Albert does not possess the powerful imagination, the rich inner universe, that makes his father so distinguished. His narrow-mindedness does not allow him to understand his father's predisposition, in the same way that the commoner's lack of sophistication makes him or her unable to inquire into the sophisticated nature of an artist. The way in which he describes his father reveals Albert's unsophisticated mind, which makes him more a close relative of Harpagon than of the Baron. Albert's desires are simple: he is a secular person whose only dream is to be accepted at court. To him, wealth is nothing but a material source, a means of obtaining worldly pleasures. Needless to say, the thought is unbearable to the Baron that a person like Albert may one day enter his sovereign kingdom of powerful visions and destroy it in the name of simple mundane pleasures:

> *Baron:* To-day I am a prince, I reign . . . But who
> My crown and scepter is to have to-morrow?—
> No other than my son, brainless spendthrift,
> Companion to a gang of profligates!
>
> (1: 111)

In comparison to these two, Molière's father and son do not have such disagreements. Molière's Harpagon and his son, Cléante, are two extremes of the same: if the father represents extreme stinginess, the son is a symbol of profligacy. Both are plain, empty creatures, typically comic personages:

> *Cléante:* How do I rob you?
> *Harpagon:* I don't know; but where else do you get the money to keep up such a style?
> *Cléante:* Why, at the gaming table; and, as I am generally fairly lucky, I spend all my winnings on Clothes. (*"Don Juan" and Other Plays* 195)

Thus, while Harpagon is a personage of farcical comedy, the Baron is a tragic character with negative value. The loss of such an original individual can only be compared to the loss of a gloomy poet whose imaginative and powerful creation is destroyed by an audience seeking simple pleasures.

"*Gobseck.*" The third type of "miser," Balzac's *Gobseck* (1830), is a tragicomic personage (DC—a combination of dramedy and comedy). Gobseck first appears to be a creature who lacks any human feelings. In the beginning, he is described as a primitive machine that functions to obtain money, even his outer look, whose "features might have been cast in bronze," amazes one with its resemblance to something inanimate. This first impression is deceptive, however, and as further analysis reveals, this is a character of strong, hidden passions. To recognize these passions, one must inquire into Gobseck's predisposition.

At this point, a story from Gobseck's past is of interest since it becomes the first step of the "stairway" leading to his sacred inner place. Gobseck tells Derville that when he was young he fell victim to an infatuation with a woman who eventually deceived him:

> There was a time when I was young, and might perhaps have been stupid enough not to protest the bill. At Pondichery, in 1763, I let a woman off, and nicely she paid me out afterwards. I deserve it; what call was there for me to trust her? (6: 15)

Gobseck does not tell Derville why he did not protest the bill, but one may assume that he was emotionally involved in a relationship with that woman. This story is included in another story about a beautiful countess whom Gobseck visited in the morning and serves to shed light on why Gobseck finally became that "stony," emotionless creature. But even Gobseck's "bronze mask" cannot hide in full measure his passionate nature, which is revealed in his descriptions of two women whom he had met in the morning. Indeed, the way Gobseck describes the countess suggests a highly imaginative, artistic mind, sensitive and flammable—the mind of a poet. His description of the countess deserves one's attention, since it reveals much about Gobseck:

> [S]he awakened desire; it seemed to me that there was some passion in her yet stronger than love. I was taken with her. It was a long while since my heart had throbbed; so I was paid then and there—for I would give a thousand francs for a sensation that should bring me back memories of youth. (6: 15)

These comments about the countess are an indirect description of Gobseck's "weak point"—his extremely passionate, spontaneous nature that may easily be taken with a strong feeling and very likely lead him to a disaster. The story of his other meeting, also related to Derville, only confirms this statement. That same morning Gobseck had had another encounter—a meeting with a young seamstress, Mlle. Fanny. Surprisingly, this simple girl has also deeply touched the "metal" heart of the "Daddy Gobseck":

> There was an indefinable atmosphere of goodness about her; I felt as if I were breathing sincerity and frank innocence. It was refreshing to my lungs. Poor innocent child, she had faith in something; there was a crucifix, and a sprig or two of green box above her poor little painted wooden bedstead; I felt touched, or somewhat inclined that way. I felt ready to offer to charge no more than twelve percent, and so give something towards establishing her in a good way of business. (6: 17)

As one can see, though different visits arouse contrasting feelings in Gobseck, he appears in both cases to be emotionally involved in the lives of his charming debtors, and he really forces himself to stop his sudden urges to support them. In describing the two women, Gobseck reveals his sensitivity to details, like an artist who takes pleasure from various hidden shades and nuances. This allows him to penetrate the psychology of his debtors and to evaluate their predisposition, which is what makes him a successful businessman. On the other hand, his extreme emotionality, combined with his readiness to spend all his money on one with whom he is infatuated, is destructive; it may cost him bankruptcy, as did happen once when he could not hold in his passions.

One can only imagine what would have happened to Gobseck were it not for his rational side, which is strong enough to find the only appropriate strategy to prevent his passionate heart from future disasters. After finally realizing that he is not a master of human relationships, Gobseck turns himself towards another extreme—a stony heart. Gobseck oscillates between two extremes all his life—a hidden struggle between a clear rational mind and a wild temper. In no way can this mighty usurer integrate these two contradictory sides of his nature. He therefore leads a double life, denying any feelings that may influence his business. He puts a placid mask on his face, which preserves him from destruction and helps him to survive in most cases. Peter Brooks writes:

> [T]he usurer Gobseck, who, through his the control of the money flow, can make all the dramas of life pass through his bare chamber, and enjoy life as a perfect spectacle of which he is both the detached spectator and the prime mover, the perfect demiurge. (115)

Gobseck acts in accordance with his concept of self-preservation, which, according to his philosophy, rules man's life. He shares his thoughts with Derville: "The one thing that always remains, the one sure instinct that nature has implanted in us, is the instinct of self-preservation" (6: 10). Such a double life gradually destroys him, however; as he ages, he degenerates, losing his ability to think rationally and eventually allowing his emotions to take over. By this time, the only passion that is left in his dried-up body is a craving for wealth. While it is true that Gobseck has great experience and a great name in the business world, he is also getting weak, and his decision to begin a new business of buying and selling eatables, which requires different tactics and strategies, becomes a fatal mistake. He applies the same tactics he used for lending money; that is, he keeps the eatables as if they were jewelry, without understanding that time works against their freshness. As a result, his room becomes full of rotten "treasures"—a powerful picture of his degradation:

> He had not disposed of the eatables to Chevet, because Chevet would only take them off him at a loss of thirty percent. Gobseck haggled for a few francs between the prices, and while they wrangled the goods became unsalable. Again, Gobseck had refused free delivery of his silver-plate, and declined to guarantee the weight of his coffees. There had been a dispute over each article, the first indication in Gobseck of the childishness and incomprehensible obstinacy of age, a condition of mind reached at last by all men in whom a strong passion survives the intellect. (6: 61)

Such an irreversible change of the potential from strong to extremely weak makes Gobseck a tragicomic figure, whose philosophy of human relationships suggests a keen mind able to generalize phenomena and things. However, I do not insist on my evaluation of Gobseck's potential as powerful—this is a subjective vision of his initial might that can be evaluated differently by different interpreters, in which case one could talk about dramecomedy (dc).

Morality and Potential: *Don Juan* and *The Stone Guest*

Both *Don Juan* (1665) and *The Stone Guest* (1830) are based on the legend of Don Juan; however, while Molière's hero is the subject of comedy, Pushkin's protagonist is a tragic hero.

"*Don Juan.*" Molière's character is a base creature with no moral values, which is in complete accordance with how his servant, Sganarelle, describes him at the beginning of the play. Sganarelle equates Don Juan with an animal, a freak that has no conscience and is cynical and blasphemous. Further scenes only confirm Sganarelle's description of Don Juan. This first of all concerns his relationship with his father, whom Don Juan treats without respect. Don Juan even wishes him death, since his father expresses (a reasonable) anger and tries to change Don Juan's way of life. There is nothing that can stop this animal from his amoral actions, though he is really vexed and bothered by the fact that the world scrutinizes him and judges his amoral behavior negatively. So he decides to convince everybody that his amoral decisions are dictated to him from on high, and he continues acting that way until one day his hypocrisy exhausts the patience of heaven; Don Juan then receives the punishment that he deserves.

The story as such does not provide the reader/spectator with a clear notion of the potential of this character because amorality can be combined with different degrees of strength and richness of the character's potential; therefore, in only analyzing this character in some particular episodes, one may only conclude on and give weight to his intellect, emotion, and system of values. To this end, the scenes with two female peasants are quite revealing. When Don Juan tells Sganarelle that he is planning to conquer a young lady whom he has recently seen with her beloved, one may assume that it is love that drives him to such a decision. Not at all! As he admits, his feelings are nothing but envy for a happy couple in love:

> *Don Juan:* The lady in question is a charming young girl, who came here in the company of the man she is going to marry. I saw her by pure chance, with her fiancé, three or four days before they set out. Never have I seen two people so happily in love. Their obvious tenderness for each other went straight to my heart, and my love found its first inspiration in jealousy. It was torture to me to see them so happy together. I was consumed with envy; and I could imagine no greater pleasure than to come between them, and break an attachment so offensive to my dearest susceptibilities. But so far, all my attempts have been unavailing; and as a last resort I have decided to take desperate measures. Her intended is to take her today for a little outing on the water. Without saying anything to you, I have already made all my preparations. I have a boat and a crew, and I don't anticipate any difficulty in carrying her off. (40)

Admittedly, envy is not love, but it may still evoke a passion of great magnitude, a fire that may burn the "arsonist" himself: not, however, in this case. Don Juan is too primitive and superficial to be consumed with any emotion for a long time. His feelings disappear as easily as they appear, leaving no trace in his heart or memory. Whether he achieves the desirable or not, he is unable to sustain his emotions, nor is he able to develop them into something strong. It is no wonder that the "victims" of his "charm" are plain country girls, naive and foolish, whose capture does not require a sophisticated strategy. But as soon as he concerns himself with women of a different potential, this womanizer ends in fiasco. He is not disappointed by the fact that he cannot conquer a noble woman who belongs to a different circle, however, for he is instantly rewarded by the admiration of two other female simpletons.

Don Juan's tactics are intended for women of low intellect, and so he never changes his simple way of "obtaining" a girl, including the words he says to them. As a decision maker, he bases his tactics on a reactive method, using the same program of capturing a new "butterfly" for his "herbarium." In the process, he values only material objects; he examines their figure, teeth, eyes, and the like, judging his beloved as if she were a horse:

> *Don Juan:* What a ravishing creature! What sparkling eyes! . . . Would you oblige me by turning round. What a pretty figure! Won't you hold up your head? Oh, what a delicate little face! Let me look right into your eyes. How beautiful! Will you allow me to see your teeth? Oh, they are made for love. And these tempting lips as well. (49)

"The Stone Guest." Pushkin's Don Juan is of a different kind. Nothing can attract him more than one's inner richness; he has never been an admirer of the empty beauty praised by Molière's protagonist. He admits to Leporello:

> *Don Juan:* The women? Why, my foolish Leporello,
> I'd not exchange—d'you hear me, stupid fellow?—
> The lowest of our Andalusian peasants
> For their most dazzling beauties—truly not.
> They pleased me to begin with, I admit it,
> Because their eyes were blue, their skins were white,
> They—modest, with the chasm of novelty!
> But soon, the Lord be praised, I realized—
> I saw quite clearly there was nothing to them—
> No life—a waste of time—like waxen dolls.
>
> (130)

As follows from this monologue, Pushkin's Don Juan most values one's inner richness, while beauty for him is that which has a predisposition for change and development. For Don Juan, beauty is not about materials or attributes but first and foremost about relational parameters; the way one looks, talks, and walks reveals to the inspired Don Juan a whole inner universe that lures his artistic imagination. It is in exactly these terms that he describes his beloved Inczа:

> *Don Juan:* It was July . . . at night. A strange enchantment
> I found in her sad eyes, on her numb lips.
> How strange. You, I remember, Leporello,
> Did not admire her. And indeed she was not
> A real beauty. It was just the eyes,
> The eyes and then—the way she looked . . . A look

> Such as I have not met in any other.
> Her voice was quiet and weak—like a sick woman's.
> Her husband was a ruthless brute, a villain,
> I found that out too late—my poor Ineza!
>
> (131)

Pushkin's Don Juan wants to be a traveler in the infinite space of his beloved's inner beauty, rather than to merely possess her body; for this, he is a poet of love. The small delicate hill under Doña Anna's long dress is not merely a part of her body, nor an object of carnal desire, but a symbol of the eternal grace and ideal beauty that never fades. His other beloved, Laura, is an extraordinary young woman with sparkling artistic talent, whose singing and acting excites her admirers; it is this talent that attracts Don Juan, to whom artistry is a necessary condition for love.

This rich nature and brilliant intellect make Pushkin's Don Juan a character of dramedy. His feelings are strong, and despite the fact that he leaves all of his beloveds, he never forgets them, nor does he lose his love for them. Moreover, when he recollects them, he seems to be as inspired and excited about their merits as he was at the time they had first met. In this sense, he is very constant and faithful to everyone he has loved—unlike Molière's Don Juan, who grows cold as soon as his goal is achieved. Pushkin's character considers all of his beloveds to be inimitable, and his next love is never a substitute for the previous one—each is important, meaningful, and unforgettable for him, since he is able to see their uniqueness. When he returns to his Laura, therefore, he is seized with the same passion that he had felt long ago.

Naturally, such a sparkling figure appearing on the horizon of daily life would not please those who are content with a stereotypical relationship. It is no wonder that the commoners feel threatened by this "burning star" lighting up their unimaginative universe. They see only his worst side, unable to appreciate that which is hostile to them—his originality. Their view of him is expressed by Leporello, who states that his master is an empty, amoral creature; with this rejection from his own servant, it seems that there is no one who would support Don Juan. Nevertheless, there is someone who does see Don Juan's extraordinary nature and who supports him a great deal—the king. The king not only shows his favor to Don Juan but also saves his life, banishing him for the duel in which he took part.

In both plays, Don Juan appears as an amoral creature who violates rules and customs; this, however, does not affect his powerful potential in Pushkin's tragedy. The loss of this rebel soul is analogous to the loss of individuality in humanity—now society is left with no bright spot, no impetus that could change that stagnant situation.

Family Relationships in Different Types of Dramatic Genre

In this section, I analyze family relationships from the point of view of their depth and strength as represented in different types of dramatic genre. The superficial character of family relationships in comedy is compared to those in dramedy and drama, based on the core of dramatic genre—the characters' potential. The main topic of discussion pertains to the *structure* of family relationships in comedy, dramedy, and drama: What principle forms the degree of *formality* of family relationships in different literary works? Why are positive comic characters considerably less involved in their family relationships than positive characters of the adjacent types, and why are they nevertheless not considered amoral or malicious? In order to answer these questions, let us refer to different systems, including chess and social systems, to see some parallels with different types of dramatic genre.

Natural (biological) relationships in chess, social systems, and literature. In the game of chess, relational (positional) parameters are not explicitly set, appearing during the game as a result of rules of interactions. The chess player creates relational parameters within a certain position and gives them valuations. In social systems, some relationships are set by nature, some are created by society, and others are invented by artistic systems. Katsenelinboigen distinguishes between three levels of relationships: natural (biological), societal, and gestalts.

The interaction between entities in social systems is more sophisticated than those in chess, since the primary biological relationships must be taken into account in the former. Underestimation of natural relationships may cause serious problems, as did happen, for example, in the Russian Communist society, in which family relationships were sacrificed in the name of ideology. In the process of dekulakizing during the civil war, and in search of enemies of the people, Russian Communists encouraged citizens to denounce members of their own families, pronouncing the Communist idea as primary over even the closest family ties. Needless to say, the underestimation of family relationships in life causes tragedy, even if society will not admit it.

In chess, on the other hand, natural relationships are not the subject of the game. When I was a little girl, my father tried to teach me how to play chess. The first lesson reminded me of a fairy tale; I was submerged into the world of royal kings, clever bishops, beautiful queens, and swift knights. In my mind, they related to each other through marriages, friendships, and the like. So I could not wait for the next day, anticipating the exciting continuation of my fairy tales. Alas! The next day was a complete frustration for both of us; I was unable to accept the logic of the game, which was against my own human logic. To my regret, I realized that the names and the shapes of the pieces were mere convention; the "king" and the "queen" could have been named the "behemoth" and the "nanny goat," and it would not have changed a thing in the course of the game.

Conversely, natural relationships are innate in literature and art, either being in agreement or in conflict with societal relationships. The involvement of close relatives in tragedy or drama makes conflicts even sharper; for instance, if Romeo and Juliet had not been the children of two hostile families but of distant relatives or even friends, the dramatic effect would have been essentially decreased. Analogously, in *A Midsummer Night's Dream*, the tension between the protagonists is primarily achieved from the closeness of the relatives involved; it is the heroine's own father who is against her marriage. If instead of her father it had been her guardian or a king whom she had refused to obey, the conflict would have had a different degree of tension.

In comedy, natural relationships are conventional—they do not essentially influence the protagonists' state, and on this point, they are similar to those in chess. In discussing the degree of importance of natural relationships in different types of dramatic genre, Katsenelinboigen and I agreed to distinguish between replaceable and irreplaceable ones. Although deep and significant in drama and dramedy, natural relationships in comedy are superficial and can easily be replaced by relationships of a different kind. A comparison between *The Servant of Two Masters* and *Romeo and Juliet* may shed light on the nature of such relationships in comedy and tragedy.

"The Servant of Two Masters" and "Romeo and Juliet." The story of Princess Beatrice Rasponi and Florindo Aretusi echoes that of *Romeo and Juliet*. Both couples are in love, both struggle to be together, and both are ready to pay a high price for being reunited. Like Juliet's cousin Tybalt, Rasponi's brother is killed in a duel by his sister's beloved. Both killers escape from the city in which they have always lived (although Romeo escapes *from* Verona while Aretusi escapes *to* Verona).

Except for these striking parallels of plot lines, there is nothing in common between the two plays. A different degree of richness of protagonists' potential causes different inflammations of passions and results in conflicts of different magnitude in the two plays. For instance, the death of Tybalt entails drastic changes in the lovers' fates, and although Juliet defends Romeo, she is deeply wounded by the fact that her beloved is also her cousin's killer. Romeo himself realizes that his action is a serious challenge to the families' relationship, and the conflict cannot be easily resolved. Hence, the killing of Tybalt becomes a turning point of the play, primarily because natural relationships are involved.

In *The Servant of Two Masters*, the killing of the heroine's brother does not become an obstacle to her marriage. Beatrice is not concerned with the problem of family relationships, nor does her beloved express remorse concerning the murder, only regretting that he may not see his beautiful bride again. Even Beatrice's monologue is written in such a way that it is focused exclusively on the description of events, rather than on her feelings and thoughts, thus emphasizing the superficial nature of her character, which is not designed for sorrow and mourning:

> *Beatrice:* You remember Florindo Aretusi? He wished to marry me. My brother would not allow the marriage. They fought a duel. Federigo, my poor brother, was killed. Florindo fled from justice. I heard he was making for Venice, so I put on some of my brother's clothes and followed him. Thanks to the letters, which are my brother's and thanks still more to you, Signior Pantalone thinks I am Federigo. I shall draw the money which he owed to my brother, and then I shall be able to help Florindo. (Goldoni 10)

Such a brief and simple narration of events is typical of traditional comedy. As a rule, comic protagonists mainly focus on the external descriptions of events in their monologues, rather than on their inner states. But even when revealing their feelings, comic protagonists confine themselves to generalized remarks, such as, "my Beatrice languishes and sheds tears because of my absence." This allows one to talk about schematic relationships in comedy, including family relationships.

In *The Servant of Two Masters,* family relationships serve merely as a motivation for the heroine's "transformations"; owing to her resemblance to her late twin brother, Beatrice is able to constantly change roles, thus creating the main intrigue. The inessential weight of the natural relationships in comedy is not comparable to that in dramedy and drama. As a comic character, Beatrice cannot be judged by her wish to marry the killer of her brother; such a judgment is inappropriate for comedy simply because the limited potential is the main condition of this genre. The comic character, whether it is vicious or virtuous, is not supposed to think in terms of unconditional values. This is the way the dramatist forms the potential of his lightweight comedic universe.

"King Lear" and "The Miser." If natural relationships are irreplaceable in drama and dramedy (unlike in comedy), then the underestimation of those relationships is a violation that results in the creation of serious conflicts between the characters and their environment. As in real life, nature severely punishes those who violate its laws, and even innocent people may automatically become victims of it. Therefore, when King Lear renounces his beloved daughter Cordelia, he is in turn abandoned and betrayed by his other children; the neglect of family relationships results in the destruction of the entire royal line.

A comparison of two fathers, Molière's Harpagon and Shakespeare's King Lear, may shed light on the different nature of family relationships in comedy and tragedy. One should agree that Molière's Harpagon is no less despotic than King Lear, whose domineering and explosive nature ultimately destroys his family. As Harpagon's son, Cléante, says:

> *Cléante:* It is really past bearing. Could anything be more outrageous than the niggardly way he treats us, the absolute penury in which we have to live? . . . I am determined to run away from home with this charming creature, and risk whatever future Fate may send us. (*"Don Juan" and Other Plays* 189)

However, while King Lear's extremism tragically influences his family, Harpagon's despotism does not destroy anything. Harpagon could easily have been Cléante's guardian, not his father, and it would not have changed the situation in essence. In *The Miser*, scenes with constant quarrels (that sometimes turn into fights) between the father and his children do not affect the family as much as they do in *King Lear*. Even when father and son raise their fists against each other, it does not result in catastrophe; this is mainly because the natural relationship is not influential. Even when Harpagon renounces his child in exactly the same way that King Lear renounces his daughter, the action does not turn into tragedy:

> *Harpagon:* Oh, you wretch! So we're starting all over again?
> *Cléante:* Nothing will ever change me.
> *Harpagon:* You villain! I'll do something. . . .
> *Cléante:* Do anything you like.
> *Harpagon:* I forbid you ever to see me again.
> *Cléante:* Delighted.
> *Harpagon:* I wash my hands of you.
> *Cléante:* Wash away.
> *Harpagon:* You're no longer my son.
> *Cléante:* Very well. (241)

In contrast to this, the family relationship in *King Lear* is the keystone of the intrigue:

> *Lear:* Let it be so: thy truth then, be thy dow'r!
> For by the sacred radiance of the sun,
> The [mysteries] of Hecate and the night;
> By all the operation of the orbs,
> From whom we do exist and cease to be;
> Here I disclaim all my paternal care,

Propinquity and property of blood,
And as a stranger to my heart and me
Hold thee from this, for ever.

(1.1.108–14)

As one can see, both protagonists express their rage towards their children, but if in *King Lear* the father's damnation ruins his children's lives, in *The Miser* it does not affect anything. Thus, seemingly identical models of behavior combined with different degrees of strength of characters' potential create different predispositions and result in different outcomes. In comedy, the violation of natural relationships causes no harm, simply because characters are limited and are not predisposed to serious emotional involvement. This is also true for the CNT, especially Chekhov's plays, in which relationships between parents and children are shown to be very superficial (as in *The Seagull* or *The Cherry Orchard*).

In general, traditional comedy stays aloof from any deep speculations and assertions hidden behind characters' statements; whatever a character says about his or her feelings towards another character is said in accordance with the role as a lover or a rival. Roger L. Cox's definition of the comic character as "lacking in self-knowledge" (171) outlines a very poor potential that influences the richness of a protagonist's inner life.

Like chess players, authors of comedy assign certain functions to their characters, being deliberately unconcerned with the creation of their characters' inner state. For instance, if comic characters are "pawns" or "queens," they must act accordingly: lovers speak of love; villains are concerned with evil. All monologues and dialogues are external, and no deep emotions are involved; however, this narrows the potential of the comic character.

It goes without saying, however, that the analogy between chess pieces and comic characters is not completely accurate; while the pieces of chess are devoid of any inner life, the comic character still possesses a certain degree of attachments, though in comparison to the character of drama or dramedy, it is very weak and superficial.

Summary

The same conflict may become the subject of different types of dramatic genre, but the degree of seriousness would be different in each of them. The analysis of works of the same or analogous topic raises the question, what makes polemics weighty—a topic or its discussants? Naturally, the significance of the polemics is determined by the degree of potential strength of the participants. In a literary work, the poorer the potential of the characters, the less significant are the conflicts they can produce. As a rule, regardless of the topic they discuss, characters of limited potential do not cross the border of local, conditional thinking, for their intellectual limitations do not allow them to elevate their speculations to the level of global generalizations.

The analysis of characters' potential cannot be limited by one or two characteristics. In order to see the differences of the "identical twins" in comedy and tragedy or drama, one must consider the diversity of parameters structuring the characters' potential and give each parameter weight.

The morality of a protagonist is not correlated with the degree of strength of his or her potential. Characters can be represented as having a different degree of strength and richness of their potential regardless of their morality or immorality, sinfulness or righteousness. Morality is just one of many characteristics forming a potential and it must be considered in combination with others.

Compared to dramedy and drama, natural relationships in comedy are replaceable and conventional. Characters in comedy are therefore closer to pieces on a chessboard, since their inner life is too simple, which influences their attachments.

A Miraculous Turn:
Fate, Chance, and Predisposition in Comedy, Dramedy, and Drama

5

The goal of this chapter is to show that the Aristotelian concept of tragedy and comedy as based on fate and chance is inaccurate and that the old paradigm of thinking based on the dichotomy of chance and program requires a modern reconsideration.

Predisposition as an Intermediate Stage of the System's Development

The question of fate and chance in literature. The question of how a system develops is fundamental for all fields, including literature and art. With regard to my study, this question concerns the problem of chance and fate in comedy and tragedy, as formulated by Aristotle and his school. From the point of view of the process, the traditional definitions of comedy and tragedy are based on a dichotomy of complete order (fate) and complete chaos (chance). According to Aristotle, peripeteia in tragedy cannot be based on chance—this is a prerogative of comedy. Such a statement presents a problem, since in some cases it is very difficult to investigate the genesis of an occurrence; therefore, the presence or absence of a "hidden design" often remains the act of one's belief. *Romeo and Juliet* is a vivid example of such difficulties experienced by scholars who unsuccessfully attempt to discover the "cause" of the chain of events that leads to the tragic outcome. Christopher Prendergast writes:

> Since Aristotle's discussion of the foundations of peripeteia in tragedy, the presence of "chance" in literature has had an extremely bad press, characteristically seen as figuring among the more disreputable or irresponsible elements of the writer's repertoire. More specifically, the device of chance or coincidence is generally defined as belonging properly to the domain of low melodrama, exploited either in T. S. Eliot's words (from his discussion of chance in the work of Wilkie Collins), "simply for the sake of seeing the thrilling situation which arises in consequence." ...

Perhaps, the most famous example of these forms of response is in the critical controversy that has always surrounded Shakespeare's *Romeo and Juliet*. Tragedy or melodrama? The question is posed, of course, because—at the level of the dramatic question—the death of the lovers is immediately dependent upon the contingent fact of the Friar's undelivered message; this dependence, in the familiar critical argument, represents either a serious violation of the inner aesthetic logic of tragedy or, at the very least, a somewhat trivial catalyst for the resolution of a dilemma whose deeper shaping forces lie elsewhere. (41)

Debates concerning works like *Romeo and Juliet* lead to the more general question of the role of outer influences on a system; namely, to what extent can a system be determined by outer influences, and is it able to absorb them in its favor? With regard to *Romeo and Juliet* the problem can be formulated in the following way: to what extent can a bad predisposition of the world absorb a chance occurrence in its favor? It seems to me that this is the basic question of Baz Luhrmann's screen version of *Romeo and Juliet* (1996), whose concept will be discussed later.

In actuality, there is a very limited number of works in which a single chance occurrence drastically changes the protagonists' lives (i.e., cataclysms or accidents whose sudden appearance cannot be absorbed by their victims). All other changes concerning human life must be considered with regard to one's predisposition and free will. As analysis reveals, in a masterful work (whether it is comedy, dramedy, or drama), the role of the characters' predisposition in interactions with chance occurrences is crucial. A chance occurrence, whether spontaneous or orchestrated, always interacts with a certain predisposition and must therefore be considered *within* the system, since it may result in a different outcome if combined with a different predisposition. This is true for any system, including artistic ones.

Stages of a system's development. As has already been mentioned, the paradigm of a system's development is traditionally represented as oscillating between two extremes—complete order and complete disorder. Katsenelinboigen states, however, that the whole process of a system's development consists of various stages, starting from complete uncertainty and ending with complete certainty. He outlines four stages of a system's development: mess, chaos, predisposition, and complete order (*Concept of Indeterminism* 25–27).

According to this concept of stages, *mess* is a "zero phase" that contains no linkages among the elements. *Chaos* is a phase that "is characterized by some ordering of accumulated statistical data and the emergence of the basic rules of interactions of inputs and outputs" (25). *Predisposition* "exhibits less complete linkages between a system's elements than *complete order*, but more complete than chaos" (26). Finally, *complete order* is the phase in which all linkages between the elements are complete and consistent.

Differentiation among the stages assists one in dealing with systems with less or more developed linkages, since stages are correlated with certain methods; this will be discussed in detail in part three. The artistic system goes through all stages of development, starting from the complete uncertainty typical of the very first stage of a creative process (when even the intent is not formulated clearly) and ending with the complete order typical of ideological works. Even in such works, however, one can find a small degree of freedom of its elements, since it is unlikely that the artist can successfully link all the artistic elements forming his system in a complete, programmatic way.

Fate and Free Will in Tragedy

Interpretation of fate and free will in modern criticism. The concept of a system's phases can easily show what stage is missing in the paradigm of fate and chance, which reflects two stages of a system's development—complete order and complete spontaneity, respectively. This old paradigm, inherited from Aristotle, is still valid in modern criticism, and so the intermediate stage (a predisposition) is generally not taken into consideration when discussing various chance occurrences in tragedy and comedy. For instance, Geoffrey Chaucer called his *Troilus and Criseyde* (1385–86) tragedy because of the presence of "necessity" in the management of the protagonists' lives. One can still find the same definition in the *Encyclopedia Britannica:* "There is always an irrational factor, disturbing, foreboding, not to be resolved by the sometime consolations of philosophy and religion or by any science of the mind or body . . ."

The influential outer force is widely represented in Greek tragedy, revealing itself through prophecies and communications with the world of gods. The question arises: do outer forces paralyze a character's will and make him or her a lifeless puppet, or does the character possess free will and make choices based on his or her predisposition? The answer to this question is that there is a diversity of types of interaction between the inner and the outer; in some cases, one may observe a complete subjugation to the outer influences when characters lose their will, as did happen with the Argonauts.

Below, we will discuss the types of interaction between the inner and outer forces, but for now it should be mentioned that such cases of a character's complete loss of will are rare, and are usually linked to either witchcraft or illness. In the majority of cases, characters are responsible for the choices they make, no matter how predetermined the situation may seem on the surface. Some ancient philosophers and writers certainly thought in these terms when approaching the question of fate and free will, though they did not elaborate a concept that would allow them to overcome the dichotomy and move further. As Winnington-Ingram states,

> [T]he terms of the philosophical debate about free will and indeterminism are modern. It is however a great mistake to suppose that the real issues of this debate were not present in the minds of Greeks and could not be expressed in their language. (154)

Katsenelinboigen's concept of free will. Before switching to an analysis of interactions between inner and outer forces, let us specify the category of free will. According to Katsenelinboigen, free will is linked to one's ability to vary one's own willpower in pursuing objectives, while a lack of free will means that one's willpower is fixed and "any change in man's behavior is categorically ruled out" (*Concept of Indeterminism* 19).

Katsenelinboigen approaches the problem of free will within the framework of different types of programs and their various levels. He distinguishes between programs that are innate, such as *behavioral zero-level program*, and those that are acquired by the individual throughout his or her life. The zero-level program that, according to Herbert Simon, is responsible for directly managing the system's behavior can be either changed or altered by the first-level program. As Katsenelinboigen notes, if the first-level program can alter the zero-level program, then one can speak of the indeterministic zero-level program. Thus, criminals may enjoy killing people, yet they are restricted by society, which imposes rules upon them. The punishment of criminals is linked to their potential capability to alter their behavior; therefore, children and people found insane are not considered responsible for their actions, for as Katsenelinboigen writes, they are unable "to internalize external constraints and to generate a proper behavioral response" (19).

> The problem of responsibility illustrates the above statement. On the one hand, the environment imposes certain restrictions upon an individual expressed in social values, such as thou shall not murder, thou shall not steal, etc. An individual may possess other values and enjoy killing others, but his liability is determined by his capacity to perceive the requirements imposed by the environment and consequently adjust his behavior. If an individual is incapable of such adjustments, he is not held responsible. Indeed, insane people are regarded as not being responsible for their actions precisely because their program of behavior fails to fulfill all or just one of the necessary conditions: to internalize external constraints and to generate a proper behavioral response.
>
> A criminal is deemed in a given society precisely because he is considered capable, at least in principle, of altering his conduct according to the

dictums of the environment, but failed to do so because of his individual values that gave him greater satisfaction from ignoring these dictates.

Punishing the criminal is the same as actualizing for him the potential system of punishment. This may prod him to change his individual values and avoid crime in the future. (19)

For example, a man may run possible consequences of his behavior in his imagination and thus induce changes in the second-level program that, in turn, may change or alter the first-level program strictly responsible for the zero-level program. In this case, such a behavioral simulation is impossible; the man may in time present a threat to himself and to society, especially when his willpower is strong and he is unable to control his psychological disorder.

The interaction between the outer force and the inner force in tragedy. In Greek tragedy, the main conflict is structured around the interaction between the outer force (fate) and the inner force (a character or a system to which the force is external), with an emphasis on the character's free will. As mentioned, only in very rare cases do characters appear in the capacity of lifeless puppets that are governed completely by outer forces. The table below is meant to provide one with a clear vision of different types of forces and their various interactions (see table 2).

As the table reveals, the outer force can be either positive (fortune, good luck, providence, etc.) or negative (bad luck, ill-chance, fatality, doom, and the like), and it may operate in the three following methods: programming, predispositioning, and spontaneity. For instance, if a positive outer force is represented through pure chance, it is called fortune or good luck or lucky chance or something similar. If the method of governing the positive outer force is programming, it can be fate or doom or fatality, depending on the sign of the outer force. The same can be said of the inner force, which can also be either malicious or benign and combine all three methods while operating the system.

The degree of strength of the forces influences the outcome; for instance, if the outer program is weak (w) and the inner is strong (s), the victor would be the inner force. When the program or chance of medium strength faces predispositioning of medium strength, however, one may talk about the advantages of predispositioning, since (as will be shown later) a good predisposition may absorb chance occurrences and use them to its advantage. Conversely, if a predisposition is weak even a lucky chance may not help—as is masterfully shown in Baz Luhrmann's version of *Romeo and Juliet* (1996), which is set in modern times.

Unlike his famous predecessor, Franco Zeffirelli, Baz Luhrmann provides his protagonists with at least three lucky chances, which, however, cannot

			Outer Force										
			Positive						Negative					
			Programming		Predispositioning		Spontaneity		Programming		Predispositioning		Spontaneity	
			W	S	W	S	W	S	W	S	W	S	W	S
Inner Force	Positive	Programming	S											
			W											
		Predispositioning	S											
			W											
		Spontaneity	S											
			W											
	Negative	Programming	S											
			W											
		Predispositioning	S											
			W											
		Spontaneity	S											
			W											

Table 2. Inner and Outer Forces

be absorbed successfully by the extremely bad predisposition. There are three episodes in the film in which fortune reveals itself: the scene of the duel in which Romeo can make his choice; the scene at the funeral when Friar Lawrence sees Balthasar who may misinform Romeo; and, of course, the scene at the tomb. In Zeffirelli's version, it is Tybalt himself who, in a rage, falls upon Romeo's sword, so that Romeo has no power over the death.

Unlike Zeffirelli's unfortunate Romeo, Luhrmann's Romeo has a choice—he is given the chance to let Tybalt go when Tybalt runs from him. This Romeo cannot use the relational parameter of remoteness to his advantage, however, since he is too furious, too desperate to think clearly. In addition, the trappings of modern civilization (in this case, Romeo's gun) facilitate the entire process, and the enemy can be easily killed from a distance. This clearly illustrates the explosive amalgam of aggressiveness coupled with technical progress, which is directed towards the immediate fulfillment of man's desires. The duel is a turning point in the film, revealing the protagonists' inability to see clearly and to change previous intentions in accordance with changing conditions. Hence, the predisposition of the scene is too bad to absorb the lucky chance and thus avoid the tragedy. Indisputably, all this predisposes Romeo's failure in the finale when he, seized by grief, pays no attention to the glimmer of life in Juliet.

Luhrmann's point seems to be the following: if the entire predisposition is precarious, if a system's inner resources are impoverished, then even providence is unable to improve it. This has nothing to do with the idea of puppets and puppeteers that is widely held in criticism as the only possible paradigm of thinking. There are certainly cases when fate may determine a character from both inside and outside, but a character's free will must not be ignored in the process of the struggle. With regard to this, determination from inside is linked, first, to the formation of such values, which would not allow the character to easily change behavior (i.e., the character's inner nature). This means that the transfer to the next-level program would be difficult for characters of this type. Difficult, however, does not mean impossible. As will be shown later, characters of this type do make their own choices and do change their actions, though it takes a lot of strength from them.

The second type of internal determination is linked to the paralysis of a character's will. As mentioned above, one can speak in this case of complete determination and inevitability, which could nevertheless be overcome by a powerful inner system. A graphic example of such a type is the myth of the Argonauts and the Sirens, who attempted to lure the Argonaut heroes to their death. The heroes lose their will when they hear the sea nymphs sing and survive only because of the music of Orpheus. But even in such a difficult case, in which the will of the heroes is paralyzed, the characters still find a way to prevent the disaster; as is known, Odysseus stops the ears of his friends and ties himself to the mast, thus saving them from disaster.

The external representation of fate in Greek tragedy is in the form of either a concrete prophecy or a general knowledge that is inherent in the protagonists. In tragedy, fate often influences a character from both inside and outside; as it does in the case of Mercutio's Queen Mab, who penetrates her victims, paralyzes their will, and governs their behavior. This means that in tragedy a rare combination of circumstances is coupled with a character's nature, which cannot withstand those circumstances. As a result, the character experiences enormous difficulties in changing his or her behavior. In Schopenhauer's philosophy, the tragic hero is interpreted as a prisoner of inner and outer inevitability, or, in our terms, as *completely* determined from both inside and outside. However, such a view of the tragic character as having no free will is questionable.

As textual analysis reveals, the tragic hero could be a victim of the explosive combination of his predisposition and circumstances but still have the willpower to change his own program of behavior. In this context, *Oedipus the King* may be of interest. Oedipus's story is based on a combination of a rare coincidence (the meeting of father and son on the road) and the protagonist's explosive nature. Oedipus is distinguished by a high intellect and physical power, combined with ambitiousness and a quick-tempered nature. Nothing can stop him from doing what he thinks is right because he has never once had to demonstrate how intelligent and strong he actually is.

Naturally, such a combination of talent, intolerance, and power makes it very difficult for such a character to reconsider his behavior in an instant. Even after hearing the prophecy from Apollo, Oedipus does not restrain himself, but merely changes his location. He naively assumes that an outer change is the right solution; his analytical ability is not directed towards his own predisposition, and despite knowing how flammable he is, Oedipus still does not try to alter his zero-level program. Moreover, after hearing the fatal prophecy, he becomes even more vexed and kills some travelers, one of whom happens to be his father.

Needless to say, a character with a different predisposition would, after hearing such a prophecy, become a hundred times more cautious; Oedipus does not, on the other hand, since he has always followed his own omnipotent nature. Although it is true that Oedipus is angry and disappointed at the moment he meets his father, he is not insane, which means that he is completely responsible for his actions. He has the option to avoid the conflict, but it is very difficult for him to make the right choice.

One who doubts in Oedipus's ability to change should refer to the end of the story, in which Oedipus changes completely; after seeing the damage he has caused his family, Oedipus makes a serious confession and swears off the destructive behavior of his past. His final revelation signifies that the program of the previous level has been altered, and as a matter of fact, he appears as a different man, a defender of Colonus, in *Oedipus at Colonus*. But what kind of upheaval must he experience in order to be changed!

A serious stroke is required to change the behavioral program of one whose greatness is high, and such a situation is typical not only of Greek tragedy. Shakespeare's characters, such as King Lear or the entire society of *Romeo and Juliet*, serve as graphic examples of the role of a catastrophic event in the transformation of characters and their environment. The same can be observed in real life, when alcoholism or killing can be stopped only under the threat of death (though there is always a question of whether or not the stabilization of one's condition is permanent).

In any case, one should not confuse changes in one's behavior with changes in one's nature, whose minor alterations, I believe, are still possible. This may concern, first of all, a degree and magnitude of initial and dual parameters structuring one's emotions. For example, alcoholics may suppress their love for alcoholic beverages, reducing the magnitude of their craving and its evaluation, thus altering their behavior, but they may not assume that they have changed in essence unless their genetic codes have been modified.

Outer forces in Greek tragedy are usually revealed through gods and prophecies. Since prophecies are usually very general, one may say that they are mostly based on characters' predispositions and subjective probability, as is the prophecy in *Oedipus the King*. Indeed, at least one part of the prophecy concerning the killing of Oedipus's father is based on Oedipus's own warlike nature and his aggression towards strangers, especially when they refuse to obey him. It is very likely that in such a dynamic world in which people constantly encounter each other, Oedipus and his cruel and powerful father would have eventually collided with each other, and consequences would be tragic given the carelessness and wildness of both.

In this way or another, even if prophecies come true, they are nevertheless unable to determine characters' future development. Even in a seemingly deterministic type of tragedy as *Oedipus the King*, the Greeks remained believers of free will. R. P. Winnington-Ingram writes:

> The gods—and particularly Zeus who is supreme among the gods—are so powerful that the decrees of fate are naturally regarded as decrees of the gods; and yet there are times when a feeling comes to the surface that even the gods cannot—or must not—abrogate the decrees of fate, particularly where the death of a man is concerned.... Why does a man suffer? Why does he fall from the height of prosperity into the pit of disaster? One does not perhaps ask these questions of a vaguely conceived *moira* or even of one's *daimon*, though one may sense hostility and express resentment. We ask such questions of gods. There are two differences indeed between a vague destiny and an operative god. In the first place, destiny is inexorable, whereas gods, it is hoped, can be moved by prayer and sacrifice. (152)

The "[vague] *moira*" can be interpreted as a very general representation of the laws of nature—the "ruling principle" that is linked to some very basic, unchangeable mechanisms, such as birth and death, inherent in all stages of life. Although these laws are fundamental and global and no one can escape them, they may not be fixed forever—nothing precludes them from change, which could be a slow-going process of development of new mechanisms of life. Everything else can be changed and altered in a shorter period of time in accordance with a predisposition of the world, and the gods' interference is a great example of such a changeableness of the primary "doom."

In this sense, the "operative god" can be interpreted as a metaphor for a changing world; if the protagonist is willing to reconsider his or her behavior (confession), the world will "change" (via the malleable gods). For instance, Antigone is aware of her destiny, but only in very vague, nonspecific terms. Unlike Oedipus, who knew the specifics of his tragic destiny, she is aware only of the fact that she will die someday (very general, common knowledge that fits anyone). Antigone says to Creon:

> Die I must, I've known it all my life—
> how could I keep from knowing?—even without
> your death-sentence ringing in my ears.
> And if I am to die before my time
> I consider that again.
>
> (Sophocles 64)

Here we see a typical representation of the "vague destiny" that has no particular plan, and Antigone herself is the one who makes decisions and chooses an untimely death. Analogously, the main characters of *Romeo and Juliet* are free in making their choices but unfortunately are not very clever decision makers. Any event in the play must therefore be considered in relation to the characters' predispositions and inclinations, which shed light on the role of chance occurrences and their interaction with characters—a significant part of the analysis that is completely neglected in criticism.

Critics are often tempted to make a conclusion based on Friar Lawrence's failure to deliver his message to Romeo, proposing a strong, successful linkage between this single episode and the final outcome, without analyzing Friar Lawrence as a decision maker. Other critics try to trace a successful linkage between the beginning and the outcome, referring to episodes with Mercutio and his friends. Jerzy Limon writes:

> Mercutio found himself quite by chance in this place that was to be fatal to him; only an unhappy sequence of events causes Tybalt to hit to him.... The fortuitousness of Mercutio's death would, moreover, be in harmony with the general character of this early tragedy of Shakespeare, in which chance and misfortune play a dominant role. (103–4)

Limon's speculations are based exclusively on a dichotomy (chance and fatality) without any attempt to discuss the intermediate stage (the predispositions of characters). It is not chance, but Mercutio's stubborn and flammable nature combined with the explosive predisposition of the world that is responsible for the tragic course of events. One should only remember how vexed Mercutio is when he appears on the square; he is full of aggression and readiness to fight, and Benvolio cannot succeed in removing him from the square in which Capulets are gathering, and into which Tybalt comes ready to start a quarrel.

The predisposition worsens when Romeo appears full of joy, paying no attention to the danger radiating from Tybalt's eyes. The excited new husband believes that he is able to reconcile everyone by saying some peaceful words, but his naive confidence is broken almost immediately when he realizes that he has underestimated the cocky determination of his friend and enemy to start a fight. The predisposition is worsened by the fact that Romeo appears in the new capacity of "Capulet-Montague," which causes confusion because no one is able to understand why he is behaving so strangely. As a result, Romeo's tactic to ignore Tybalt's assaults vexes both parties even more, and Mercutio decides to take revenge for his insulted friend.

All these factors, multiplied by Romeo's own unstable nature (that often oscillates between sadness and excitement and blinds him, negatively affecting his decision making), are not taken into account by Friar Lawrence when he decides to let Romeo go out on the streets after the marriage. Friar Lawrence's decision is based on the simple assumption that Romeo is a peaceful young man who never participates in stupid fights. This is a perfect example of how assumptions based on probability may not work if the situation is unique. As I already mentioned, the uniqueness of the situation is that relational parameters (love) form "new objects"—"Capulets-Montagues"— that cannot be approached probabilistically, since there are no prior statistics available. Therefore, all the parameters must be analyzed and given weights before making any decisions. Friar Lawrence takes into account neither the predisposition of the entire situation nor Romeo's predisposition and attachment to both families. Though in love with Juliet, Romeo is obviously still more attached to his own friends; as a matter of fact, as soon as his friend is killed, he takes up a sword and forgets his other obligations.

It is much easier to blame fate or chance than to analyze the entire predisposition and the cause of the unexpected outcome. It is especially justifiable because a sense of fatality is conveyed in the prologue and in Romeo's monologues, in which he often refers to stars and fortune. One must not forget, however, that this is the characters' interpretation of the event, which may signify a simplistic vision of the world rather than reveal the "truth." Like Romeo's speculations on the matter of life and death, the story told in the prologue represents one of various possible interpretations of the outcome—a simple one. Only a thorough analysis of characters and the way they make decisions may reveal the nature of interactions between the inner (society) and the outer (fate, chance, etc.).

In Luhrmann's *Romeo and Juliet,* a sense of the existence of the outer force is conveyed through Romeo's visions. Before coming to the party, Romeo has a momentary, drug-induced dream in which he is walking along lights and crosses—a dream that partly corresponds to the final scene, in which Romeo does walk along the lit church in which his Juliet lies. The dream does not show the outcome, however, nor does it reveal the circumstances in which the event will occur. This suggests an incompleteness of linkages, gaps between events and consequences—a typically indeterministic situation. Thus, despite an early awareness of Romeo's final "destination," the whole "plan" is still obscure; and though Romeo is "shown" the place in which his fate will be decided the final score is still unknown, since it involves the character's predisposition to be attentive and careful.

Chance in Comedy, Drama, and Dramedy

What is the role of chance occurrences in comedy and funny drama? Does a chance occurrence completely influence a character's life? or does it also appear in combination with the character's predisposition and so must be considered *within* it?

I proceed on the assumption that in comedy and in dramedy and drama, chance cannot be considered without regard to the entire predisposition, and therefore the outcome is a combination of both. In tragedy, dark comedy, and unhappy drama, chance is combined with an explosive, dangerous predisposition; in succedy, funny comedy, and drama, however, the predisposition is not explosive, making it possible to absorb a chance occurrence in its favor. As in tragedy and unhappy drama, therefore, it is not a chance occurrence as such that must be discussed, but the predisposition with which it is combined.

"The Servant of Two Masters." In succedy, funny comedy, and drama, the entire predisposition is so auspicious that even unfavorable chances are absorbed successfully. In *The Servant of Two Masters,* Truffaldino succeeds not because he is lucky or smart (for he is obviously not) but because he interacts with characters who are confused and upset; he would otherwise have been easily caught in his lies. The happy ending occurs in spite of Truffaldino's "merits," however, and is a result of a favorable predisposition that saves the protagonists, whose passions are not as explosive as those in dramedy or drama.

This concerns both main characters and secondary ones, such as Silvio and Clarice. The scandal between the "rejected" lover and his unfaithful beloved is nothing but farce; when Silvio tells Clarice that he would rather see her die than betray him, Clarice draws a sword, pretending that she is willing to commit suicide. It is clear to everybody, however, that she just wants to startle her cruel sweetheart. This scene echoes the "suicidal" scene between Beatrice and Florindo at the end of the play; after hearing the "news" of each other's deaths, both lovers draw their swords to commit suicide in the presence of their servants, who, of course, attempt to stop them.

In general, characters and circumstances predispose the situation to a successful ending. The two lovers live in the same hotel at the same time and know the same people, and the only person who could spoil the situation is their loyal servant, Truffaldino. But this clod is not a villain, and so even he is unable to do any real harm.

"Much Ado about Nothing." This play represents characters of average and above average potential. Here, not only the heroes but also the villains are keen and observant, making them all successful in their enterprises. It is only owing to a good predisposition that evil is not allowed to triumph over good and the truth is finally celebrated. By the good predisposition, I first and foremost mean Hero's strong reputation and the honesty of the watchmen; though the watchmen are represented as comical figures with apparently limited scope, their orientation towards the good, combined with excellent experience and responsibility, makes them helpful tools in catching the conspirators. It is not by chance that they are able to catch the cheaters.

Friar Francis also demonstrates his astuteness in analyzing the psychology of the villains and their predispositions, which would make them confess. His unusual plan to keep secret the fact that Hero does not actually die works very well; Conrad and Borachio, the followers of Don John, finally admit their participation in the conspiracy against the innocent Hero and deeply confess. This only confirms the strong potential of Friar Francis, who appears to be a very smart decision maker in combining different methods and styles to realize his plan. In some way, Friar Francis's plan echoes that proposed by Friar Lawrence *(Romeo and Juliet)*, however, the game depends on the player, and even a great combination can be spoiled if the player is immature.

Miracle and Predisposition in Comedy, Drama, and Dramedy

"A Little Fool." Chance sometimes appears as a miracle that changes the whole situation as if with a magic touch. Even in such cases when a miracle seems to be the only impetus that changes lives and determines the outcome, however, one should nevertheless inquire into characters' predispositions to find some less mystical and more realistic explanations of a "miraculous" turn, remembering that even a magic chance interacts with certain predispositions.

A Little Fool by Lope de Vega seems to be a pure case in which a miracle instantly turns a complete fool into a brilliant individual. Indeed, there is no detail, not a single feature at the beginning of the play, that may suggest that the young and beautiful Finea—the incarnation of stupidity and blockheadedness—would ever become one of the most sparkling and enviable women in Madrid. In the beginning, the two daughters of old Oktavio, Nisa and Finea, are represented as opposites: Nisa is a symbol of perfection on all levels, including her sparkling appearance, while Finea combines a beautiful appearance with complete idiocy.

Liseo, who is on his way to Oktavio's house to meet his fiancée, Finea, receives shocking information about the peculiar stupidity of his future bride. Deeply upset, Liseo still hopes that this is just a rumor, a lie. Alas! As soon as he meets Finea, who is a genuine laughingstock in her household, his hopes disappear forever—the primitive, brutal, animal nature of the girl astonishes those who first meet her. The only person who believes in Finea's transformation is a young poet, Laurencio, who states that love is a genius that carries world reason and transfigures the universe. According to the young poet, whoever (or whatever) is touched by love acquires intellect and creativity. He states that love not only endows one with reason but also polishes one's mind, improving one's talents.

Finea's magic transformation is perfectly grounded in Laurencio's explanation of the nature of love that is omnipotent. This certainly explains the sudden change of the little fool, but it does not explain Finea's ability to fall in love. Analogous to this is Eve's tasting the forbidden fruit; true, the fruit has the power to transform a simple creature into a powerful being able to continue the creation of the universe, but what made Eve taste the fruit in the first place? It would be too simplistic to blame the poor serpent, especially because it was not able to succeed with Adam, who showed no interest in the tree.

The same thing happens with Finea, who is always very much predisposed to fall in love. First of all, love concerns strong emotions, which are required for one to experience that majestic feeling; it goes without saying that a cold and indifferent person can hardly fall in love, nor can he or she truly experience any other passion. Finea is a character of strong emotions, and though in the beginning her temperament is primitive and wild, it only predisposes the heroine to be open to the divine "flame." In this context, the scene in which Finea fights with her teacher is very revealing; even the threat of punishment cannot stop Finea from defending herself from one who humiliates and abuses her. There are also some other details (such as her love for hot food) that indirectly suggest Finea's predisposition to strong feelings. In addition, Finea adores cats, and she expresses great excitement when listening to a story told by her servant Clara about the birth of kittens by Clara's cat. All this reveals a passionate, yet tender, soul ready to share feelings with others.

The dramatist thus creates a predisposition of his wild heroine to fall in love, and as soon as she does her potential changes drastically from limited to powerful. As a result, Finea obtains a mind that allows her to win over her sister, who is known for her extraordinary intellect and wisdom. Finea gains her beloved and masterfully avoids a conflict between her father and herself owing to her new ability. The play therefore appears to be a *come-succedy* because of the potential of the main heroine, which changes from limited to powerful.

"*A Midsummer Night's Dream.*" Magic forces that affect protagonists' potential play a considerable role in *A Midsummer Night's Dream*. Oberon, King of the Fairies, the almighty ghost whose power can change people's will, tells Puck that he had seen Cupid aim his bow at "a fair vestal throned by the west," but that his "love-shaft" had not pierced her. Oberon had noted the place where the arrow fell, and now decides to use his the arrow and his magic to play a joke on Titania, Queen of the Fairies, to teach the shrew queen a lesson. Meanwhile, he overhears a conversation between Helena and Demetrius, who rudely rejects the young beauty's love. Oberon asks Puck to give some of the love potion to Helena's beloved, so that when Demetrius wakes he will fall madly in love with Helena.

Everything that happens with Titania is the subject of a funny comedy, for the love potion drastically changes the potential of the fairy queen, and she falls madly in love with a comical monster. Titania is unable to see clearly; the ugly appearance of her new "sweetheart" amazes her, she listens with admiration to his false voice and vulgar songs and vows that she has never heard or seen anything better than him:

> *Tit.* [*Awaking*] What angel wakes me from my flow'ry bed?
> *Bot.* [*Sings.*]
> The finch, the sparrow and the lark,
> The plain-song cuckoo gray,
> Whose note full many a man doth mark,
> And dares not answer nay—
> for, indeed, who would set his wit to so foolish a bird? Who would give a bird the lie, though he cry "cuckoo" never so?
> *Tit.* I pray thee, gentle mortal, sing again.
> Mine ear is much enamour'd of thy note;
> So is mine eye enthralled to thy shape;
> And thy fair virtue's force (perforce) doth move me
> On the first view to say, to swear, I love thee.
>
> (3.2.128–41)

The scenes with the bewitched queen, who used to be a very powerful creature, may serve as a graphic example of the affliction of a potential from the inside. The magic transforms the characters from being mighty to being limited and makes them completely lose their intellectual strength. The trick played on Titania does not seem to be harmful, for no one is hurt and the future is not affected. Conversely, the mistake Puck makes during his attempt to help Helena may cause a tragedy, since it also interferes with Hermia and Lysander's relationship. Therefore, a sense of possible disaster is constantly in the air.

Though it may seem that it is only owing to Oberon's magic force that potential tragedy turns into succedy, the happy ending is actually predisposed by the characters' inner strength, which allows them to withstand all the unexpected turns. Indisputably, Oberon has the power to bewilder and the power to undo the charm; nevertheless, the tragedy may have easily occurred even before Oberon realizes what kind of mistake Puck had made. Remembering only Hermia's distress after she finds out that her beloved has betrayed her—this would be enough to turn everything into a disaster.

As in *A Little Fool*, magic forces in *A Midsummer Night's Dream* only support the further development of a predisposition, but they do not prevent the heroine in the very beginning when she faces horrible changes in her beloved. So the question is, is it just a lucky chance, or is it something in Hermia that does not allow the tragedy to take place right at the beginning?

In order to answer this question one should refer to the first act; namely, to the scene in which Hermia and Lysander discuss their future. Hermia complains that she cannot reach an agreement between her father and herself, which upsets and frightens her a great deal because she understands that her love is in danger. Lysander then tells her that it is natural for lovers to struggle for their happiness and that "the course of true love never did run smooth":

> *Lys.* Ay me! for aught that I could ever read,
> Could ever hear by tale or history,
> The course of true love never did run smooth;
> But, either it was different in blood—
> *Her.* O cross! too high to be enthrall'd to [low].
> *Lys.* Or else misgraffed in respect of years—
> *Her.* O spite! too old to be engaged to young.
> *Lys.* Or else it stood upon the choice of friends—
> *Her.* O hell, to choose love by another's eyes!
> *Lys.* Or if there were a sympathy in choice,
> War, death, or sickness did lay siege to it,

Making it moment any as a sound,
Swift as a shadow, short as any dream,
Brief as the lightning in the collied night,
That, in a spleen, unfolds both heaven and earth;
And ere a man hath power to say, "Behold!"
The jaws of darkness do devour it up:
So quick bright things come to confusion.

(1.1.132–49)

This dialogue plays a significant part in the creation of a favorable predisposition, for it prepares the lovers for future difficulties and predisposes them to patience and fortitude, which will eventually save them from catastrophe. The clear understanding of what they should expect in the future helps them to find their strategy and to prepare themselves for all possible ordeals. This conversation is especially helpful for Hermia, who is more vulnerable and emotional than Lysander. In the beginning, she seems to be very upset with reality, which is in disagreement with her idealistic notion of life; however, she later comes to a very strong conclusion that influences her future decisions:

Her. If then true lovers have been ever cross'd,
It stands as an edict in destiny.
Then let us teach our trial patience,
Because it is a customary cross,
As due to love as thoughts and dreams and sighs,
Wishes and tears, poor fancy's followers.

(1.1.150–55)

As the monologue reveals, Hermia recognizes the negative possibilities but accepts everything as it is, giving her the strength to fight for her happiness to the end. Such awareness of the real state of affairs has improved the whole predisposition and made the potential of the couple even stronger. When Lysander "betrays" her, therefore, Hermia does not lose heart; in fact, she continues to struggle for her love.

The sudden turn does not kill her mostly because she has been prepared to retain her love since the moment she discusses it with Lysander. Unlike Romeo and Juliet, who are constantly disoriented by Friar Lawrence's promises of great success, this couple survives the tragedy owing to its strong predisposition. As the text reveals, magic does not work alone; it interacts with a certain predisposition and is absorbed by it. When all the mistakes are corrected, therefore, it is not too late for the combination of a favorable predisposition and help from the Fairy King to result in a happy ending.

Summary

The question of fate and chance is linked to the concept of chaos and order as two extremes of a system's development. There are four stages inherent in a system's development: mess, chaos, predisposition, and complete order. Each stage is distinguished by the degree of coherence of its elements. Outlining stages assists one in differentiating among methods of approaching the system.

Chance occurrences in both tragedy and comedy must be analyzed within the frames of the characters' predisposition. Therefore, while analyzing the role of a chance occurrence, even if miraculous, one should refer to the potential of the system rather than try to find out whether or not the chance is incidental; in some cases, this would be impossible to detect. As Katsenelinboigen states, any chance occurrence appears in a system and is absorbed by it in accordance with the system's predisposition.

The interaction between the system and outer forces involves three basic methods: programming, predispositioning, and spontaneity. With regard to outer forces, these methods are associated with different types of supreme interference, such as fate, chance, doom, and the like. Only in some very rare cases is the inner force completely suppressed by outer influences. As a rule, any entity has a mechanism of inner development and is distinguished by free will.

Part Three
The Comedy of a New Type:
The Integration of the Part and the Whole

This part of the book is dedicated to the theory of the CNT with a special emphasis on Chekhov's four major plays, which I discuss at a much more detailed level of engagement than any other works mentioned in the present study. This format allows not only a better illustration of some general statements but also a detailed discussion of the interaction between the space of action and the implied space and their integration in the mytholiterary continuum. The goal of this analysis is to reveal the weight of Chekhovian characters and their universe based on mythological and literary structures, forming the potential of Chekhov's plays.

Chekhov and Balzac as the Pioneers of the CNT 6

The Quasi-Strong Potential as a Prerogative of the CNT

Innovations in the structuring of characters' potential in the CNT. The appearance of Balzac's and Chekhov's comedy posed new questions concerning the formation of protagonists' potential, namely, the integration of the part and the whole. The new development in comedy is linked to an elaboration of the quasi-strong potential of the protagonist. A traditional comic hero is distinguished by an apparently weak potential that is structured from homogeneous characteristics that do not create a spectrum. Therefore, traditional comedy does not require a special technique for detecting the degree of strength of its simple-minded characters since their weight is apparently small. The need for a new methodology appears when contradictions arise between a traditional view of comedy (as linked to the idea of the laughable and survival) and its development into something quite the opposite. This first of all concerns innovations in the structuring of characters' potential; characters of the CNT often remind one of characters of drama because they possess isolated strong features that may mislead the reader/spectator, who often perceives the characters as endowed with average or above average potential. In order to see the characters' genuine strength, one should consider these isolated features within the whole, applying a technique that will be discussed below. As a rule, characters' good abilities are immersed in a weak whole—a very limited potential that eventually affects their future development.

The comedy of a new type highlights the question of integrating the part and the whole. Most importantly, such integration cannot be done intuitively; it requires an analytical approach to characters' potential and predisposition. This is in disagreement with traditional comedy, which requires an immediate and intuitive assessment of the comic. The spectator of traditional comedy must not wonder if the character is comic, he or she must immediately see it and react to it in accordance with the rules of the comedic genre. All the efforts of the dramatist, director, and actors would otherwise be wasted. In other words, no intellectual, analytical thinking with regard to the characters' potential is required from the spectator of traditional comedy, whose feedback is expected to be reactive. This is the main reason why many critics do not agree with Chekhov's description of his four major plays as comedies (since, on the surface, his main protagonists resemble characters of drama). Needless to say, a new theoretical approach to comedy is required to see the ingenuity of Chekhov's works.

Chekhov's comic mode was close to that of Balzac. The fact that one of Chekhov's plays, *Uncle Vanya*, is subtitled "Scenes from Country Life" speaks for itself; surely, it echoes one of Balzac's subtitles, "Scenes from Provincial Life." Neither is the mention of Balzac's name in *Three Sisters* accidental—it may suggest a parallel to *The Human Comedy*, whose integral idea is the lack of global vision in humankind and that presupposes the vanity of humankind's desires and oblivion. Though Chekhov deals mostly with provincial life, he also finds a way to generalize his vision of the entire country, giving it global ambitions in a world of local importance. Like Balzac, Chekhov creates major characters (such as Trigorin, Treplev, and Astrov) who are seemingly intelligent, gifted, and able protagonists. They are all so far away from the cliché of simpletons who inundate traditional comedy that any doubt concerning the strength of their potential may seem ridiculous. Therefore, without approaching their potential from the point of view of the whole, it would be impossible to see their essential limitations, which are the main subject of the CNT.

Unfortunately, Chekhov's innovations were well received by neither directors nor theatergoers. Nor did they receive proper treatment from critics. Chekhov always insisted that he created cheerful, funny short stories and dramas, while critics labeled him a creator of dismal works: "Chekhov's play makes a hard, if not to say, oppressive impression on the audience" (*Sochineniia* 13: 449; trans. John Holman); "*Three Sisters* appears to be a heavy stone on one's soul" (13: 449; trans. John Holman); "I do not know another work that could 'infect' one with such a heavy, obsessive feeling" (13: 449; trans. John Holman). That Chekhov intended his work to be seen as a farce has not yet received a comprehensive evaluation.

His first comedy, *The Seagull*, failed. And no wonder! Spectators who anticipated vaudevillian scenes became extremely angry with the dramatist for misleading them with the subtitle and for representing, instead, a depressing story that ends with the suicide of a main protagonist. The same fate had befallen *The Cherry Orchard*, a play that was planned to be a farce (as reflected in Chekhov's letters to his wife, Olga Knipper). In 1901, he wrote to her: "The next play that I am going to write will definitely be funny, at least by its concept" (*Sochineniia* 13: 478). Critics accused Chekhov of lacking skill; they naturally did not see anything funny about the distressing plays that Chekhov called comedies. But what happened to *Three Sisters* was even worse.

A struggle for the CNT: conservators and innovators. Just as any other innovator, Chekhov suffered for his pioneering changes of the comedic genre, which he unfortunately never discussed in a more logistical way. As Savely Senderovich states, "Chekhov was the most misunderstood Russian writer—be it his prose or drama. Everybody misread him—be it friends, admirers, or arrogant ideologues" ("*The Cherry Orchard:* Chekhov's" 226). Up to now his major plays have been defined by critics as something between melodrama, drama, and tragicomedy.[1] An interesting phenomenological analysis on *The Cherry Orchard* was done by Senderovich. In regard to dramatic genre, Senderovich states that *The Cherry Orchard* "is a comedy in a very special sense: it is a burlesque, a travesty in its self-referential game" (230). In some cases, Chekhov's plays are also considered satire, which in criticism is interpreted as an equivalent of comedy.[2] As has been mentioned, however, Chekhov was against such an interpretation of his plays and always stated that he wrote "funny comedies" not satires (*Sochineniia* 13: 397, 491). Nevertheless, his statement was nothing but a solitary voice crying out in the wilderness, the best evidence of which is the struggle around *Three Sisters*.

Regardless of Chekhov's genuine comic intentions, the opinion that *Three Sisters* was written as a drama still exists in criticism. Moreover, even after reading the evidence presented below, some scholars still refuse to accept the fact that Chekhov was working on a new type of comedy in creating his stories and plays.[3] Critics justify their belief by the absence of documents showing that Chekhov wrote the subtitle "comedy" by his own hand and that someone else crossed it out, thus changing the genre designation of the play.[4]

In its first edition, *Three Sisters* was subtitled as "drama"; the fact that Chekhov insisted that he created comedy, even vaudeville (which he seriously argued about with Stanislavsky and Nemirovich-Danchenko), sank into oblivion. In this regard, the first question that I want to answer is, when did information about the genre of *Three Sisters* first appear? The very first evidence of it comes from fall 1900. On October 14, 1900, a month before the censored version was registered, V. M. Lavrov—who heard from newspapers that Chekhov was working on a comedy—turned to him with a request to "give that comedy to Russkaia mysl" (*Sochineniia* 13: 434). The name of those newspapers and the sources of the "rumors" about Chekhov's new comedy require further investigation. However, Lavrov's letter is one of the first written proofs that Chekhov was working on a comedy, not a drama.

Two weeks later, on October 29, Chekhov visited the Moscow Art Theater (MAT) to have his first reading of *Three Sisters*. This meeting unexpectedly became a quintessence of disagreement between the author and the actors, as well as the directors. According to Stanislavsky, the main conflict occurred because of the genre of the play; while Chekhov considered it to be vaudeville, "everybody else took it for drama and wept" (*Sobranie sochinenii* 1: 235; trans. John Holman). As Stanislavsky stated in his memoirs, this lack of understanding of his comedies amazed Chekhov, who was unable to learn to accept it. Stanislavsky writes: "What shocked him most of all and what he could not reconcile himself to was that his *Three Sisters* and, later, *The Cherry Orchard* were perceived as heavy dramas about Russian life. He was sincerely convinced that he wrote cheerful comedy, almost vaudeville" ("A. P. Chekhov" 394; my trans.).

Later, while working on *The Cherry Orchard*, Chekhov, who remembered his previous experiences with his comedies, wrote the following to M. P. Alekseeva (Lilina) in 1903: "It turned out to be not drama, but comedy, sometimes even farce, and I am afraid that you will 'get it for that' from Vladimir Ivanovich" (*Pisma* 11: 248; my trans.). Thus, though writing in a jocular manner, Chekhov strongly emphasized that his new play was not a drama and that he wanted it to be considered a comedy—no matter what.

Returning to *Three Sisters*, there are some other remarks scattered in letters and memoirs that suggest that Chekhov called this play a comedy among his friends and acquaintances. For instance, M. M. Kovalevsky, who visited Chekhov in Rome when he worked on proofreading *Three Sisters*, remarked that Chekhov told his friends to wait until "his comedy" was directed on the stage to see its genuine mastery (365). So when and how did the subtitle "drama" appear?

Before moving onto the next part of our investigation, I should admit that I was unable to find a direct answer, and the only thing that I managed to do was to trace some facts that allowed me to make some speculations and hypotheses concerning the predisposition of the whole situation. These facts revealed some essential disagreements (and even a hidden conflict) between Chekhov and Nemirovich-Danchenko, who was ultimately responsible for the numerous "misreadings" and "mistakes" that occurred in the first published version of *Three Sisters*.

In his memoirs, Nemirovich-Danchenko remarks that at the first reading (which, as has been mentioned, occurred on October 29, 1900) no one was able to perceive the play as comedy, especially because "in the manuscript it was subtitled drama" (169; trans. John Holman). Nevertheless, this statement about the subtitle seems to be questionable. It remains unclear as to when and how the subtitle "drama" appeared on the front page of the manuscript. The first censored, theatrical version that was registered in November 1900 had only the title of the play, with neither the name of the author nor a subtitle. The final version appeared in December 1900 as a result of discussions and disputed readings *(raznochteniia)* between the dramatist and the director. The edited version prepared by Chekhov for publication in December 1900 had been hidden in Nemirovich-Danchenko's archives for many years. As Chekhov's *Polnoye sobranie sochinenii i Pisem* (*PSSiP;* [Complete Works]) suggests, Nemirovich-Danchenko not only kept the corrected version in his archives but was also responsible for *raznochteniia* (different interpretations) and other distortions that occurred during the play's publication in *Russkaia mysl'* (Chekhov, *Sochineniia* 13: 434–37). All subsequent editions of *Three Sisters*, including that of Marx, were based on the defective version published in *Russkaia mysl'* under the supervision of Nemirovich-Danchenko (13: 439–40).

A short article by E. Kostrova, "K istorii teksta 'triokh sestior,'" appeared in *Literaturnaia gazeta* in 1954, in which the story of the final draft of the manuscript was first discussed.

> The play *Three Sisters* has been performed on the stage of the Moscow Art Theater (MAT) for more than fifty years. How strange it is that, up till now, nobody has gotten it into his head to check the stage text of the MAT performance against the editing of the play as it was published in its final form in the last edition of the author's collected works published in his lifetime. Whereas there are in these texts, especially in the third and fourth acts, significantly different readings. But how can one succeed in establishing this fact? This year, in connection with the fiftieth anniversary of the death of Chekhov, a film was made, *The Notebooks of A. P. Chekhov*, which revealed to the audience the "creative laboratory" of the great Russian writer. The author of the screenplay, S. Vladimirsky, while searching out material for the film, began to listen to gramophone recordings of the MAT performance, while holding in front of himself the text of the play, which was published in the twenty-volume collected works of A. P. Chekhov. At first the texts seemed identical. But, the further it went the more often variant readings were detected. It was impossible to admit the idea that in the MAT (which so carefully referred to every authorial remark) there could have been permitted any kind of "ad-libbing" in relation to Chekhov. Consequently, there had to have existed some kind of authorial (or author-authorized) stage edition of *Three Sisters*. It merely remained to be found. Research led to the MAT museum. With the assistance of the director of the museum, F. Mikhal'skij, an archive was brought up, and in the Chekhov safe there came to light a thick cardboard folder bearing the inscription "not to be examined without the director's permission." The folder had

been kept there from the time of the museum's founding, in the early 1920s. In the folder there turned up two little black oilskin notebooks, containing the author's manuscript of the first and second acts of *Three Sisters*, as well as a manuscript of the third and fourth acts, which had been sent from Nice at the end of December, 1900 (O. S.). It is known that Chekhov, having finished the play in the Fall of 1900 and having then turned it over to MAT, continued to work on it nonetheless. After having corrected the first two acts in Moscow, Chekhov left for abroad and while there he "made drastic changes" to the third and (especially to the) fourth acts, as he wrote to O. L. Knipper. The fact was also revealed that the folder contained a second version of *Three Sisters*. The first (typewritten) version of the play was also kept in the safe; this turned out to be the director's copy. It is marked throughout with insets, inserts, and corrections made in accordance with the clean copy. According to one such director's copy—that belonging to K. S. Stanislavsky—it is possible to judge which "drastic changes" the author had made.

In researching these materials, S. Vladimirsky, the young Leningrad philologist A. Mervol'f, and Professor G. Byaly came to the conclusion that apart from this working, director's copy, there existed yet one more clean, original text of the play. It appeared to them to be the censored copy, which was also kept in the theater's museum.

Although there is no mention of the play's genre, this article reveals the constant disregard for the author's version and thus indirectly supports the speculation that the genre could be also have been altered "a bit" by some anonymous "editors."

To continue the story, according to *PSSiP*, when Lavrov first contacted the MAT to request the text of the manuscript, Nemirovich-Danchenko replied in bewilderment that he did not have a copy and that it was some kind of misunderstanding. Judging by later discoveries, however, Nemirovich-Danchenko did keep the manuscript and for some reason did not want to give it to Lavrov. As a matter of fact, Lavrov succeeded in getting the manuscript a few days later and informed Chekhov of the incident: "Finally, I 'confiscated' from Nemirovich-Danchenko your *Three Sisters* and set it in type" (*Sochineniia* 13: 435; my trans.). All this suggests that Nemirovich-Danchenko might have had his own secret ambitions while hiding and "editing" Chekhov's manuscript. As Chekhov writes to Knipper-Chekhova, *Russkaia mysl'* published *Three Sisters* without his proofreading it and Lavrov "states that it was Nemirovich who 'corrected' my play." (*Pisma* 9: 207; my trans.).

In this way or another, *Three Sisters* lived through a rough time, being corrected by editors other than Chekhov. In 1901, *Three Sisters* was first published by Marx Publishing House (St. Petersburg) as a single edition with photographs of the first performers who played the three sisters—Savitskaia (Olga), Knipper (Masha), and Andreeva (Irina). As I previously mentioned, this edition is based on the distorted version published in *Russkaia mysl'*, which was subtitled "drama" and also was designed with portraits of the first three performers who played the leading characters. Naturally, with these portraits of the dramatic actresses, the subtitle served to emphasize Stanislavsky's staging of *Three Sisters* as a drama. The Chekhovian subtitle "comedy" would not work at this point. It is still unclear, however, whether Chekhov himself decided to compromise and give his permission to subtitle his play "drama" or if it was done without his knowledge (as did happen with the last two editions released before Chekhov's death, over which he had very little control) (*Sochineniia* 13: 439). Thus, there is a very high possibility that Chekhov, who constantly blamed his publishers for the mistakes and distortions of his original text, might not have noticed or had no chance to change the subtitle that contradicted his definition of the genre of *Three Sisters*.

Though we cannot disprove Nemirovich-Danchenko's statement that the play was subtitled "drama" in the first place, we may confirm that it was in complete disagreement with both the description of the censored version and with Chekhov's own statements. As a matter of fact, the further editing of *Three Sisters* was intended to clarify the vaudevillian character of the play. To this end, Chekhov introduces some traditionally comical remarks that are intended to enhance the sense of vaudeville within the frames of his innovations and to facilitate one's "digestion" of his comedy. For instance, Chekhov introduces the line "Ne ugodno l'etot finik vam prinjat'?" (Would you like to eat this date as your medication?) and explains that this is a song from a vaudeville that he wants Chebutykin to sing (*Sochineniia* 13: 439). At the beginning of the first act, Chekhov introduces ironical remarks for Solyony and Tuzenbakh as a background for the sisters' conversation, which essentially reduce the lyricism of their dialogue. In addition to this, numerous other remarks, jokes, and stage directions are scattered throughout the play to emphasize the author's comedic intention (*Sochineniia* 13: 431). Hence, from beginning to end, Chekhov worked on a comedy and not a drama when he created *Three Sisters*; and even if he himself once subtitled the play "drama" (we still leave this possibility open), it could be meant in the sense of dramaturgy.

To understand Chekhov's innovations required a shift in conceptual ground. Unfortunately, Chekhov did not like giving explanations, naively believing in his readers' intuition; this failed in most cases because simple intuition was not enough to understand the new type that he created. Stanislavsky writes: "When we began to read the play and turned to Anton Pavlovich for explanations he, being extremely confused, refused to give any, telling us, 'Listen, I wrote there everything I knew'" ("A. P. Chekhov" 394; my trans.).

As follows from his correspondence, Chekhov believed in the "obviousness" of what he was doing and confirmed that anyone who carefully read his texts would interpret it in the same way. Such an underestimation of subjectivity in the interpretation of artistic texts caused constant disagreements between the innovative vision of the author and the traditional mind of his reader/spectator. Stanislavsky writes about *The Cherry Orchard:* "I was crying like a woman; I wanted to restrain myself but I could not. I hear you saying to me: 'Excuse me, but this is just farce.' No, for a simple person this is a tragedy" (*Sobranie sochinenii* 7: 226). Stanislavsky was absolutely right; it was ridiculous to expect from a traditional reader—"a simple person"—complete comprehension of the sophisticated design of Chekhov's new comedy. Chekhov's old dream of a congenial reader was utopian, for it was, according to *Moskovskie vedomosti,* "an excessive demand of working fantasy not only for the reader but also for the spectator" (qtd. in *Sochineniia* 13: 375; my trans.).

Notably, the comic nature of *Three Sisters* was obvious to Lanford Wilson, who subtitles his translation of the play, "a Comedy in Four Acts." Though Wilson does not give any theoretical grounds for such a "free" translation of the subtitle, his artistic intuition leads him in the right direction.

The Macrolevel of CNT: Order and Chaos

Chekhov and Balzac constitute two levels, micro and macro, on which the potential of humankind is formed. Both levels are structured in the same way, representing strong features immersed in a weak whole. This concerns both a particular individual and his society. For example, there are characters in Balzac's novels whose creativity and human qualities are very high; at the same time, they are surrounded by a society whose destructive, aggressive nature ruins everything noble and sublime. Luciene de Rubempre's friends, David and d'Arthez, incarnate spiritual purity, fortitude, and devotion to their work. However, they become isolated seeds that do not sprout in that garden of weeds. David's life may serve as a graphic example of how best intentions are destroyed by the mercantile world. Pure and naive, this talented young man becomes a victim of errant swindlers who appropriate his innovations. Nevertheless, the swindlers are not the issue, but rather the world is—the world that allows them to thrive at the expense of those who are able to contribute new developments.

In this next section, I focus on the macrolevel of Chekhov's and Balzac's works, approaching their characters as a system; that is, from the point of view of their interactions. As is known, Chekhov was the one who changed the tradition in drama and introduced a group of characters instead of a single protagonist as the central figure. Naturally, the question arises, how does one evaluate the potential of Chekhovian groups? As a rule, characters of Chekhov's major comedies are intelligent, gifted people who suffer from their inner weakness and inability to develop. If approached as an aggregate, they represent an above average potential; however, if analyzed as a system, their potential appears to be weak.

Let us analyze how the system of relationships is structured on the macrolevel, using as an example two of Chekhov's plays, *Three Sisters* (1901) and *The Cherry Orchard* (1904).

"Three Sisters": the world of the uniform and ill chance. In *Three Sisters*, relationships on the macrolevel can be described as complete disorientation and confusion on the one hand, and a complete subjugation to order on the other.[5] Such a dichotomy suggests a very poor, primitive relationship with the universe typical of characters in comedy.

The universe in *Three Sisters* exists as a world of extremes, formed by complete balance and complete unbalance. The symbolism of the uniform becomes vital in the structuring of protagonists' relationships on the macrolevel. It appears as a frontier between the civil and military worlds (including officials paid for by the government) and becomes a reliable shield for its bearers. All characters in the play are divided into those who wear a uniform and those who do not. In the former category are the troops, teachers, post officers, and the like; they are distinguished by their ability to survive any cataclysm. The transition from the world of the uniform to the free, civilian world is risky and results in characters' death or failure.[6]

The wild, spontaneous expansion of the world beyond the uniform is symbolically represented by Natasha's weedy sprouting along the house. It is important to stress that such a dichotomy echoes a totalitarian mentality that, though suppressed, cannot tolerate freedom and, moreover, sees it as a disaster. Therefore, Chekhovian protagonists, who were happy to be rid of their father's domination, switched to another pole—a chaotic existence with no orientation, no mentor, and no program. According to Chekhov, such an inability to overcome a dichotomy and elaborate a degree in existence suggests a very primitive method of thinking, which is unfortunately typical of Russians. In his diary, Chekhov writes:

> Between "there is God" and "there is no God" there exists a huge space that even a great thinker overcomes only with much difficulty. The Russian knows only one of the two extremes, the middle ground between them is not interesting to him; that is why he usually knows either nothing or too little. (qtd. in Derman 318)

The characters in *Three Sisters* oscillate between the world of strict order and the world of chance (which turns out to be ill chance). Chance rules their lives as the uniform once did. They have no power over either because they always flow with the stream, no matter which pole they belong to; this is true not only for the characters but for all of the creatures in the play.[7]

"The Cherry Orchard": relationships at the fair and the lucky avos'. If switching to chaotic freedom in *Three Sisters* brings nothing but ill chance and misfortune, spontaneous farcical changes in *The Cherry Orchard* often result in happy outcomes with profits for some of its lucky protagonists. Regardless of Ranevskaya's superficial sentiments, the smell of good luck and fortune tickles the nostrils of Lopakhin, Pishchik, and Petya Trofimov, who anticipate a happy future in their own manner. Metaphorically speaking, if in *Three Sisters* the protagonists lose at cards, gambling with fate in *The Cherry Orchard* leads to gains in merchandising in the fair of life. Nevertheless, from the global point of view, their momentary gains lead to destruction of their world.

The allusion to the fair in *The Cherry Orchard* appears with regard to particular names and characters whose function predisposes a carnival atmosphere of purchasing and buying typical of the fair, with its folk merriment.[8] In general, the nature of relationships in the play, combined with the symbolism of performances at the fair, echoes the rules of interaction at a fair. The difference between a market and a fair is that the former is based on planning and legal agreements between negotiating partners, while economic relationships expand chaotically in the latter—their momentary changes are dictated by purchases and sales. This liberates the negotiating partners from any responsibilities—they are not obliged to make any promises or to keep their word. Consequently, profit cannot be planned at a fair, and all decisions are based on participants' intuitive conjectures.

A lack of responsibility and naive, intuitive attempts to approach the future are the basic features distinguishing the protagonists of *The Cherry Orchard*. Some of them proclaim radical changes in their life and the life of their society, but all these statements are nothing but empty words. One such "theoretician-practitioner" is Lopakhin, who creates a groundless theory of a rising "working class," *dachniks*, that is formed by people living in summer houses *(dacha)* during the summer. It is his intuition that "whispers" to Lopakhin that he may completely count on the dachniks while making his plans.

So he buys the cherry orchard convinced that the *dachniks*, who traditionally rent the plots during the summer vacation to have fun by drinking heavily in noisy nocturnal parties, will do nothing but work hard in taking care of the orchard. The date of the estate sale—August 22—"predetermines" its dark future.[9] As one of my students suggested, the last name of the new owner of the estate, Lopakhin, can also be interpreted as derived from *lopukh* (Lopakhin as distorted Lopukhin)—a sort of weed (burdock) and also a synonym for "a failure" in Russian slang.[10] Both interpretations perfectly fit the idea of the cherry orchard's ruin in the hands of incompetent owners.

Lopakhin is often considered in criticism as a practical character in contrast to Gaev and Ranevskaya, who are called impractical. However, it seems that in comparison to those two characters, Lopakhin represents the opposite of practicality, for if a practical man is one who succeeds in achieving his goal, then he is a complete failure; his goal to build a great future on the laziest part of society is completely utopian.

Superficiality, irresponsibility, and egoism are the features structuring relationships in *The Cherry Orchard*. This concerns everything from the estate to friends and relatives. For example, Anya is left alone in the estate by her mother, Ranevskaya, who egoistically justifies her actions with the fact that it would be painful for her to live in the estate in which her youngest son had died; the feelings and needs of her only daughter are not taken into consideration. Ranevskaya does not even care that her daughter is going to build a future with such a bankrupt character as Petya Trofimov.

Petya Trofimov appears to be a revolutionary ideologist, who barely distinguishes between the notions of freedom and anarchy (in common sense of this word). For him, freedom is liberation from responsibility, and as both a student and a teacher, he ends in fiasco; he cannot finish his education in college, and his student, Ranevskaya's youngest son, drowns in the river. Now Petya asks Anya to follow him, to build a future together. But what kind of future awaits her? Petya's ridiculous "revolutionary" speeches in which he "exposes" all "exploiters," combined with his name, evoke an association with Petrushka—a popular Russian puppet who was a cocky character through which revolutionary ideas were proclaimed. As the Russian encyclopedia describes, "Petrushka performed in the fairs, markets, and neighborhoods. A street artist spoke for Petrushka, using a so-called *pishchik*, a thing that made his voice metallic and shrill" (*Bol'shaia sovetskaia* 19: 499; my trans.).

It is no accident that another character in *The Cherry Orchard* has Pishchik as his last name. In prior criticism, this last name has been associated solely with the verb "to squeak" *(pishchat')*, but this is insufficient.[11] Vera Gottlieb even suggests that "in *The Cherry Orchard* Simeonov-Pishchik's name might be translated as 'Simeonov-Squeaker'" (29). The meaning of the last name Pishchik cannot be linked directly to this character since this protagonist does not emit any squeaky sounds (unlike, for instance, Epikhodov). This last name contributes to the creation of a fair atmosphere and is the focal point that serves to establish the basic paradigm linked to the fair. In other words, by means of such names a predisposition of the fair is created.

With regard to Pishchik as a character, he also predisposes the allusion to the carnival atmosphere that reigns at the fair, the farcical world in which everyone tries to capture the "wheel of fortune." The idea of spontaneous changes is linked directly to this character, whose success is based on the philosophy of *avos'* (a Russian word for "lucky chance")—a typical philosophy of the fair. Pishchik is the one who believes in fortune, and at the beginning of the play he tells everyone that his daughter Dashen'ka "is going to win 200,000 . . . she has a lottery ticket"[12] (*Chekhov: Four Plays* 226).

After the estate is sold, the fair is closed and everyone leaves in a hurry, abandoning the old firs; these are seen as a "walking encyclopedia" of their life, which no one needs. Again, all are emotional, sharing their feelings with others, expressing their love and sadness, bursting into tears; but in actuality no one really cares for anything but his or her own welfare. The depraved nature of these relationships is parodied in a scene in which Charlotta enacts the abandonment of a child:

> Charlotta: *(Picks up a bundle, resembling an infant in swaddling clothes.)* My sweet little baby, 'bye, 'bye . . .
> Poor baby! I feel sorry for you! *(Throws the bundle down.)* (263)

To conclude, the macrolevel assists in observing the system of relationships from the global perspective, which allows one to better see the rules of interaction among protagonists and to holistically approach the predisposition of the given artistic universe. As the analysis reveals, the system of relationships can be so weak that even some relatively strong characters are unable to change the sign of its development. The characters may have good intentions and a positive way of thinking, but they are not able to influence the system in its essence, and their isolated voices are eventually devoured by the whole that is predisposed to disintegration.

Microlevel: The Formation of the Segmental Strength

Switching to the microlevel requires approaching a character's various isolated features as a system; likewise, the analysis of a group of characters requires a consideration of their relationships as a whole. Thus, at the microlevel, in place of a group of characters, there are a number of characteristics belonging to a particular character, and in place of a system of characters there is a minisystem (a single character whose potential is measured in accordance with the same rules).

Like a society that consists of various types of individuals, characters are woven from different features, some of which can be strong. It is not enough to possess some isolated strong features to develop successfully, however, since a rich potential is required to support those strong sides revealed in a character. Therefore, the appearance of some seemingly able characters in the works of Balzac and Chekhov saves neither society nor its individuals, for the potential as a whole is weak. By the same token, individual strong features structuring the microlevel of the CNT cannot prevent a character from degeneration.

Segmental strength: "*Old Goriot*" *(1835) and* "*The Grasshopper*" *(1892).* The segmental strength of a potential signifies some ugly discrepancies between a well-developed part and the weak whole.[13] Such representation of a system becomes a subject of the CNT, whose seemingly gifted protagonists suffer from an inability to progress in their personal relationships and professional skills. They may sparkle among their friends and colleagues; they may strike others by their brilliance in a certain field, but as soon as they cross these borders, their limitations come to the surface. And they often do cross it; their disadvantages arise, and misfortunes begin when they are unable to see their own constraints and ambitiously think that they can successfully wield the whole world.

The formation of a character's segmental strength is perfectly illustrated by a famous Balzacian character, the Old Goriot—a formerly great businessman who once earned vast amounts of money and spent it all on his daughters. The depiction of this personage requires a detailed analysis:

> It was during this year that Goriot made the money, which, at a later time, was to give him all the advantage of the great capitalist over the small buyer; he had, moreover, the usual luck of average ability; his mediocrity was the salvation of him. He excited no one's envy; it was not even suspected that he was rich till the peril of being rich was over, and all his intelligence was concentrated, not on political, but on commercial speculations. Goriot was an authority second to none on all questions relating to corn, flour, and "middling"; and the production, storage, and quality of grain. He could estimate the yield of the harvest, and foresee market prices . . . Anyone who had heard him hold forth on the regulations that control the importation and exportation of grain, who had seen his grasp of the subject, his clear insight into the principles involved, his appreciation of weak points in the way that the system worked, would have thought that here was the stuff of which a minister is made. Patient, active, and persevering, energetic and prompt in action, he surveyed his business horizon with an eagle's eye. Nothing there took him by surprise; he foresaw all things, knew all that was happening, and kept his own counsel; he was a diplomatist in his quick comprehension of a situation; and in the routine of business he was as patient and plodding as a soldier on the march. But beyond this business horizon he could not see. He used to spend his hours of leisure on the threshold of his shop, leaning against the framework of

the door. Take him from his dark little counting-house, and he became once more the rough, slow-witted workman, a man who cannot understand a piece of reasoning, who is indifferent to all intellectual pleasures, and falls asleep at the play, a Parisian Dolibom, in short, against whose stupidity other minds are powerless. (14: 84–85)

Describing Goriot, Balzac first outlines a very narrow field—"all questions relating to corn, flour, and 'middling'; and the production, storage, and quality of grain"—in which his character achieves perfection. Goriot demonstrates extraordinary capability in estimating harvest yields and in making prognoses concerning market prices. It is not only his sharp mind that is highly praised but also his human qualities such as patience, energy, and an ability to appreciate others. The comparison to the minister only enhances the impression of the brilliance of this man, who succeeded in a very difficult and dangerous time, when even his friends and colleagues failed. Reading all this, one can do nothing but admire this genius who found an original way of interacting with the world. Such an extended description of Goriot's best qualities, however, is provided to a different end, for the author's next step is directed towards the representation of how the powerful sides of his characters are correlated with their other sides. It is now the reader's moment to shudder, facing the ugliness of the entire picture; here is a man with a mind disproportionately developed for business, a skill that grows like a tumor and suppresses the development of the rest of his brain.

As further examination reveals, the comparison to a tumor is quite accurate; Goriot's great abilities to count and to love are distorted by his limited potential (as Quasimodo's body is disfigured by the narrow space in which it is incarcerated) and eventually turn into a sickness. I will provide an analysis of Goriot's failure in the next chapter. For now, it is important to stress the technique of integrating the strong part and the weak whole, which in most cases is not explicit and requires strong analytical skills from the interpreter working on the evaluation of a character's potential. The latter is typical for Chekhov's artistic system, which is based on the contextual representation of characters.[14] This hinders one's understanding of Chekhov's intent because, like Balzac, he often emphasizes explicitly some positive qualities in his protagonists, while making their essential limitations the subject of the context.

In a letter to Suvorin, the editor of *Novoe vremia*, (December 30, 1888), who insisted that Doctor L'vov (a protagonist of Chekhov's play *Ivanov*) was a "distinguished man," Chekhov explained his approach in the following way:

This is an honest, open, emotional, but limited and straightforward man.... The broad vision of life and spontaneity of feelings are foreign to him. He is an incarnation of a cliché, of a current tendency. Any phenomenon and face he considers within his narrow perspective and he is very biased. He praises one who proclaims the "honest work" and he disparages one who doesn't. There is no golden middle. (*Pisma* 3: 112; trans. John Holman)

Such an exhaustive characterization of a character is not typical of Chekhov who, as I mentioned above, did not like explanations and assumed that the reader would be intelligent enough to see those things. However, this is important evidence of Chekhov's method of structuring his protagonists' potential, which he deliberately endowed with segmental strength. In this short letter, he also showed exactly how one must approach his seemingly "positive" protagonists and what characteristics must be taken into account in considering their potential as a system.

It is not only Doctor L'vov but also Doctor Astrov, whose patronymic name is L'vovich (a hint on Doctor L'vov), who does not see "the golden middle" and proclaims that "everything about a person should be beautiful: face and dress, mind and soul" (*Chekhov: Four Plays* 112). At the same time, he himself is extremely vulgar in approaching beauty—no, not the abstract beauty he constantly expounds about but a concrete person who bewitches him, Elena Andreevna. He finds nothing better than proposing a one-night stand with her in his forest district, calling her "my beautiful little beast of prey"—the peak of vulgarity and cheap taste. As a rule, people like Astrov are good at some abstract, ideal notions, but as soon as they turn to concrete situations, they reveal their complete bankruptcy.

The hidden limitations of Chekhovian characters are sometimes similar to those inherent in Balzacian protagonists. For example, a comparison between Balzac's Goriot and Chekhov's Dymov ("The Grasshopper") enriches one's understanding of both authors' system of values and their basic positions from which the judgment of their characters is made. Like Goriot, Dymov is a loving husband and a good professional who, at the same time, is highly insensitive to art. His assessment of artistic creation is based exclusively on pragmatism, on the market that establishes the "genuine" price of the artist:

> "You are a clever, generous man, Dymov," she used to say, "but you have one very serious defect. You take absolutely no interest in art. You don't believe in music or painting."
>
> "I don't understand them," he would say mildly. "I have spent all my life in working at natural science and medicine, and I have never had time to take an interest in the arts."
>
> "But, you know, that's awful, Dymov!"
>
> "Why so? Your friends don't know anything of science or medicine, but you don't reproach them with it. Every one has his own line. I don't under-

stand landscapes and operas, but the way I look at it is that if one set of sensible people devote their whole lives to them, and other sensible people pay immense sums for them, they must be of use. I don't understand them, but not understanding does not imply disbelieving in them."

"Let me shake your honest hand!" (*Essential Chekhov* 88)

Dymov's criterion—"immense sums"—assists him in accepting the importance of art, which he is otherwise unable to grasp. His narrow, pragmatic, and unimaginative mind attempts to justify this deficiency with a comparison to natural science, which, as he claims, is unknown to most artists. Though such an explanation seems reasonable to his "thoughtful" wife, who immediately agrees with him, it is nevertheless inaccurate. Literature and art belong to a general education and are required for one's intellectual and spiritual development, along with the development of one's professional skills. A medical doctor himself, Chekhov was highly skeptical concerning the pragmatism of his colleagues, whose narrow perceptions of life as a complex of physiological processes did not allow them to enjoy flights of human fantasy. The role of art is to develop one's imagination, which then broadens one's scope and makes one generate "crazy" ideas that are always ridiculed by common sense. Most distinguished scholars are known for their rich imagination and sensitivity to art.

The main focus of art is the sophisticated relationships between characters and objects, relationships that create new dimensions and invite one to an ever-developing universe of forms and meanings. This is an endless process of change, a "perpetual mobile" whose existence becomes possible owing to the interpreter's imagination, which has been improved and cultivated for ages. Chekhov's characters, however, are of a different kind—they are unable to fly high, being too close to the ground to overcome the laws of gravity. Chekhov's "man in a case" is afraid of any changes going around; he feels safe, wrapped in his narrow earthly logic of the commoner, and nothing can convince him to leave his shell.

Traces of such consciousness can be found in many Chekhovian characters. The scientist Dymov defends his dissertation in pathology and spends most of his time with corpses—a metaphor for dealing with stasis, for the anatomizing of corpses signifies a static analysis of dynamic processes. This is correlated with Dymov's inability to comprehend dynamic changes in life and his failure to "diagnose" problems before they are irreparable. Being extremely primitive in the sphere of relationships, he naively believes that everything will stay the same; this is the mentality of one who only deals with corpses. The "pathology" of his relationship with his wife is not clear to him until it is too late, at which point their marriage becomes a dead "body" that he can "anatomize." But the problem is that he cannot revitalize the "deceased," and so the "anatomization" will not help him rescue the situation. Dymov pretends that nothing has happened, just hoping that the dead "body" will not decompose too quickly. Dymov's memory of having once cut himself while dissecting a corpse now comes to light, and the reader anticipates a repetition of the same mistake that will result in Dymov's death. The irony, however, is that Dymov dies not from the cut of the corpse but by being infected by the living; metaphorically speaking, he dies *because* of life, which is fatal for those whose immune systems are not designed to deal with change.

More insight concerning the formation of the quasi-strong potential is revealed when other characteristics are taken into consideration. Among them, the formation of goals and types of vision becomes an important step forward in approaching characters' predisposition.

Types of goals. In general, goals are divided into close, or short-term goals, and remote, or long-term goals. Both types can be as local as they are global, as material as they are positional. Setting material goals is typical of the combinational style; likewise, setting positional goals is a prerogative of the positional style. For example, the development of art through new forms and concepts is a remote global positional goal formulated by such protagonists as Balzac's d'Arthez, who sacrifices his well-being in the name of art, and Chekhov's Treplev, who proclaims the creation of new forms. Conversely, obtaining prestige for money and well-being is a remote global material goal that is explicitly expressed by Nina and Luciene, to whom art is the ladder to a luxurious life. No matter what his friends say to him, Luciene stubbornly seeks a way to sell his "treasure" at a great profit, making his gift a means of achieving his material goal.

Different types of potential are designed for different types of goals. For instance, a limited or quasi-strong potential is good only for short-term local or intermediate goals. Characters of comedy, both traditional and the CNT, can be successful in achieving such goals as long as they are not complete simpletons like Truffaldino. This explains why Goriot succeeds in his field but fails in a broader sense, wasting the money he has earned for nothing.

As a decision maker, Goriot is distinguished by a local disjointed vision that works only for limited tasks, and as soon as a holistic vision is required, he ends in fiasco. He therefore approaches his relationship with his daughters as if he were a buyer and the girls were goods—demonstrating the mentality of a merchant who values only materials. So, instead of making a positional goal of developing a strong relationship with his daughters, he sets the local, short-term material goal of buying their presence for the moment. He wins locally—they come to him each time they need money—but this only enhances their hidden hatred and disgust for him. His house of cards eventually collapses and buries him.

Another character who does not much care about the feelings of her own prodigy, but whose happiness one can only envy, is Chekhov's Arkadina *(The Seagull)*, a star of the "first magnitude" on a provincial stage in Kharkov. The secret of her cheerful mood is that she is always good with her local material goal, which is to retain her audience and admirers. She believes that a bird in the hand is worth two in the bush, and so she never changes her local "Olympus." Conversely, those who pursue global goals fail; Nina's global goal to conquer the world ruins her, and Arkadina's rising talent of a son, Treplev, despises local achievements and proclaims radical changes in art, thus ending in fiasco.

Treplev's global goal is to reform art by finding new forms that will assist in revitalizing the theater and literature, but he does not know how to elaborate a strategy to achieve the desirable end. Setting a goal is just a part of the sophisticated process of decision making, and one must possess other skills and the ability to realize an intent. Global vision is necessary in solving tasks and is linked to strategic thinking, which combines strategy and tactics. As Katsenelinboigen mentions, "Due to this versatility, the strategic positional play merges strategy and tactics. The reverse is not true, meaning a good strategy can be corrupted by poor tactics but poor strategy cannot be salvaged with good tactics" (*Concept of Indeterminism* 66). According to Katsenelinboigen, global vision is defined by the three following conditions:

- Setting a goal or a direction
- Defining the initial conditions
- Elaborating a strategy to link the former to the latter. As a result of this, a trajectory of development can be formed.

Like characters of drama and dramedy, characters of the CNT may set global goals, but their lack of global vision predisposes their failure. In formulating his goal of reforming art, Treplev *(The Seagull)* does not know how to elaborate a strategy and, moreover, does not even have any tactics to link his initial position to the final goal. In the end, therefore, he admits his complete bankruptcy:

Treplev: Forms. For so long I've been going on and on about the need for new forms. And now, little by little, I'm falling into the same old rut myself. ... Now Trigorin has technique, it's easy for him ... He's got a "broken bottle neck gleaming on the bank," a "mill wheel casting a somber shadow"—and presto—there's his moonlit night right there. And what do I have—"the shimmering light," and "the soft twinkling of the stars," and "the distant sounds of the piano receding into the fragrant air" . . . I mean, it's unbearable! (*Chekhov: Four Plays* 85)

As follows from Treplev's monologue, his rival seems to be successful in finding a technique of creating the artistic image. Trigorin has no strategy as a writer; his local disjointed vision of things results in an inability to approach the world from a global, philosophical perspective. He "hunts" for local, isolated ideas (such as a cloud that resembles a piano or the smell of heliotrope in the air) and he masterfully introduces all those details into his works, as one can conclude based on Treplev's remarks. Trigorin's frustration comes when he tries to switch to a field that is foreign to him. This new field requires different abilities from him; namely, to become a thinker, a teacher, and a preacher, representing all aspects of life. This makes his status unbearable, and he complains to Nina, "I love this lake, the trees, the sky, I feel nature, it arouses a great passion in me, an uncontrollable urge to write. But . . . I feel that since I am a writer, I am obliged to write about the people, about their suffering, about their future" (*Chekhov: Four Plays* 62).

Like Arkadina, Trigorin sets local goals and elaborates tactics to realize his intent, but the lack of global vision upsets him because this is the requirement that he is unable to fulfill. Arkadina, on the contrary, does not have such requirements and so nothing can cloud her life as the prima donna of the secondary stage. Conversely, the young couple representing art (Treplev and Nina) is united in their global goals, which neither can achieve by virtue of their inability to think strategically. Nina sets a global, remote positional goal to become famous but nevertheless acts as if it were a short-term, local material goal. Instead of developing her relationship with Arkadina to learn some important things, which any novice actress should know, she applies a combinational style and tries to capture the "king," Trigorin, in the hope that their marriage would introduce her to the circle she needs. Needless to say, 99 percent of her infatuation with this man is about his fame, and she is "in love" with him even before she meets him.

One must admit that Nina is excellent in achieving her local intermediate goal—she does get the "king"; moreover, she receives the opportunity to make her debut at a summer theater outside Moscow. It is difficult to say what the reason is for her failure and return to the provinces, and whether it is a lack of experience or a lack of talent, but one thing is obvious: her goal requires positional strategic thinking, which would include establishing good relationships with critics, actors, directors, and influential admirers. As a beginner, she needs tremendous professional and personal support from them, which would come in the form of professional discussions, teaching, proposals, and so on.

As the analysis of Nina's predisposition reveals, however, she is very narrow-minded when it concerns her desires, and she does not pay much attention to human relationships. Nina practically ignores Arkadina, who tolerates her impudent behavior, and she has absolutely no sympathy for Treplev, for whom she is a source of great pain. Her goal is the most important thing to her, and she smites everything in her way to attain it. Therefore, it is not a surprise that she is unable to build her circle in Moscow, and, conversely, she acquires more enemies than friends there. I provide a detailed analysis of Nina's predisposition in the next chapter. Here I just stress the fact that her local vision in combination with global desires and an aggressive nature create an explosive mixture that destroys not only the people around her but also herself.

Characters of traditional comedy are rarely provided with global goals; as a rule, they think in terms of local pragmatic objectives linked to short-term tactics. On the other hand, characters of the CNT often set long-term global goals, and readers who do not differentiate between setting global goals and possessing a global vision may be deceived about the ability of these characters. As shown above, it is not enough to have global desires—to realize them, one must possess an ability to think strategically and involve unconditional evaluations.[15] The neglect of strategic constraint, which "aims to prevent us from succumbing to the tempting gains dictated by tactical considerations," destroys pragmatically thinking characters, no matter how sophisticated they may seem in their tactics (Katsenelinboigen, *Concept of Indeterminism* 146).

Such are Balzac's powerful characters, who eventually become victims of their immoral behavior, which disfigures their souls, affects their minds, and leaves them in spiritual poverty and genuinely cosmic loneliness. Rastignack, Luciene de Rubempre, Gobseck, and Goriot—this list of locally thinking protagonists who only pay attention to material goals, gradually destroy their relationships with the world, and ruin their own souls, can be continued. The same can be said of Chekhovian characters, who are united by their lack of holistic vision and inability to think globally, though some of them attempt to set global goals. Astrov *(Uncle Vanya)* is one of them.

This bright character bewilders the reader with his energy, attractiveness, and noble intentions, but he demonstrates a typically disjointed vision in the correlation of the global and local steps in his everyday life. Practically, he is unable to save even one bush in his forest; his patients die, and moreover, he ruins his own life, drinking heavily and engaging in nocturnal debauchery. This character represents a disjointed system of values, having no idea how to integrate his high ideals with his way of living. In her monologue, Elena Andreevna outlines that lack of integrating vision inherent in all the protagonists:

Elena Andreevna: It's just as Astrov said: You're all recklessly destroying the forests, and soon there will be nothing left on earth. Just in the same way you're recklessly destroying human beings, and soon, thanks to you, there will be no purity, no devotion, no fidelity left on earth. (*Chekhov: Four Plays* 102)

Astrov is a typical representative of a group of characters whose global goals are not appropriate to their intermediate steps. Petya Trofimov, whose best intentions are expressed in the hackneyed writing style of revolutionary newspapers, actually moved some of Chekhov's contemporaries unable to see Chekhov's irony. His speeches, intended to excite only naive girls such as Anya, excite the entire countryside, which unfortunately does not ask the simple question of how such an irresponsible type could become the ideologist of a new life. If they blame anyone, it is mostly the practical Lopakhin, whose remote, local material goal to develop the cherry orchard is not greatly appreciated by a society whose world-renowned "spirituality" keeps it safe from any pragmatic tactics. As shown above, however, Lopakhin's practicality is an exaggeration, and his limited potential does not allow him to find a way to link his local goal to the initial conditions.

In the same way, the Chekhovian sisters are unable to realize their local remote goal of moving to Moscow because, as shown above, they have never been trained to elaborate on any tactics or strategies. Nor do they understand that in their case the goal must be reformulated from local to global; namely, from changing their location to reconsidering their lives, for this would be the only way for them to seriously approach the question of the future. Furthermore, it seems that the Prozorov family should focus on finding a direction rather than on setting a goal, since the latter may appear only after they clarify which way to go, and the only "transportation" that may carry them to Moscow is their clear vision of themselves.

To conclude, the comedy of a new type represents different types of goals set by the protagonists; however, the lack of integrating vision does not allow them to succeed in the infinite scheme of things.

Summary

The CNT introduces the notion of a quasi-strong potential, which is a combination of some isolated strong features (a segment) and a weak whole. The integration of the part and the whole assists in the valuation of a character's potential.

The analysis of an artistic system should be performed on both the macro- and the microlevels. The macrolevel allows one to approach the system from a global point of view, taking into consideration the relationships forming the whole. The microlevel allows one to approach a potential of a single character in order to evaluate his or her predisposition for future development. Both levels are important in considering the dramatic genre of a literary work.

The types of goals set by characters shed light on the degree of strength of their potential. Goals are divided into close and remote, each of which can be either local or global, and positional or material.

To elaborate a trajectory of development of a system one should possess a global vision that can be as teleological (goal) as nonteleological (direction). The global vision comprises a global goal or direction, initial conditions, and a strategy of linking the former and the latter. The presence of the global vision signifies a high degree of strength of one's potential.

Quasi-Dramatic Effects in the CNT 7

Words, Deeds, and Predisposition of Characters

"Words, words, words!" says Hamlet. "Words, words, words!" echoes Treplev, watching Trigorin walking with notebook in hand. "Words, words, words!" exclaims the reader after them, listening to all these extended monologues on the meaning of life, beauty, and the role of labor.

The question of what one should primarily take into account in analyzing characters has been debated for decades; some critics say that Chekhovian characters must be judged by their actions; others insist that it is important to focus on what they say rather than on what they do. My approach to this problem is that both words and deeds are aspects of behaviorism that do not allow one to penetrate deeply into the motivations and psychology of characters. Characters may often say and do things that could deceive the reader, who might be misled by the protagonists' seemingly generous words and decent actions. Therefore, it is important to reformulate the problem; it is important to know *who* is speaking, not only *what* is being said, and *who* is acting in a certain way, not only *what* kind of action is being performed. This approach requires an instant switch from behavioral analysis to the analysis of characters' potential and predisposition, by researching their decision making, values, and everything else that may not be revealed explicitly in the text.

As a student, in the past, I discovered how many professors, leading scholars, and witty interpreters were trapped by the profound speeches of main Chekhovian characters and built interpretations on praising the protagonists' credibility and blaming their environments. Indeed, if only words were taken into account, what could be wrong with the statements, "one must work" *(Uncle Vanya)*, and "our grandchildren will have a more successful life" *(Three Sisters)*? Indisputably, the statements are correct, but the problem is that the words about work belong to Uncle Vanya, who would not do a thing were it not for Sonya, and the speculations about the bright future are made by

Vershinin, who is helpless and cannot solve the problems in his own family. Furthermore, the belief in the grandchildren's happiness is expressed by Andrey Prozorov, whose paternity of at least one of his children is questionable. So, all positive statements are made by powerless, helpless characters, which must essentially decrease the weight of their words.

Characters' self-evaluations. The turning point of characters' various good-natured statements is in the way they represent themselves to others. The self-images they want to create often have very little similarity with their real selves; but this is the way they desperately want to be seen by others, and they truly believe that they are what they say. They sound so sincere, so honest, so convincing that one must be a block of wood not to be touched by their revelations. Harvey Pitcher builds his whole approach to Chekhovian characters based on their statements and the way that they sound. He states that the interpreter "should always be sensitive to the emotional coloring of what is said, as well as to the meaning of the words themselves" (101).

Although it is true that the emotional coloring of a speech may say a lot about the character who delivers it, this may not necessarily be linked to the verification of the truthfulness of his or her statement; rather it may indicate unfulfilled ambitions and an inability to see the self from the outside. The character may truly believe that he or she deserves a better life, but it may not be in accord with the real state of affairs. For instance, when Uncle Vanya at the breaking point of his nervous tension, cries out that he would have been a Schopenhauer were it not for Serebryakov, he sincerely believes that the world has been unfair to him. This would not be taken seriously, however, unless other indications in the play directly or indirectly suggest that Uncle Vanya had the potential to become a distinguished figure. In the same way, the emotional statements of Balzac's Goriot that he loved his daughters more than anything else—as "confirmed" by his actions of spending all of his money on them—may only deceive one if considered in isolation, without regard to his predisposition.

Most of Chekhov's characters simply repeat popular ideas, enacting the life and thoughts of someone else. Emphasizing the histrionics of Chekhovian characters, Morson writes: "Voynitsky wants to enact a grand and dramatic crime, but he manages only one more petty squabble" ("'Sonya's Wisdom'" 69). Such constant dramatizing is typical of a considerable number of Chekhov's characters, among whom Nina Zarechnaya *(The Seagull)* is not of the least importance.

Nina certainly believes that she is becoming a great actress. And who would blame her for this? She is young, attractive, full of energy and ambitions, and she is not willing to give up her dreams. But does it mean that her opinion on her self-improvement corresponds to reality? To decide to what extent Nina's self-evaluation is adequate, one should inquire into her predisposition. It would be especially interesting to analyze her final monologue, in which she asserts that she has already achieved some considerable results on the stage, from the point of view of the style in which Nina expresses her thoughts.

Characters' monologues, except for the information about their way of thinking and their way of feeling, consist of words, expressions, and exclamations that allow one to speculate about their nature. For instance, the word *provoronit'* ("to let slip by") in Voynitsky's angry monologue against Serebryakov may add much to the understanding of Voynitsky's psychology if combined with the other features inherent in his character. In some cases, even the order of the words matters to the interpreter sensitive to positional parameters as independent variables, since the ordering is a positional characteristic. In Nina's monologue, the way she describes how she feels on the stage now is indicative: "I'm a true actress now, and I perform with joy, with ecstasy, I'm intoxicated on the stage, and I feel beautiful" (*Chekhov: Four Plays* 88–89).

"Ecstasy" and "intoxication" are characteristics of Nina's bohemian nature that are first revealed during her conversation with Trigorin, to whom she admits with excitement, "[I]f I were a writer like you, I would give my entire life to the multitude, knowing that their happiness lay only in reaching my heights, so that then they could draw me in my chariot" (62). No, it is not about art but about Nina's vain desire to sparkle, to excite a crowd, to become a pagan priestess of orgies in her honor. And she truly feels intoxicated on a provincial stage when they give her an ovation, and she may finally feel her long-awaited superiority. But this has nothing to do with talent.

Art does not exist for Nina as a source of inspiration and development but as a step towards her bohemian Olympus. It has no independent value for her and is just an intermediate stage in achieving her material goal. Nothing matters to Nina but an unsatisfied pride that obscures her mind and soul. Appearing at the estate after a few years of absence, she talks only about herself and her illusory advantages, absolutely ignoring the man whom she once wounded so deeply. One who attempts to speculate about Nina's professional quality based on her final monologue in the fourth act should realize that it is first and foremost about her personal qualities, about her predisposition, which has never changed since she was a young, inexperienced girl craving a "noisy glory."

The formation of the degree of talent in the CNT. Despite all this, the question of Nina's talent must still be answered, for even such negative characteristics as vanity and conceit do not preclude the possibility that one can be gifted and make a contribution to the development of one's field.

136   *The Comedy of a New Type*

At the beginning of the fourth act, Dorn asks Treplev for his opinion of Nina:

> *Dorn:* And her career?
> *Treplev:* Worse, I'm afraid. She made her debut at a summer theater outside Moscow, and then she went away to the provinces. At the time I wouldn't follow her. She played all the big roles, but she overacted badly, gesticulating, ranting and raving. There were moments when she showed some talent—she played hysteria and the death scenes well—but those were only moments.
> *Dorn:* Still, she had talent, didn't she?
> *Treplev:* Difficult to say. Probably. (79–80)

It is not only Treplev who experiences difficulty in answering Dorn's question but the reader as well, because the dichotomy (talented or not) requires further elaboration to allow speculation on such a delicate topic. Most likely, this heroine has *some* talent, but it is not as great as she states. Talent is a combination of various qualities, including a strong will, the ability to develop one's gift, and a complete dedication to work. Though Nina appears to be a very persistent person, her will and energy are directed towards flighty desires. She does not express interest in what she performs, nor is she eager to improve her qualifications as an actress by discussing her performing skills with an experienced actress such as Arkadina. In the beginning, she reveals a complete lack of concern for Treplev's playlet, which she finds boring and undeserving of her attention. When, in the second act, Masha asks Nina to read something from the playlet, Nina seems to be very surprised. She asks Masha, "Do you really want me to? It's so uninteresting" (55). At the same, she does not mind appearing on the domestic stage in order to perform before Trigorin. One can only imagine what kind of performance it is—an immature actress playing a role that she does not understand and does not like. It is only the fact that *she* is on the stage that inspires her deeply; nothing else matters to her. At this point, Treplev's remark in the fourth act that Nina takes up only "all the big roles" on the small stage once more confirms what her urges are.

On the other hand, Nina sounds like a very dedicated person when she expounds on the importance of one's belief and says that she now understands that for the creator the most important thing is "not the glory, not the glitter," but "the strength to have faith" and "to bear your cross" (88). Nina's monologue is woven out of contradictions that do not allow one to link all her statements successfully into a complete and consistent picture of her character. This is typical of the indeterministic representation of a heroine, whose characteristics create an incompleteness that can only be approached by applying predispositioning as the method of evaluation. Only after ascribing weights to Nina's various characteristics and integrating them into a whole can one conclude to what extent these last words about faith and strength are true. In my interpretation, they are nothing but a melodramatic cliché to Nina's taste, which does not contradict her histrionic nature exposing itself in a provincial manner.

Nina's love of affectation is briefly mentioned by Treplev when he tells Dorn that Nina signed her name "Seagull": "She would sign her name 'Seagull.' You know, the way the miller said he was a raven in Pushkin's *Rusalka*—so she kept saying in her letters, that she was a seagull" (80). Treplev astutely outlines the imitative nature of this heroine, who is inclined to act as a martyr, using literary personages as her role models. Such mention of Nina's signature with regard to stage performances creates a predisposition for perceiving her further behavior through the prism of theatricality.

Treplev turns out to be the only spectator before whom Nina has the chance to make her "benefit performance," and so she does. It does not mean, however, that she fakes her feelings concerning her past and present—it is much more complicated than simple imitation. She truly suffers from everything she goes through, but at the same time, she cannot help acting because it is the only way she can establish herself in the eyes of others and herself. This sensitive young woman is certainly not devoid of artistry, but the degree of her talent seems not to be as high as she claims.

Among Balzac's protagonists, whose degree of talent is essentially insufficient for their ambitious desires to conquer the world, Luciene de Rubempre plays a considerable part: he becomes a character-mediator between the spiritual and mercantile worlds. At the beginning of his career, Luciene oscillates between complete dedication to the art of the word, requiring seclusion and concentration on his work, and giving into the temptation of being accepted by the crowd, which requires an absolutely different lifestyle. He finally makes a choice, which leads him to the desired (though questionable) success; he sparkles in the salons of aristocratic society, but the price he pays is too high, killing the creator within himself. Momentary pleasures and promises of fame and glory seize him completely so that he becomes indulgent in secular amusements, intrigues, and scandals. After all, he blasphemously betrays those who have helped him, who have shared in his worst days and who have supported his talent endlessly. He eventually loses his gift, his friends, and his love and finds himself in spiritual and physical poverty, abandoned by those who once loved him and betrayed by those to whom he has sold his soul for illusory treasures.

The story of his talent's decline is sad, but it would be too rash to mourn it since the loss is not truly great. Balzac does everything in order to be clear concerning the degree of talent of this protagonist, and towards this end he introduces Daniel d'Arthez's circle of poets and writers, whose literary talents and willingness to sacrifice their well-being in the name of the creative process only outline the sparkling but superficial ability of Luciene.

From the beginning, Luciene is shown as capable of creating a promising draft; but as soon as he embarks on editing, he reveals a complete inability to improve his work. This suggests that his talent is neither strong nor deep enough to develop rough ideas into rich artistic concepts containing weighty images and thoughts. His friend does this for him generously, polishing his novel so that it becomes a masterpiece—a fact that excites Luciene when he receives his edited manuscript:

> At the present time Daniel d'Arthez was correcting the manuscript of *The Archer Of Charles IX*. He reconstructed whole chapters, and wrote the fine passages found therein, as well as the magnificent preface, which is, perhaps, the best thing in the book, and throws so much light on the work of the young school of literature. (9: 89)

This passage is revealing, for it shows the segmental strength of Luciene's potential as a writer. When Luciene is later asked to criticize his dear friend on the pages of his newspaper, he is also incapable of producing anything weighty because his literary gift is sufficient only for writing piercing critiques of works by mediocre writers. Among his journalist colleagues, Luciene is a star of the first magnitude, whose articles embellish the front pages of leading newspapers, but in his circle of thoughtful writer friends he is a moth flying close to the flame. Luciene's talent is an instant impetus of wit and imagination, a gift that fits only short-term goals such as writing sharp but superficial critical essays for public amusement.

Luciene's literary talent is completely correlated with his political ability, which is perfect for staging numerous intrigues and playing offstage games. He uses his pen to solve his momentary political tasks and he always succeeds—his is the mind of a schemer, and it is his best adviser on how to use his literary skills to good advantage. As soon as serious, thoughtful topics are involved, however, his mediocrity is revealed. He faces the height of his intellectual impotence when he is asked to write a devastating critique of a novel by his dear friend d'Arthez. For the first time, Luciene faces his inability to write an adequate criticism on a book that is not one of the trashy novels he is used to masterfully "disembowelling" with his "knife" (which now turns out to be a kitchen knife that is fit only for the dirty kitchen of political games). Knowing that this would be the end of his career, he turns to his friend for help:

Luciene held out the manuscript; D'Arthez read, and could not help smiling.... "Will you leave it with me to correct? I will let you have it again to-morrow," he went on. "Flippancy depreciates a work; serious and conscientious criticism is sometimes praise in itself. I know the way to make your article more honorable both for yourself and for me. Besides, I know my faults well enough." (9: 305)

The appearance of this article brings about Luciene's new wave of popularity. At the same time, it utterly debunks the myth of Luciene's omnipotence and his status as a god on Olympus. In actuality, this article that brings him so much success is also the beginning of his end.

Victims and villains. The impression of the dramatic is intensified when characters of the CNT act as victims. Such an impression may appear as a result of one's disjointed vision of a character, whose various features require a holistic approach. For instance, when Voynitsky accuses Serebryakov of his ruined life and claims that he has spent his years in supporting the old professor, or when Nina blames Trigorin for her misery, one should inquire into their predisposition in order to see what kind of mentality lies behind the accusations. The protagonists' "philosophizing" often becomes a clue to their psychology; this is because the artist's main concern in the CNT is not the philosophical concept as such, but the type of mind that adheres to a certain philosophy. For instance, Ragin, the main protagonist of Chekhov's "Ward No. 6" (1892), philosophizes about death in the following way:

Why should we not let people die if death is a normal, legal end for everyone?... First, as they say, suffering leads man to perfection, and, second, if mankind finds out, indeed, how to decrease its suffering with the help of pills and drops, then it will abandon religion and philosophy which not only defend it against numerous misfortunes, but give it happiness. Poor Pushkin suffered a great deal before dying. Heine had been paralyzed for several years. Why then would a certain Andrey Efimovich or Matryona Savishna, who live a senseless, empty life, resembling the life of amoeba, not tolerate their illness for a while? (*Sochineniia* 8: 85; trans. John Holman)

Such a philosophy is obviously generated by a passive type who wants to comfort his conscience with a "lullaby," for he is unable to change anything in essence. As a matter of fact, Ragin is described as one who "extremely loves intelligence and honesty. However, he has not enough will and self-confidence to surround himself with such an intelligent and honest life. He absolutely cannot order, forbid or insist" (*Sochineniia* 8:84; trans. John Holman). Thus, Ragin's "philosophizing" becomes a shield for his sluggishness; it is his self-justification, a straw that he grasps at tightly in order to avoid sinking to the bottom of his swampy nature. His attempts to survive under the wing of his philosophy fail, however, and he becomes a victim of his own demagogy.

Among Balzac's "victims," Father Goriot is number one. Traditionally, Goriot is considered to be a loving father who suffers his daughters' indifference and pragmatism. Janet L. Beizer writes that he is "[a] powerless father figure ruled by his children[;] he is a *deus abdicatus*, a would-be god who has relinquished his authority" (137). But is Goriot really as powerless as he appears to most critics? Is he a puppet ruled by his daughters, or does he himself manipulate his family?

As is mentioned in the previous chapter, this character is no less a monster than his daughters. Goriot's love for his daughters is really strange—one would hardly call it parental love, for there is much more to the ugliness and hidden depravity than warm fatherly feelings. There are some descriptions in the text that make one shudder to think about the sick nature of these relationships. For instance, it is mentioned that in Goriot's house his daughters "lived as the mistresses of a rich old lord might live," and this allusion to mistresses is persistent (14: 86). It first appears at the beginning of the novel, when the daughters visit their father at the lodging house of Mme. Vauquer and everyone immediately suspects that the beautiful young ladies are Goriot's mistresses:

> At that time Goriot was paying twelve hundred francs a year to his landlady, and Mme. Vauquer saw nothing out of the common in the fact that a rich man had four or five mistresses; nay, she thought it very knowing of him to pass them off as his daughters. (14: 26)

There are numerous other details in the text that hint at an abnormal, strange relationship between the father and his daughters, who "had only to express a wish, their father would hasten to give them their most extravagant desires, and asked nothing of them to return but a kiss" (14: 86). But perhaps the most revealing detail is the mention of Goriot's keeping his daughters' hairs in a little locket and wearing it on his breast "as the symbol of his own heart" (14: 265); this is a thing that may befit a lover, but not a father. Thus, the perverted nature of this relationship stems from the wild instincts of this father-"lover," who himself makes courtesans of his daughters. In turn, they manipulate him and are concerned only with gifts, as befits courtesans.

Goriot indulges his daughters in every way but has only one goal in mind—to comfort himself. He corrupts them in order to satisfy his own selfish desire to have that which delights him most of all, agreeing to pay any price for his own satisfaction. If Goriot loves anyone on Earth it is, first and foremost, himself.

Goriot's fiasco is a result of his lack of holistic vision, which does not allow him to elaborate a strategy that could help him develop his family relationships. This initially concerns his status in society (without an aristocratic title), which bothers his daughters because in nineteenth-century Europe it is title, not money, that allows one to enter high society. Goriot is very well aware of this, and he knows that his appearance at parties embarrasses his daughters, who are very sensitive to the position of their father. He does not care much about their feelings, however, and does not want to undertake anything to change this situation. He could easily buy an aristocratic title and hire tutors to receive an education, but he is too primitive to understand the role of a positional sacrifice in the development of a position. It seems that he even enjoys scandalizing people by coming to parties arranged by high society; he would otherwise never make shocking appearances that deeply wound the daughters whom he claims to love.

As he himself admits, he knows perfectly well what kind of reputation he has: "So these grand folks would ask in my son-in-law's ear, 'Who may that gentleman be?'—'The father in-law with the dollars: he is very rich" (14: 253). But perhaps the role of cash dispenser suits him fine and even convinces him of his power over the material world, which, because he can buy anything, frees him from the need to think about relationships. Ironically, even on his deathbed, Goriot is still convinced that money is the only powerful thing in the world. His cynicism and primitivism are revealed perfectly in his final monologue, which appears to be the apotheosis of his pragmatism and local thinking:

> Ah! If I were rich still, if I had kept my money, if I had not given all to them, they would be with me now; they would fawn on me and cover my cheeks with their kisses! I should be living in a great mansion; I should have grand apartments and servants and a fire in my room; and they would be about me all in tears, and their husbands and their children. I should have had all that; now—I have nothing. Money brings everything to you; even your daughters. My money. Oh! where is my money? (14: 253)

This monologue reveals in full measure his selfishness and disregard for the feelings of others. He spends the last minutes of his life trying to retain his "toys" at any price, bribing them as only an old profligate lover could do; in exchange, he wants them to pretend that they love him back—a dangerous game that destroys both sides. He is very well aware of his daughters' feelings, but he wants to buy their illusory love anyway, and he cries out on his death bed, "Millions, tell them; and even if they really come because they covet the money, I would rather let them deceive me; and I shall see them in any case. I want my children! I gave them life; they are mine, mine!" (14: 256) Reading this monologue, it is hard to imagine how some critics can make a saint from this devil incarnate.

Goriot nevertheless finds sympathy and appreciation in criticism; critics usually interpret this character as "a victim, the object of his daughter's exploitation" (Pasco 28). Hunt places old Goriot in opposition with Balzac's other characters:

> The ex-manufacturer of vermicelli, Jean-Joachim Goriot, is not like Félix Grandet and Balthazar Claés, an egocentric whose mania inflicts unmerited suffering on his family. He himself is the victim of the idolatrous love he bears his two daughters, a passion natural enough in its origins, since it is the transference to them of a "religious adoration" formerly lavished on his now defunct wife, but one which in course of time has become exclusive, uncritical, monstrous. (86)

Moreover, some critics view old Goriot as an "unfortunate modern Lear" (Dargan 19). However, there is a big difference between these two protagonists. In the sphere of human relationships, Lear, like Goriot, reveals a very weak ability to understand human psychology. As a dictator, Lear is not concerned with the relational aspect simply because his power is great enough to solve any problem. In addition, Lear has smart, loyal people, such as Kent, who appreciate his brightness and political talent and are willing to follow him in sickness and in health. In building relationships with people, Lear applies the same methods he uses in being a ruler; in this sense he is analogous to Goriot, who uses business methods to establish his relationship with his daughters. But this is the only thing that is in common between them. Unlike Goriot, Lear is distinguished by a great intellect, philosophical mind, and ability to think in general categories even in madness. He cannot be satisfied with a primitive, illusory love from his daughters and seeks real feelings and true respect in exchange for his generosity; at this point, he represents a powerful potential, a potential typical of dramedy.

The Momentary and the Eternal in the CNT

Deaths and losses. As previously mentioned, deaths and losses, though not typical, were still subject matters of some traditional comedies. However, the clearly manifested limited potential of the protagonists in traditional comedy never deceived the reader/spectator concerning the type of genre of the work. For instance, Alfred de Musset's comedy *On ne badine pas avec l'amour,* which ends with the death of one of its heroines, represents traditional comical characters, primitive and superficial, who have no impact on their surroundings. Perdican, a main character, is described as the most educated and brilliant creature that ever existed in the world; however, the one who gives such a characterization of Perdican is his former teacher, Metr Blazius, a heavy drinker (a "wine barrel") whose words cannot be taken seriously. No special analytical skills are required to realize that the "learned" Perdican is a banal, vulgar creature with very pragmatic feelings and no imagination. The comedy ends with the death of a secondary character, the heroine's younger sister, Rosetta, who commits suicide because of the heartless Perdican. This does not change the apparently farcical nature of the play, however, because the characters' limited potential makes them resemble two-dimensional puppets.

The deaths of protagonists in the CNT have quite a different impact on the reader/spectator, who wonders if the dramatist was serious in defining his work as comedy. The most common reaction is to accuse the author of cynicism, as some conservative critics did with regard to death in Chekhov's major plays. Less conservative critics tried to explain Chekhov's "insensitivity" by his medical background, stating that, as a doctor, Chekhov perceived death as something natural and unavoidable and thus saw no reason to "weep" over his heroes' demise. Thomas Winner writes: "His early study of medicine undoubtedly affected his own artistic views" (66). Similarly, I. N. Sukhikh states that for Chekhov, "life, death, oblivion—this process is unavoidable and universal" (75). In general, critics deny Chekhov his global philosophical vision, stating that eternity "is a concept that is almost absent from Chekhov's work," and death "is simply the end-point of each human life" (Turner 84). Chekhov is thus often represented as a cold-minded pragmatist who simply accepts the law of nature and denounces regret and compassion as ridiculous and senseless. Indisputably, such a narrow interpretation impoverishes his rich artistic intent, whose focus cannot be exhausted by the "medical" mentality.

By introducing death into his works, Chekhov raises the question of oblivion as a universal phenomenon linked to the degree of one's influence on the development of the world. The quasi-strong potential of his characters, whose physical disappearance is combined with their vanishing as individuals from the surroundings and from the memory of friends, only sharpens the significance of the traces they leave after they are gone. This becomes a primary subject of Chekhov's philosophy of death, in which one's demise plays the role of a litmus test, revealing the unconditional value of one who has gone forever. Therefore, the main questions that must be answered with regard to the death of a Chekhovian character are, what was the meaning of the character's life and did he or she influence the development of society, friends, and family? The answers to these questions serve to reveal the character's weight on the scales of eternity.

Significantly, the technique of juxtaposing a character's conditional and unconditional valuations was elaborated at a very early stage of Chekhov's work and was successfully introduced in his satirical articles and short stories. One such humorous short story, "At the Cemetery" (1884), may serve as a graphic example of exactly how conditional and unconditional values are formed in Chekhov's works. An obscure actor, a certain Mushkin, dies; his colleagues collect money to erect a memorial for him but cannot help spending everything on drinks: "Actors and newspaper boys collected money for his memorial but . . . they spent it all on vodka," recounts Mushkin's colleague. "Cheers, angels!" he adds, finishing his story. On Mushkin's tombstone his colleagues place an inscription: "In the memory of our unforgettable friend, Mushkin." However, two letters fell down and instead, one reads another inscription: "In the memory of our forgettable friend, Mushkin." "Time erased the particle 'un' and, in so doing, changed a human lie," concludes the narrator (*Sochineniia* 3: 76; trans. John Holman).

The question of transience and timelessness becomes central to the story, which makes the reader think about why such a "misfortune" befalls poor Mushkin and whether or not it is his predisposition that makes him sink into oblivion. An analysis of this early short story sheds light on Chekhov's late poetics, in which the cemetery and death become a scale upon which characters' unconditional value is weighed and measured—a value that is established regardless of the characters' momentary status in society. But what exactly does the term "unconditional" mean, and how can one apply it to the measurement of the potential? In order to answer these questions let us first refer to the concept of the degree of conditionality of values, elaborated by Katsenelinboigen for the measurement of the system's potential and then see how they can be applied to the literary character.

A formation of the degree of conditionality in chess and social systems. According to Katsenelinboigen, game pieces in chess are evaluated from two basic points of view: their weight with regard to a certain situation on the chessboard and their weight without regard to any particular situation, only to the position of the pieces. The latter are defined by Katsenelinboigen as semiunconditional values, formed by the sole condition of the rules of piece interaction. The semiunconditional values of the pieces (such as queen 9, rook 5, bishop 3, knight 3, and pawn 1) appear as a result of the rules of interaction of a piece with the opponent's king. All other conditions, such as starting conditions, final goal, and a program that links the initial condition to the final state, are not taken into account. The degree of conditionality is increased by applying preconditions, and the presence of all four preconditions fully forms conditional values.

Katsenelinboigen outlines two extreme cases of the spectrum of values—fully conditional and fully unconditional—and says that, in actuality, they are ineffectual in evaluating the material and so are sometimes replaced by semiconditional or semiunconditional valuations, which are distinguished by their differing degrees of conditionality. He defines fully conditional values as those based on complete and consistent linkages among all four preconditions. Accordingly, fully unconditional values are free of the preconditions; the introduction of the first preconditions, which is linked to the formation of the scale of positivity/negativity, results in the appearance of unconditional values. Semiconditional values are those based on some conditions, while semiunconditional values are formed by complete and consistent linkages between the rules of interactions, taking no other conditions into consideration.

The formation of the degree of unconditionality is dictated by the necessity to evaluate an entity in *uncertainty* (when the future is unknown) and when *conditions cannot be specified,* or, as Katsenelinboigen defines it by using the famous expression, when "time is out of joint." This means that in cases in which it is impossible to elaborate an algorithm giving a global evaluation of the position at each local stage—an evaluation that would provide one with information concerning the impact of a given position on the final outcome—the holistic effect should be determined by establishing the degree of unconditionality (through evaluating the material and relational parameters of the system).

The game of chess often reveals the impossibility of a player's complete and consistent linkage of his or her current move to the final outcome. This explains why it has been divided into stages such as opening, middle game, and end game. The middle game represents the greatest difficulties in problem formulation, and the prevailing style of this stage is the positional style, which is based on an unconditional evaluation of positional and material parameters. The lack of information on the total value of the pieces, crucial for evaluating a position, is compensated for by the establishment of the semiunconditional values of pieces and their relation to other pieces. The parallel to life is clear: if the creation of an algorithm that links an initial position to the final outcome is impossible in a game with a finite number of combinations and a determined goal, how can we expect the creation of such an algorithm for an open-ended system such as life? This question becomes vital in social and economic systems, amongst others. Applying his concept of values to social systems, Katsenelinboigen shows how the degree of unconditionality forms morality and law. According to him, the moral values represented in the Torah as the Ten Commandments are analogous to semiunconditional values in a chess game, for they are based exclusively on the rules of interactions.[1]

According to Katsenelinboigen, moral statutes are linked to the idea of a posthumous reward or punishment. Conversely, the legal system is based on mainly pragmatic values and establishes a judicial apparatus for rewarding and punishing during life; laws are intended to better indicate conditions under which one should be executed. However, the premise for forming fully conditional values is only partially accepted because life provides one with a richer diversity of situations. As Katsenelinboigen notices, "In order to achieve explicit results (legal expression), moral statutes usually pass through pragmatic values. This is, however, not obligatory" (*Concept of Indeterminism* 138–39).

Conditional and unconditional valuations in the literary work. The formation of values is vital for the literary work, which is a source of diverse valuations represented by the artist through a gallery of characters. Each character is distinguished by his or her own particular set of values, which assists him or her in making decisions. At the same time, the character is a subject of the artist's evaluation, which is based on the spectrum of unconditionality discussed above. Thus, a literary character can be analyzed from two different perspectives: from the point of view of the character's conditional importance (revealed through aspects of everyday life, such as his or her status in society, current position, and relationships with friends and family) and the character's semiunconditional weight (appearing as a result of interactions with the universe in the capacity of demiurge). The integration of these two types of evaluation gives a richer understanding of the character's predisposition, which cannot be exhausted by examining his or her momentary advantages or disadvantages.

The conditional evaluation of a character is based on his or her function in particular episodes. In chess, this analysis is described as "equivalently situation-specific valuations [that] incorporate all the constituent elements of a given position relative to the set goal" (Katsenelinboigen, *Concept of Indeterminism* 24). The semiunconditional values are often conveyed through characters' names and/or their juxtaposition with those whose unconditional weight has already been determined. Such are various mythological or historical figures with which a character could be associated, and whose contribution to the development of society, civilization, or the universe may serve as a scale upon which the protagonist's unconditional importance can be measured. For instance, in "The Last Leaf" (O. Henry), the mention of Michelangelo's Moses with regard to Behrman creates a scale of unconditionality upon which the potential of the old artist should be weighed. As shown in part one of this book, the contradictory nature of Behrman's characteristics does not allow complete and consistent linkages that would otherwise create an algorithm of this character's behavior. This explains the necessity of referring to an analysis of the character's predisposition with the subsequent establishment of his weight function.

The lack of programmed linkages between various characteristics is the main feature of the artistic work that is "complete incompleteness."[2] Characters can be judged completely by neither their words nor their actions because sometimes even antagonists may behave analogously—as Natasha Rostova, for instance, whose behavior resembles that of Helen Bezukhov (*War and Peace*), as Natasha is seized by a "sinful sensuality" being suddenly infatuated with Helen's brother Anatol. If approached only from the point of view of their behavior at the moment, these heroines may seem to be of one and the same kind, and it would be impossible to explain why one confesses deeply, while the other remains cynical and cold. It would require an evaluation of all the diverse characteristics structuring Natasha's character in order to see why her emotional, and sometimes impetuous, nature is nevertheless predisposed to inner purity and chastity, which eventually overcome her momentary lust. The analysis of her predisposition would also affect one's conclusion of the outcome, which, as is shown above, always raises questions of the characters' development in the future, which cannot be answered in a programmatic way.

In returning to Mushkin, Chekhov's worst "sin" with regard to his comic characters is that he shows a discrepancy between their conditional and their unconditional/semiunconditional weights, which is not typical of traditional comedy. The Chekhovian character is distinguished by a very low unconditional value combined with a middle conditional value that is sometimes perceived by the character's friends as high, which makes them proclaim the character as "very talented"; such is the case of Dymov in "The Grasshopper" or Mushkin, who was a very famous actor in his town. As Mushkin's colleague says, they brought ten or more wreaths to his funeral, which indicated his important local status; however, he was completely forgotten by his friends and admirers soon after, and only his enemies remembered him for his foolishness and irresponsibility. Such a quick disappearance from the memory of those who once supported him is in accordance with the meaning of Mushkin's last name, which is derived from *mushka* ("a small fly"), indicating his very low unconditional value. At this point, Mushkin's last name is equivalent to the notion of a piece on a chessboard; namely, to a pawn that in some particular cases may have considerable weight but in general is of the lowest weight.

In addition to the character's name, some other details may serve as a scale for measuring the character's potential. One of the questions that often puzzles Chekhov's readers is whether or not Chekhov held a cynical view of humankind in general, because none of the Chekhovian characters represent a solution for a better life, no matter how much they talk about it. All the Chekhovian scientists, artists, and doctors end in fiasco, blaming either their friends or society. This does not, however, preclude Chekhov's appreciation of talents contributing to world progress, which explains the appearance of such names as Shakespeare and Tolstoy along with the fictitious names of his characters. The real and created worlds coexist on the pages of Chekhov's short stories and plays, permeating each other and thus building a scale for measuring the protagonists' creative power. In describing Ragin's inert character ("Ward No. 6"), ignorance, and ridiculous references to eastern philosophy (which serve to shield him in his helplessness), Chekhov adds:

> On the other hand, he knew very well that a magical change had taken place in medicine during the last twenty-five years. When he was studying at the university he had fancied that medicine would soon be overtaken by the fate of alchemy and metaphysics; but now when he was reading at night the science of medicine touched him and excited his wonder, and even enthusiasm. What unexpected brilliance, what a revolution! Thanks to the antiseptic system operations were performed such as the great Pirogov had considered impossible even *in spe*. Ordinary Zemstvo doctors were venturing to perform the resection of the kneecap; of abdominal operations only one per cent. was fatal; while stone was considered such a trifle that they did not even write about it. A radical cure for syphilis had been discovered. And the theory of heredity, hypnotism, the discoveries of Pasteur and of Koch, hygiene based on statistics, and the work of Zemstvo doctors! (*Essential Chekhov* 141)

The introduction of such names as Pasteur, Pirogov, and Koch establishes a hierarchy that sheds light on the role of the Chekhovian characters in the development of the universe. Within the frames of unconditionality, their local importance becomes apparent, and the reason why they all eventually sink into oblivion becomes clear. The same can be said of the Balzacian universe that was intended as a parody of Dante's *Divine Comedy*; at this point, *The Divine Comedy* serves as a scale on which the momentary passions of Balzacian protagonists reveal their genuinely low weight.

Above all, the scale of unconditionality can also be formed through the symbolism of various objects whose notions may suggest the unconditional weight of characters. For instance, Treplev's suicide is followed by Dorn's remark that a small bottle of ether has exploded; this immediately generates an idea of a momentary existence, of a life that will vanish as quickly as ether evaporates from the exploded bottle—a fate that befalls all of the Chekhovian Mushkins.

After the degree of conditionality is established, the next task is to integrate the character's conditional weight with his or her unconditional valuation.

Integration of values in the artistic work. The integration of the local and the global requires the ascription of weights not the establishment of the average of given characteristics. The magnitude of the initial parameter ("small fly," for instance) and the value (insignificant) must be taken into account because the process of integration requires a general assessment. Taking Mushkin as an example, his hind forms a gestalt that is an aggregation of material and relational parameters. The gestalt represents the object in general, as a whole. Thus, a general perception of Mushkin's character is a gestalt of a fly. The next step is to analyze some particular features and episodes and then to synthesize them into a new wholeness.

Synthesis requires a juxtaposition of each concrete characteristic with the unconditional/semiunconditional value of the object. For instance, the last name Dymov may suggest a vanishing into the air (*dym* in Russian means "smoke")—another metaphor for oblivion. Therefore, in approaching Dymov as a character, the interpreter may either ignore the scale of unconditionality, finding the average of Dymov's qualities, or integrate them into a whole. The latter requires a consideration of Dymov's characteristics in regard to their interaction with the notion of smoke. This would assist one in better understanding the magnitude of Dymov's talent and the richness of his human quality.

Dymov's limited scope and primitivism in the sphere of human relationships have been discussed earlier. Concerning his professional quality, which is often overestimated in criticism, one should pay attention to what kind of characters praise Dymov as a scientist. Ironically, the one who proclaims Dymov's great significance, his friend by the name Korostelev, is himself small fry in both the literal and figurative sense; his last name alludes to *korostel'*, or "corncrake," which is a small bird.[3] As a matter of fact, Korostelev is described as a small man with a short cut and a rumpled face, which only intensifies the sense of his insignificance. In his monologue, Korostelev insists that Dymov is a man with an unusual gift; but the question arises, in comparison to whom? Korostelev's answer is "in comparison to all of us." Dymov's position as Gulliver among the Lilliputians makes his status equal to that of gods in comedy; he is unable to change anything in his personal life, and even his attempt to save a patient at the cost of his own life is ridiculed by his colleague Shrek, who considers it to be a senseless sacrifice.

Two different approaches to a character—finding the average and integrating valuations—will result in two different conclusions concerning the character's potential, which may oscillate between average/strong and limited. Neglecting the unconditional valuation may not only distort the representation of a character, but also hamper one's understanding of genre as defined by the artist. It therefore seems to be extremely important to create a scale of measurement of the characters' potential and to establish a degree of unconditionality while approaching their predisposition.

Summary

Names often take the place of unconditional valuations of characters. The symbolism of names conveys a notion of the characters' influence on the development of their universe and their ability to leave a trace in the memory of society.

Conditional valuations of characters are revealed through the analysis of characters' current achievements, their relationships with others, their present status in society, and the like.

To integrate conditional and unconditional valuations of the character, one must compare all particular information with the unconditional weight of the character.

The CNT represents some essential discrepancies between the conditional and unconditional weights of characters. As a rule, characters of the CNT are distinguished by their average or strong conditional valuations and a very low unconditional weight.

In defining the dramatic genre of his work, the artist draws one's attention to the unconditional valuations of his or her artistic universe.

In the CNT, death becomes a litmus test of characters' unconditional importance. It outlines the degree of a character's significance from the global perspective.

Myth and Symbol in the CNT: *The Space of Action and the Implied Space*

8

Styles and Methods of Approaching the Artistic Space

As has been discussed in part one, the differing degree of abstraction in the interpretation of metaphors forms the space of action and the implied space. The transition from one level of abstraction to another goes through intermediate stages forming the implied space. As a rule, such a sophisticated design is not a prerogative of traditional comedy, though this also has a level of generalization and abstraction on which the artist's concept of the world is revealed; however, if the implied space is present in traditional comedy, it is very simple, obvious, almost allegoric in the sense that all linkages and allusions appear as one-step programmed correspondences—a subject for textual analysis.

The appearance of the CNT changes this rule, and the extended network of various mythological allusions and associations in combination with the author's own mythological notions weave a rich and sophisticated implied space. As in Gogol's works, the symbol in Chekhov's plays first appears as a detail structuring a particular scene, then its meaning attains further generalization and is elevated to the level of the textual context (the space of action). As the degree of abstraction is increased, the intermediate level is formed. On this level, one can discuss some concrete mythological plots and their interactions with literary structures. Further abstraction from particular myths and references to their more general notions signify a complete transition to the implied space.

The formation of a predisposition in the space of action. Let us analyze in detail how material and relational parameters contribute to the formation of a predisposition in the space of action, taking *The Seagull* as an example. In the space of action of *The Seagull*, the description of the stage contributes both to the design of a particular scene and to the description of the potential of the Chekhovian universe. The play begins with a description of the stage on which Treplev's playlet is performed: "A part of the park on Sorin's estate. A broad avenue leads away from the audience deep into the park toward the lake. The avenue is obstructed by a stage, hastily constructed for a home performance, and the lake is therefore not visible" (*Chekhov: Four Plays* 39).

Two things are important here. First, the remark that the stage was constructed "hastily"—a relational parameter evaluated negatively—suggests the momentary orientation of its builders. Elevating this observation to a more general level of assumption, one can say that we here discuss the categories of the eternal and the momentary from the point of view of the psychology of the decision makers designing the Chekhovian universe. Treplev's appeal to the "eternal questions" from this temporary scaffold only emphasizes the incongruity between his abstract intentions and its concrete realization, highlighting the poor potential of his brainchild that is doomed to die while still in its infancy. Hence, from the point of view of the contextual analysis, the creator in *The Seagull* appears to be a "seasonal worker" who is concerned only with momentary achievements and who lacks holistic vision.

Second, the stage obscures the lake, thus depriving one from a beautiful sight. Here the positional parameter of closeness is analogous to the doubled pawn in chess.

> [T]he function embodied by such a positional parameter as *connected pawns* is that of mutual aid—an item which is assigned a positive value. The *doubled pawns* parameter reflects the piece's ability (or lack thereof) to maneuver while hindered by obstacles in its path; it also reflects the pawns' lack of mobility. Consequently, this parameter is assigned a negative valuation. (Katsenelinboigen, *Concept of Indeterminism* 76)

From the point of view of their local meaning (in a concrete scene), the relationship between the stage and the lake represents Treplev as a bad chess player who "situates" his "pieces" in unfavorable way. His local disjointed thinking does not allow him to observe the picture as a whole and to see the ugliness of the relational parameters structuring his landscape. This makes one speculate on a more general level about the relationship between the creator and his creation, which often suffers from the limitations inherent in its creator (as does the stage, which is gradually transformed into a ghost).

At this point, the stage and the lake may symbolize an opposition between art and nature; this is linked to the problem of plausibility in art. Treplev's criticism of contemporary art is that the modern theater does not cross the border of "our daily domestic consumption" (*Chekhov: Four Plays* 42). He therefore attempts to show his spectator something that will reveal the world from a global unconditional perspective, using the landscape as scenery. He naively believes that the majestic picture of the rising moon, combined with the "majestic" monologue of his heroine and seasoned with the smell of sulfur, will have an irresistible effect on his audience. Alas! The realization of his intent only shows his artistic immaturity and his inability to understand the problem of conventionality in art. As a result, such a vulgar, direct "application" of nature works against Treplev, who is mocked and humiliated in front of those to whom he wanted to teach a lesson. This must be associated with a real story from Chekhov's life, which indirectly sheds light on Chekhov's attitude toward "Treplevs." As Meerhold recollects, the following conversation occurred between Chekhov and an actor concerning scenic conventionality:

> One of the actors tells Chekhov that in *The Seagull* during the performance frogs will croak behind the stage, dragonflies will chirp, and dogs will bark.
> "What for?" Chekhov asks with a displeased voice.
> "To create a sense of reality," the actor answers.
> "Reality," Chekhov repeats, grinning. After a small pause he says: "Theater is art. Kramskoy has a painting in which he masterfully depicted faces. What if we were to install a real nose instead of the drawn one on one of these faces? The nose would be real, but the whole picture would be spoiled. (120; trans. John Holman)

Exactly the same effect is observed in Treplev's play, in which only nature is real; the whole picture is spoiled because of this immature attempt to integrate the realistic part into an artificial whole. Nature in the play rejects the stage as a foreign body that hinders its development. As a matter of fact, the stage is transformed into a skeleton that frightens the tenants in the fourth act:

> *Medvedenko:* It's dark in the garden. Someone really should have that theater torn down. It's standing out there, bare, and ugly, like a skeleton, the curtains flapping in the wind. Last night, when I was passing by I thought I heard someone crying. . . . (*Chekhov: Four Plays* 75)

Gradually, the theme of the dying stage becomes a leitmotif of the entire play—it symbolizes the limited potential of the Chekhovian universe and attests, on a very abstract level, to the inner bankruptcy of the actresses and the writers of both generations. From a global point of view, Treplev is no better than Trigorin, and Arkadina is no better than Nina; they all belong to the same category of mediocre artists sentenced to oblivion. As I mentioned before, Arkadina is a prima donna in Kharkov, but she is no Sarah Bernhardt, whose talent was highly appreciated by Chekhov. Furthermore, no matter what it was in reality, Kharkov in the Chekhovian universe symbolizes a provincial city. One has only to remember what kind of protagonists inhabit the Chekhovian Kharkov! Among them are Lopakhin, who departs for Kharkov at the end of the fourth act *(The Cherry Orchard);* an off-stage personage, Pavel

Alekseevich, who sends his strange brochure to Voynitsky's mother; and some others that make the Chekhovian Kharkov a city of mediocre people.

Formation of inconsistent linkages in analyzing a predisposition in the implied space. The same characters and objects form both the space of action and the implied space; for instance, the lake is not only a part of the landscape of Sorin's estate (space of action), but it also contributes to the creation of the implied space through its link to mythology. During his explanation to Nina, Treplev uses a metaphor of water streaming into the ground, a metaphor that relates to the mytholiterary continuum of the play. He says: "You're cold to me, and it's so terrible, so incredible, it's as if I woke up and saw that the lake had suddenly dried up, or drained into the earth" (58). In this monologue near the lake, the monologue about the *oblivion* of feelings, the mention of water streaming underground evokes an association with the mythic rivers of the underworld,[1] namely, the river Lethe. But before developing this allusion, let us discuss first the methodology of establishing semiefficient linkages among the parts of compared systems.

As has been explained in part one, the interpreter (including the artist) uses different styles and methods in analyzing a predisposition. However, this fact is not very well understood in contemporary literary criticism. That is, most intertextual analysis is based on the reactive style and a programming method; in other words, only associations that generate *immediate* and *efficient* links between the analyzed structures are accepted by editors and reviewers. No established scholarly journal of literary criticism publishes intertextual analyses based on semiefficient linkages and a selective style because the method of using subjectivity and predispositioning has not yet become a paradigm in literary criticism.[2]

The need to understand that different stages of a system's development require different methods of approaching it becomes a primary task for contemporary literary criticism. A work of art (whether it is a painting, music, or literature) comprises all stages of development and cannot be approached through a single, unified method of programming of all its parts, as most scholars believe. Even a completed artistic work consists of different degrees of coherence of its artistic elements at its different stages, some of which are occupied with complete and consistent linkages, while others create semiefficient or inefficient linkages. To the former belongs the formation of focal points, which are intended to create a direct allusion through a reactive style and programming. In *Uncle Vanya*, the names Elena and Sonya immediately allude to the cosmogonic opposition between Helen and Sophia, which on a more abstract level refers to the paradigm of chaos and cosmos. The allusions appear reactively, since Elena's name, her beauty, and the scandal that it causes, are all linked in a complete and consistent way to the myth of the

Trojan War. However, such linkages would be sufficient only if the artist is concerned with the creation of an *analogy* to mythology or to any other structure that he or she has in mind; but since the artist's goal is not to *imitate* but to *imply* a relation to other texts (either artistic or nonartistic), and since such an implication is only the first step towards creating his or her own, original artistic structure, one must refer to the predispositioning as a method.

In returning to the symbol of the lake, one can see indirect allusions to Lethe, a river of oblivion at which the souls of the dead come to drink and forget all earthly burdens connecting them to the past. Here, we are dealing with a selective style in choosing this allusion among many others, concerning the lake in the play. In selecting an allusion (or a group of allusions), the interpreter is guided by his or her ability to successfully develop it into a concept, that is, to discover the way that the chosen associations are linked to each other and to the whole. At this point, the allusion to the river of oblivion seems effective to me because it pertains to the leitmotif of oblivion that encompasses all of the main characters in the play.[3]

In addition to the allusion to the Lethe, the lake evokes another association with the river Styx that seems very significant to me in the understanding of *The Seagull's* implied space. When approaching the lake from the point of view of its relation to the major characters, one notices a very interesting correlation between the utterances expressed in front of the lake and their realization in the future. Indeed, all of the statements made in front of the waters come true: Treplev threatens to kill himself as he had killed the seagull, and he eventually does so; Trigorin tells a story of a man who abandons a young girl, which becomes his reality; and Nina states that for the honor of becoming an actress she would give up her happiness and joy, which she eventually realizes:

> *Treplev places the seagull at her feet.*
> *Nina:* What does it mean?
> *Treplev:* Today I have done something despicable—I have killed this seagull ... Soon, in the same way, I shall kill myself. (*Chekhov: Four Plays* 59)

> *Trigorin:* An idea for a short story: Once upon a time there lived a young girl, on the shore of a lake, a young girl like you; she loved the lake, like a seagull, and she was happy and free, like a seagull. But one day, by chance, there came a man, who saw her, and, for lack of anything better to do, destroyed her, just like this seagull. (63)

> *Nina:* For the happiness of being a writer or an actress, I would endure rejection of my loved ones, poverty and disillusionment, I'd live in a garret, and

eat only black bread, I'd suffer discontent and disappointment in myself, but in return for all this, I shall have fame . . . real, resounding fame . . . (62)

Though Nina has not had yet attained the fame she craves, she receives everything else in full. But what is the link between all those words and their realization later on? The answer can only be given from the point of view of the mytholiterary continuum of the play. In Greek myth, the river Styx is connected to the Underworld and is the sacred river of the dead by which the gods seal their oaths. The allusion to gods appears with regard to Trigorin and Arkadina in Treplev's monologue, in which he ironically calls the members of the establishment the "high priests of our sacred art" (42). Nina also evokes an association to a priestess of the mob when she talks about a chariot and her glorification. Finally, Treplev himself acts like a rebellious demiurge who strives to change the laws established by the "high priests" of art. So, with regard to the lake, the "Olympian" atmosphere predisposes a humorous allusion to the gods, who seal their oaths by the river Styx.

According to myth, the Styx flows in the territory of mythic Arcadia: a fact that is significant in my interpretation of the basic mythological paradigm forming the mytholiterary continuum of this play.

A holistic approach to intertextual analysis: combining various methods and styles. To establish a whole, one must first define a focal point suggesting a certain paradigm to which structures in the text can be compared. The process of evaluation will result in a variety of opinions concerning the notion of the whole, and the interpreter should support his or her hypothesis in each case by using different methods of approaching the whole. In my interpretation, the focal point that suggests a relation to myth is Arkadina's last name, whose meaning immediately evokes an allusion to Arcadia, the mythical land. Arcadia is the "bear country," which was named after its king, Arcas, the son of Jupiter and a female bear. This reactive method of establishing a connection between the space of action and myth becomes the initial step in creating a network of associations (through all the styles and methods inherent in systems analysis).

The mention of bears in the myth generates another reactive association linked to the Chekhovian couple, Masha and Medvedenko.[4] As I show in my book on the mythopoetics of this play, owing to direct and indirect associations, Sorin's estate is gradually transformed into a Chekhovian "bear country"—a Chekhovian Arcadia.

The most effective evaluation is achieved when each protagonist is approached from a multidimensional perspective; including the character's structure, function, genesis, and the way he or she operates. This provides a broader vision of a character and his or her relationship with the space of action and the implied space and serves to highlight the character's genuine weight. One of the most challenging tasks for me was to interpret Shamraev within the mythological paradigm of the Arcadian space.

From a structural point of view, this character appears to be a "centauric" figure; Shamraev cannot be separated from his horses and should therefore be considered to be in structural unity with them. From a functional point of view, Shamraev is the manager of the estate. From the point of view of processing, he takes greater care of the horses than of people, including his own relatives. Not only does he refuse to give horses to his son-in-law, Medvedenko (who must therefore walk home at night in stormy weather), but he also refuses Arkadina's request for them, thus running the risk of being fired from the estate for such behavior. Such an exaggerated modus operandi requires an explanation. My first question was, why horses? And my next question was, what is the connection between these animals and the Arcadian space?

In order to approach these questions, I attempted to inquire into the meaning of Shamraev's last name (the genetic aspect), of which there are no previous explanations in criticism. Initially, I was very disappointed because no dictionary could give me any hints, and I wondered if the last name had any meaning at all until I referred to a Russian encyclopedia of the nineteenth century. I discovered that Shamraevka was a Russian village famous for its stud farm, Shamraevskaya stadnitsa. This information completely reinforced my speculation that horses are a significant part of this character. The search for the mythological structure linked to both notions began.

I started with the myth of Peloponnesus, since Arcadia was a district of mid-Peloponnesus. The mythic founder of Peloponnesus was Pelops, who was Poseidon's favorite pupil and who was taught how to ride and train horses by the sea god (whose gift to humanity was the horse). Shamraev's function as manager of the estate and his mysterious love for horses allows the establishment of a semiefficient linkage between him and his mythological counterpart, Pelops. The first name of Shamraev, Il'ia, alludes to the family of gods linked to both Poseidon and to horses: Holy Eleyah is a counterpart of Perun, the god of rain and storms, who appears in Slavic myth in a miraculous chariot with wild horses, and is the early version of the Greek Poseidon. Il'ya's patronymic name, Afanas'evich, which in Greek means "the blossoming," is in accordance with Poseidon's other role as a god of fertility.

Shamraev's relationship with his wife and daughter can also be interpreted within this mythological frame. In the myth, Pelops's seed is cursed because of his indecent behavior, and some myths tell of the Pelopponeds' inability to recognize each other as relatives, thus causing their deadly feuds.

The motif of Pelops's "cursed seed" is represented in such a way that Masha constantly calls herself Mar'ya of forgotten origin, and Shamraev's wife behaves as if she had no husband at all.

Disjointed and holistic vision. As one can see, only a combination of evaluative methods proves effective in approaching the literary work that is an indeterministic system. In general, a system can be approached from the point of view of the variety of its structures and from the point of view of its holistic design. Both methods, though equally important, represent different stages of analysis (see appendix 3).

Disjointed incrementalism is a prerogative of the initial stage of approaching the diversity structuring a system. If the interpreter's goal is to show the richness of a system that generates many allusions, then he or she will limit analysis to the initial stage. On the other hand, if the interpreter's focus is on an integration of the many, then he or she will switch to the next level, which is linked to the establishment of a whole.[5] It is important to understand, however, that neither method is better; the best method is that which is appropriate to the interpreter's goal. Furthermore, both methods have advantages and disadvantages: a disjointed vision "cuts" the global meaning; a holistic approach reduces the diversity discovered by a disjointed analysis. In order to reduce the "damage," I always admit that my interpretation is only one of many possible approaches to the whole. Moreover, I attempt to find more than one global paradigm in my analysis and establish two or more equivalent systems in order to see how they interact and enrich each other. This is the basic concept of my book on Chekhov's plays (1997), and the current research introduces some elaborations to clarify my previous statements.

At the same time, one must understand that a disjointed analysis cannot exhaust all the possible allusions; this is simply because some of them appear only as a result of a holistic approach. For example, without regard to Arcadian myth in its various representations, I would never have answered the question of Nina's name and her role in the implied space. Nina is not a common name among the Chekhovian heroines; there are only a few heroines in his works who possess this name, and the meaning of Nina remains a puzzle in criticism. To me, therefore, only when approached from the point of view of the whole can the meaning of this name come to light.

Thus, structurally, the holistic vision requires a consideration of Nina in the context of Arkadina, since both create an opposition that can be conventionally defined as the innocent and the bohemian. Nina initially appears as an innocent provincial girl who secretly comes to the estate in spite of her father's ban from entering the bohemian society gathering in Sorin's estate. The chief of this bohemia is Arkadina, who is described ironically by her son, Treplev, as a priestess of art. With regard to the myth of Ages, the opposition between the "innocent" and the "bohemian" is associated with the mythological opposition between the universes of Jupiter and Kronos (all the more so because energetic and warlike Arkadina is also called "Jupiter" in the play). As previously mentioned, the end of the Golden Era came with Jupiter, whose activity destroyed the peace and stillness of Kronos's times.

From the point of view of genesis, Nina's name could be interpreted as derived from Ninus, one of Kronos's sons. King Ninus, together with his brave, sharp-witted wife, Semiramis, the queen of Assyria for forty-two years, founded Nineveh. In the myth, Ninus and his wife are often interchanged, and one of the Seven Wonders of the World, the Gardens of Semiramis, is also known as the Gardens of Nineveh. With regard to Nina, she spends her entire life trying to establish her "Nineveh," which she finally does in Elets, a provincial city of Russia in which, as she claims, she finds acceptance and success.

But greater insight into the connection between Nina and the myth of Semiramis is provided when it is approached from the point of view of processing. From this perspective, Nina compares herself to the seagull, which becomes first and foremost symbolic of her. A striking parallel to the myth of Semiramis is that after her death, Semiramis was transformed into a dove and then worshipped as this bird. From a functional point of view, Nina functions as a seeker of praise and worship.

Thus, an indirect allusion to Kronos's times resulting from the myth of Ages generates a network of associations that allows one to interpret Nina's name within the framework of the mythological paradigm, enriching the field of associations with new aspects. Needless to say, none of these allusions would have appeared in disjointed analysis; the establishment of semiefficient linkages requires the presence of a basic structure that can direct intermediate steps towards the creation of a predisposition to certain allusions. In modern criticism, unfortunately, such an approach is often called "a stretch" because there is a general underestimation of the indeterministic nature of a literary work and a lack of theory in dealing with indeterministic systems.

Myth as a Scale of Measuring Protagonists' Potential

Myth as a scale of unconditional valuations. The next question to be considered with regard to the implied space concerns the degree of its importance in the analysis of a literary work's potential. Does the implied space provide us with a new understanding of the degree of strength of the universe represented by the artist, or does it only serve to add new features to it?

My answer to this question is linked to my own definition of myth as an abstract representation of mechanisms that rule the universe. In my book on Chekhov's four major plays, I state that (unlike legends or fairy tales) myths "[are] concerned with the general mechanisms that rule the universe rather than with particular principles that organized human relationships and daily life" (Zubarev, *Systems Approach* 23). In other words, by *myth* I refer to an abstract model of universal development that is measured in unconditional, global values; therefore, gods in classical myths are, first and foremost, incarnations of elemental forces that rule the universe.

Conversely, in legends and fairy tales, a character that is an embodiment of a human characteristic (e.g., vice or virtue) often appears as an element (for instance, a dragon—an incarnation of greed and violence—often appears as fire). At the same time, one may interpret a character in a legend as a mythological figure, thereby elevating its notion to the level of a more abstract notion. This suggests that myth, in addition to legends and fairy tales, is a way of representing a system that is linked to a more abstract vision of its process, structure, and the like. The abstract representation of the development process is revealed through the typology of myths, which is divided into large groups (such as cosmogonic and calendar) that in turn generate various types and branches. In general, therefore, myths tell us about the process of universal development and what the unconditional weights of events and entities are. At this point, myth is a structure that operates with an unconditional representation of the universe.

At the same time, mythology is a collection of stories that illustrate general principles through specific examples. In this sense, myth combines unconditional values with conditional ones, revealing the weights of mythological figures in certain conditions (which may not always be in agreement with their unconditional valuations). Jupiter, for example, is considered to be a supreme god with a high unconditional value, though he does not appear as an almighty figure in every episode; as a matter of fact, he cannot prevent the death of his beloved Semela of which he himself is the cause. Such an integration of conditional and unconditional valuations of mythological figures corresponds to the evaluation of pieces in and out of a chess game, as I discussed in previous chapters. The semiunconditional values of gods in myths are their representations as elements from the point of view of their interaction with the universe (rules of interaction).

A direct allusion to myth in a literary work serves to build a scale of unconditionality upon which the characters and their actions can be weighed. The original structure of the myth informs the interpreter of the way everything should operate, and deviations from this structure reveal the true state of affairs. References to mythology in Chekhov's works highlight the local importance of his characters, who sometimes consider themselves to be stars of the first magnitude. The primary mythological pattern appears as an ideal to which the mytholiterary structure can be compared.

It is important to note that the shifts in mythological paradigms that can be observed in Chekhov's works are directed towards revealing the limited nature of Chekhovian, not mythological, characters. In other words, Chekhov's plays do not so much parody myths as they exploit mythological paradigms in order to establish the unconditional weight of the characters. Even in his early works, Chekhov refers to myth as a scale of measurement of the potential strength of his contemporaries and his characters.[6] Chekhov's early uses of myths are as funny combinations of names belonging to Greek history and mythology and to Russian culture; this serves to underscore the triviality of Russian daily life and the insignificance of its "heroes" when compared to the legendary ancient Greeks. This early principle finds further elaboration in Chekhov's late works (such as in his short story "Ariadne")[7] and achieves perfection in Chekhov's four major plays, so that despite further changes and development of technique, Chekhov's main device remains recognizable.

The integration of the space of action and the implied space in the mytholiterary continuum. In my book on the mythopoetics of Chekhov's plays, I introduce the notion of a *mytholiterary continuum*[8] in order to outline the interaction between mythological and literary structures, and their development into a new wholeness:

> The mythological pattern attains its new concretization in a particular literary structure that, in turn, is enriched by universal mythological values rather than subjugated to a mythological narrative. Hence the mytholiterary continuum is the continuous, uninterrupted unity of the interactive mythological and literary patterns that can be taken apart only through analysis. (Zubarev, *Systems Approach* 25–26)

Since the original structure is affected by outer influences that change the weight, sign, and even outer appearance of the associated patterns, one should investigate all direct and indirect correspondences arising within the text, give them weights, and consider them from the point of view of the whole. There is no other way to do so but to apply a systems methodology of measuring the predisposition of an artistic structure; the analysis would otherwise be limited to the initial stage and the picture of the whole would fade. Therefore, a combination of efficient, semiefficient, and inefficient linkages is needed in order to receive a holistic effect. This is the way the artist creates the predisposition of his or her work, and this is the way the predisposition of the artistic work must be approached.

In terms of the present analysis, the mytholiterary continuum appears as a result of the integration of the space of action and the implied space. The integration is such that it changes the sign and vector of the mythological or any structure that is considered to be mythological in the analysis. Outlining the similarities between the structures is therefore the first step in establishing a basic paradigm to which the mytholiterary structure can be compared. The next step is to find deviations between the paradigm and the continuum, which would assist in the integration of both spaces.

In comparing the bird symbol in *The Seagull* to that in the myth of Semiramis, one should first point out the differences between the two types of bird. If the dove is a symbol of peace, the seagull belongs to the class of scavengers; in the space of action, Nina, who is associated with the seagull, is herself such a scavenger (a fact that has been widely discussed in criticism). In the myth, Semiramis is resurrected as a bird, while in *The Seagull* the bird is stuffed and the "deity" is forgotten.[9] This changes the sign of the mythological paradigm from positive to negative and allows one to talk about a new mytholiterary structure that appears as a result of integrating the classic paradigm appearing in the implied space with the literary structure forming the space of action.

When making a parallel between Nina's and Kronos's times of innocence, one should take into account Chekhov's irony concerning Nina's "innocence" in order to see the change in the sign of the mythological allusion. From the very beginning, Nina appears to be an aggressive young girl whose intentions are not clear only to such simpletons as Sorin. Her provincial "Nineveh," Elets, in the mytholiterary continuum appears to be Chekhov's biggest irony; the name of the city is the Russian name of a fish of the carp family. Thus, in the mytholiterary continuum, Nina-seagull lands a "catch," which she nevertheless "eats" with disgust.

Integration of several basic paradigms into the mytholiterary continuum. The task becomes more complex, however, when more than one mythological paradigm is considered. In my analysis of *Three Sisters*, I state that in addition to the calendar myth, there is at least one more paradigm forming the implied space; namely, the myth of the Holy City (Sacred City), which is the eschatological myth of Rome as a symbol of the world (Zubarev, *Systems Approach* 102–20). The integration of various metaparadigms requires the same sequence of steps as the integration of literary and mythological structures into a mytholiterary continuum. The first step is to search for isomorphisms in order to find compatibility between the structures. The next step is to outline their differences, which would then suggest a new metaparadigm.

From the point of view of processing, both calendar and eschatological myths are united by the idea of the cosmic cycle, represented as the movement of the universe toward its end with its subsequent revival.[10] In the myth of Rome, the concept of cosmic rhythm as ruling the world is basic for its tales; this includes the myth of the Great Year, according to which Rome is predestined to burn to ashes.[11] The allusion to the myth of Rome in the implied space appears as a result of some direct and indirect allusions to Romans and interactions between the notions of fire and the city, as observed in the space of action.[12]

Thus, in the mytholiterary continuum, the town is a combination of three cities that have fire as common denominator: Moscow, Rome, and the city of three sisters. Fire in the implied space appears in the form of a great fire symbolizing the end of the world (Act 3) and a Shrovetide fire symbolizing the end of a winter season (Act 2). The integration of all the notions of the fire in the space of action and the implied space creates a new paradigm that in the mytholiterary continuum becomes the burning of a "straw-universe"—a paradigm that serves to highlight the limited potential of a Chekhovian "Sacred City."

In conclusion, the integration of several basic paradigms into the mytholiterary continuum serves to highlight the *weight* and *sign* of the universe represented by the artist in a global way.

Summary

The quasi-strong potential in the CNT can also be approached through symbolism and mythological allusions, which form the semi-implied and the implied spaces. The network of various intertextual correspondences is established through a combination of styles and methods, including the formation of efficient, semiefficient, and inefficient linkages.

The diversity of associations can be approached from a holistic point of view. To this end, a focal point referring directly to a certain paradigm must be established. The establishment of the focal point facilitates the creation of a general paradigm, through which all isolated structures can be integrated into a whole.

Myth becomes a scale of measurement of protagonists' potential. Allusions to mythological figures facilitate the discovery of the unconditional value of protagonists in particular and their universe in general. The same can be said of any literary or nonliterary structure that appears as a result of intertextual associations. In establishing intertextual parallels, one must also outline deviations, since they are important in approaching the mytholiterary continuum of the play.

The integration of the paradigms forming the space of action and the implied space results in the creation of the mytholiterary continuum, in which characters and their universe attain a new structural and semantic quality. The mytholiterary continuum may consist of more than one basic paradigm whose integration further highlights the potential and predisposition of the characters' universe when approached from the global point of view.

Conclusion

Dramatic Genre as a Multidimensional Category

In conclusion, the primary question concerning the notion of dramatic genre is, what does this term mean to writers? What structures, processes, functions, and the like are represented by dramatic genre? To answer this question, let us define dramatic genre as a systems phenomena, using a multidimensional perspective.

Structurally, dramatic genre is linked to the degree of strength of protagonists' potential. In this book, I approach the problem of dramatic genre from the structural point of view because it seems to be the most effective way of investigating the peculiarity inherent in this category. A discussion of the structure of characters' potential is therefore the initial step in my analysis on the various types and branches of dramatic genre.

Functionally, dramatic genre represents the degree of influence a protagonist wields over the future development of his environment. Unlike the character of dramedy, the comic personage is unable to make drastic changes to his universe because he has insufficient potential to influence its global development.

From the point of view of *processing*, dramatic genre represents a correlation between a potential and a result (by means of fate, chance, and predisposition).

The *operator* (any interpreter of the text, including the artist) gives weight to protagonists' potential in defining the genre of a literary work.

A *genetic* approach helps one understand an artist's values, to clarify the reason why an author defines the genre of his or her work in such a way.

Genetic Approach

Traditionally, the genetic approach is used to research the circumstances under which a certain dramatic type has appeared. However, descriptions of external circumstances, which are seemingly responsible for the appearance of a certain type or branch, do not provide one with a holistic vision of this category.

Using the genetic approach, I attempted to consider dramatic genre from the point of view of its philosophical basis. I investigated what kind of philosophy lay beyond the spectrum of the character's representation—from the insensitive, inanimate creature whose failure evokes only laughter, to the highly sensitive, unique individual whose suffering shocks the spectator. At this point, it is worth considering Aristotle's observation on the harmless nature of deformity in comedy (namely, his assertion that "a mistake or deformity" is "not productive of pain or harm to others" in comedy), which implies two things (1459; 1449a, 35). First, deformity in comedy does not have the potential to cause any drastic changes, including harmful ones; this has been discussed in previous chapters.

Second, the spectator is not supposed to *feel* for the comic character as deeply as he or she is supposed to feel for the tragic character. In other words, as follows from the Aristotelian definition, deformity and ugliness in the comic character does not cause the spectator any pain; regardless of the number of blows on the back of the comic hero's head, this character is supposed to evoke laughter (which may even be combined with light pity) but not compassion. Here, we are actually facing the age-old problem of the human being's attitude toward the strong and the weak. It is an attitude of differential treatment that is especially typical of children, who tend to mock weaker peers; as soon as children see others who are inferior to themselves, they immediately take advantage of them, making jokes and laughing at the weaker children's deficiencies. The differing degrees of the spectator's compassion in comedy, dramedy, and drama formulated by the Aristotelian school reflect a more general paradigm; namely, the relationship between diversity and singular variety.

In accordance with Katsenelinboigen's argument, the need for diversity in a system is dictated by the degree of indeterminism.[1]

Uncertainty demands a long-term strategy of maintaining diversity in a developing system. As Katsenelinboigen writes, "Changing conditions may cause one class of objects to decrease and another to increase in size, so the universe as a total ecological system will have ample opportunities for further development" (*Selected Topics* 287).

Katsenelinboigen applies his concept of diversity to his analysis of the Torah, namely, to the legend of Noah. He states that in saving both clean and unclean animals, God (who in Katsenelinboigen's interpretation is indeterministic and developing) deals with a multitude of objects (287). Furthermore, in a *mid-term strategy*, diversity is usually exchanged for *variety*, which is a "set of prioritized elements, but with all the elements of the set preserved" (*Concept of Indeterminism* 110). And finally, in short-term tasks, one primarily deals with a *singular variety*, which is "a set of prioritized elements, with all elements outside of the select subset being banned" (110).

In societal systems, the idea of diversity and singular variety is linked to the problem of integrating different ethnic groups. A democratic society therefore develops manifold varieties, while totalitarian regimes prefer a singular variety. Katsenelinboigen writes:

> The described principle of integration of manifold, variety, and singular variety in societal systems is also illustrated by the perennial debate between the radical liberals and radical conservatives centering on the coexistence of different ethnic groups. As racists, conservatives not only underscore ethnic distinctions, but claim the superiority of the ethnos over another based on certain indicators. . . . On the other hand, liberals who recognize the need to preserve diverse ethnic groups are unwilling to acknowledge a *variety* . . . Perhaps, inadvertently, the radical liberals seem to advocate only *uniformity*. (*Concept of Indeterminism* 113)

This paradigm is in complete accordance with the principle structuring the types of dramatic genre. Indeed, the way in which tragic and comic heroes are represented suggests that the dramatist thinks in terms of singular variety, holding preferences toward one kind (the tragic hero), which he or she pronounces highly valuable, while completely neglecting another kind (the comic character), which the dramatist portrays as something not even human. Therefore, the traditional comic character is represented as lacking deep feelings and thoughts; in this sense, the character is a block of wood that is unable to suffer and can only be the subject of one's mockery. In other words, the comic hero is made ridiculous even in circumstances in which the typical human being seeks compassion. The character is represented in exactly the same way that totalitarian regimes represent minor ethnic groups, which is that harmful and destructive treatment of these groups is valid.

Conversely, the hero of dramedy is one who is chosen and whose failure must be mourned, not mocked. Drama as an intermediate type consequently conveys the idea of a diversity; in combining a wide range of characters whose potential vary from average to strong, drama attempts to show that all characters are equally important and must be treated as human beings. Moreover, drama often represents characters with quasi-weak potential in order to emphasize the inner richness of all human beings, who under no circumstances can be treated as a piece of wood. A marvelous example of such drama is *The Other Sister*, directed by Garry Marshall (1999). This love story between two semiretarded teens (played by Juliette Lewis and Giovanni Ribisi) is a masterful representation of the inner richness and beauty of apparently limited characters.

At this point, "the little man" also can be interpreted as a literary type whose genuine potential is hidden and whose humiliating position in society is not befitting of his rich inner quality. Another view of "the little man" is that this type is distinguished by a limited and poor potential that may evoke pity in the reader/spectator. Depending on the interpretation, this type may belong to either drama or to comedy (a sad comedy). As I mentioned before, giving weights and establishing the degree and magnitude of initial and dual parameters, as well as their integration into a whole, is a matter of one's interpretation.

All types of dramatic genre can generally be considered a *variety*, for each time they keep "situational priorities" of one type over another as "judged on the basis of certain criteria."

Structural Approach

The core of dramatic genre is the degree of strength of protagonists' potential. Limitations inherent in the comic character have certainly been discussed before in criticism; as the *Encyclopedia of Aesthetics* summarizes, "Throughout comedy, the emphasis is on human limitations rather than greatness" (Kelly 1: 401). The structure of these limitations has never been analyzed as independent from the laughable and laughter, however, and it has never been considered to be the core of dramatic genre.

In accordance with the analysis, the structure of dramatic genre comprises three basic types—comedy (limited potential), dramedy (powerful potential), and drama (average/above average)—with each type divided into branches. Tragedy and comedy are not opposite types in dramatic genre. Tragedy is a branch of dramedy whose other branch is succedy. I also introduce the notion of the comedy of a new type (the CNT), which is based on a quasi-strong potential and elaborate a new technique of analysis for it.

In defining the notion of the potential, I use a systems approach, which allows one to define a system or an object from various perspectives to reveal its different sides; these are independent in most cases and cannot be determined from a single angle.

Processing

First, processing assists in an inquiry into the integration between the part and the whole, which is linked directly to the analysis of the quasi-strong and quasi-weak potential.

Second, this aspect reveals different types of interaction between the potential and the laughable/funny. I differentiate between the notion of the comic and the laughable in the following way: the comic is linked to a limited potential, which must not be confused with the laughable. A limited potential may evoke diverse feelings in the observer, including sympathy and tears, but the degree of one's emotional involvement in each type is different.

I also propose to differentiate between the comic and the comical in the following way: whereas the comic is a manifestation of a limited potential, the comical is a combination of the laughable and the comic. One may call the entity "comical" if its limitations are represented in a laughable way. Nevertheless, laughter does not assist in differentiating between entities with strong or weak potential, nor does it influence their quality. As has been mentioned, the tragic hero may sometimes evoke a reaction of amusement without losing his or her regal, elevated status (the hero's strong potential); analogously, the comic character is able to arouse sympathy and compassion without changing his or her comic nature. The term *comedic* signifies a relation to comedy, not to the laughable or funny.

Appendixes
Notes
Works Cited
Index

Appendix 1:
Variety of Basic Types

As one can see in table 3, there are eighteen varieties of dramatic types. The naming of varieties is conventional—it can change in accordance with the interpreter's taste and vision. For example, it seems to me that the degree of criticism is increased when the discrepancy between the inner and outer strength of protagonists is revealed. Satire and farce appear as a result of discrepancies between the character's inner ability to develop and his or her outer influence on society; the more such discrepancies exist, the stronger is the criticism. To me, farce represents a lesser degree of criticism than satire; it therefore occupies cells with positive evaluations of the discrepancies in the matrix. There is always a degree of freedom in interpreting these combinations, however, in the sense that one may feel that farce is linked more to negative evaluations and so one may rename the cell while keeping to the basic idea. I just want to stress once more that naming is not a topic of my discussion, but the idea of doing so is. Those who are concerned with the sound of certain types or branches is welcome to propose their own names for them.

As the matrix reveals, there are cases when a certain variety does not seem to have been introduced yet in literature, such as a powerful potential with an evaluation that is merely important (positive or negative). The inner significance and outer significance of the powerful potential traditionally coincide with or are represented as extremes such as travesty (if by "travesty" one refers to characters with genuinely powerful potential who are treated in a humiliating way). However, if the character is just an imitation of his or her powerful counterpart—an empty shell—then we talk about a complete correlation between the intrinsic and the extrinsic.

Appendix 1

			Evaluation of Characters' Outer Strength
			Weak		Strong		Powerful
		Positive	Negative	Positive	Negative	Positive	Negative
Inner Strength	Weak	Funny comedy	Farce	Idyllic comedy	Satiric comedy	Comic utopia	Satiric comedy
	Strong	Farcical drama	Satirical drama	Optimistic drama	Pessimistic drama	Melodrama	Melodrama
	Powerful	Farcical dramedy	Travesty	Ironic dramedy	Sarcastic dramedy	Optimistic dramedy	Pessimistic dramedy

Table 3. Variety of Basic Types

Appendix 2:
Mixed Types and Branches

In accordance with this, the following twelve mixed types can be outlined:
1. (C): A combination of comedy and dramedy; a change from limited to powerful potential in a group of protagonists or in a single main character;
2. (DC): A combination of dramedy and comedy; a change from powerful to limited potential;
3. (D): A combination of drama and dramedy; a change from average or above average potential to powerful;
4. (DD): A combination of dramedy and drama; a change of the potential from powerful to average or just strong;
5. (CD): A combination of comedy and drama; a change from limited to average or above average potential;
6. (dc): A combination of drama and comedy; a change from average or above average to limited potential on either macro or microlevel;
7. (DCD): A reversible change of a powerful potential (dramedy) that is temporarily limited (dramedy-comedy-dramedy);
8. (CDC): A reversible change of a weak potential that is temporarily limited (comedy-dramedy-comedy);
9. (dcd): A reversible change of a strong potential that is temporarily limited (drama-comedy-drama);
10. (cdc): A reversible change of a weak potential that is temporarily average (comedy-drama-comedy);
11. (DDD): A reversible change of a powerful potential that is temporarily decreased to strong (dramedy-drama-dramedy);
12. (ddd): A reversible change of a strong potential that is temporarily increased to mighty (drama-dramedy-drama).

Theoretically, all types can be represented within a literary work. As awkward as these names may sound to the ear, they fully represent the *idea* that is behind them. I do not insist on this terminology, I am only explaining my typology.

Like pure main types, pure main branches can be mixed to create a considerable number of mixed branches, for example, tragedy-unhappy comedy (a change of the rich but explosive potential from powerful to weak with the subsequent death of the protagonist). One may create various unusual combinations of branches, some of which have not been yet introduced in literature.

In addition to the characteristics discussed above, one may add some new ones, thus enriching dramatic genre with new subbranches and subtypes. For instance, one may also consider the degree of the laughable (the funny, the sad, and the normal) and combine it with types or branches. As a result, some interesting combinations may appear such as unhappy funny comedy (which also generates black comedy) or funny tragedy—works in which the degree of the laughable is very high despite the tragic outcome that may not necessarily be perceived as funny. Not every unhappy funny comedy can be considered a black comedy, however; Alfred de Musset's comedy *On ne badine pas avec l'amour*, which ends with the death of one of the heroines, or Sukhov-Kobylin's comedy *The Death of Tarelkin* belong to black comedy, while Molière's *Don Juan* serves only as an example of unhappy funny comedy. The formation of a black comedy most likely requires one more dimension that is linked to the degree of negativity in one's evaluation of the characters. This explains why Molière's *Don Juan* has never been interpreted as a black comedy; the main character is evaluated in a highly negative way, and his death evokes neither sympathy nor compassion in the spectator. In addition, satire is sometimes confused with black comedy, which in my opinion is linked to nondifferentiation between the degree of strength and richness of characters' potential and the degree of their criticism. To me, satire is linked only to the degree of criticism that can be applied to any type of potential.

Appendix 3:
Text, Context, Subtext, and the Literary Work

Let us briefly discuss table 4. As one can see, there are different techniques in literary analysis that are based on the degree of one's holistic vision of the space of action and the implied space (Vision) and the types of the interpreter's conclusion about the two spaces (Conclusion). In accordance to this, a "two-story" table can be drawn. One of the "floors," which I conventionally call *vision*, is linked to the degree of holistic vision. This outlines two types of approach to the whole: from the point of view of its individual, disjointed elements (text) and from the point of view of its design (context). Another "floor" is linked to the types of conclusion about two spaces, which can also be made, based on either disjointed (textual subtext) or holistic approach (contextual subtext).

Vision	
Disjointed	Holistic
Text	Context
Conclusion	
Disjointed	Holistic
Textual subtext	Contextual subtext

Table 4. Text, Context, Subtext

In accordance with this, four types result:
1. Disjointed vision of the elements of the artistic work—the text
2. Holistic vision of the elements of the artistic work—the context
3. Disjointed conclusions about the artistic work—the textual subtext
4. Holistic conclusion about the artistic work—the contextual subtext

Below is a brief description of each cell in the table.

1. *Disjointed vision—the text.* Textual analysis deals with more or less obvious correspondences between literary structures, with the creation of stereotypes, direct parallels, and the like. One who is occupied with the analysis of individual elements, sometimes integrated into isolated gestalts, performs textual analysis. Textual analysis is typical of linguists, who often attempt to establish one-two-step correspondences between textual units, mostly within a limited textual space such as a sentence, a phrase, or a small paragraph. Remote elements of the artistic structure can be the subject of textual analysis if they are not considered within the whole. Textual analysis is the early stage of the literary analysis, dealing with a diversity of isolated observations of structural elements inherent in textual segments. For instance, in *Uncle Vanya*, Astrov's name can be interpreted as an allusion to either Asteria, Astarte, or Astraea (Zubarev, *Systems Approach* 18). In the textual analysis, all associations exist as isolated observations and no integration is required.

2. *Holistic vision—the context.* The context results from the attempt to create a holistic vision of artistic structures through a multistage analysis. The context pertains to an extensive system, and it usually takes more than one step (even a large one) to establish a network of artistic units. Multistage associative links among various artistic images cannot be appreciated through formal textual analysis; they require a more sophisticated approach to diversity. This may seem overly complex to those who prefer local and obvious chains of associations based on the reactive method and programming. In order to create the context of a literary work, the interpreter synthesizes the most distant elements and structures, generating a whimsical network of associations. In so doing, the interpreter attempts to design a new wholeness. In the contextual analysis, one deals with incompleteness and inconsistencies in the artistic system by outlining some conflicting characteristics and ascribing weights to them.

3 and 4. *Disjointed and holistic conclusions—the textual and contextual subtext.* All the above is also applied to the types of conclusions that can be based either on some isolated segments of the work or the attempt to comprehend the whole.

Notes

Preface

1. By *traditional comedy*, I mean comedy in which the apparently poor and weak potential of protagonists is combined with a great proportion of the laughable and a happy ending.
2. It is necessary to distinguish between the potential of characters and their worlds and the potential of genre and the author. For example, poor and weak potential of characters does not preclude the wit and talent of an author, for example, certain obtuse Shakespearean and Chekhovian characters. Such characters only enrich the comedic genre with new developments. In general, any dramatic genre is potential-filled, and the degree of satisfaction of this potential depends on the creativity of an author.

1. Dramatic Genre: *A New Classification*

1. Aron Katsenelinboigen proposed a following parallel to economics. In order to evaluate a field, economists go to a micro-micro level (see Leibenstein), which is represented by a single firm, and analyze its isolated parameters. Then they synthesize these parameters and make their decisions concerning the credibility of the field. Therefore, cases exist in which the field appears to be weak, but the promising potential shown by the analysis and synthesis of its individual features means that the field is maintained to develop.
2. For information about the quasi-strong potential in CNT, see part three.
3. The discussion of mixed types and branches is provided in appendix 2.
4. *Conditional thinking* is a term introduced by Katsenelinboigen in regard to his structure of values. See part two for a detailed discussion of types of thinking.
5. It is beyond the scope of my research, but I am aware of theoretical and applicational works in game theory. See, for instance, works by Robert Wilson and Mihai Spariosu.
6. The new definition of styles and methods was provided by Katsenelinboigen during our discussions concerning the difference between styles and methods.
7. A discussion of the meaning of unconditional values is in part three.
8. Literary criticism distinguishes between "narration" and "description": narration is linked to collisions, clashes, and dynamic plot development; description is concerned with introduction of various images and lyrical digressions, which do not link directly to plot development. For many years Russian literary criticism has distin-

guished between two types of narrative—*roman* and *povest'*. It is well known that western European literary critics prefer to use the common term *novel* for both notions. The term *povest'* is a specific Russian term for novels characterized by a prolonged plot development and a lack of glamorous conflicts that are more inward in nature. In contrast to this, a completely different style exists that is distinguished by intrigues and hot collisions, which create a "dynamic" narrative; expressive dialogues are typical for what we here call *roman*. In *The American Collection of Literary Terms*, the term *novelette* is an equivalent to the Russian term *povest'*. West German literary criticism offered terms *erzahlung* and *kurzgeschichte* to distinguish between "dynamic" and "static" novels; according to West German critics, stasis is a property of *erzahlung* while dynamism belongs to the realm of *kurzgeschichte*. In attempting to distinguish between these two styles in literature, Russian critic Victor Shklovsky introduced a new term *ornamental prose*. While analyzing Andrey Bely's prose, he proposed to distinguish between *form (stroi)* and *swarm (roi)*. Shklovsky wrote: "'Swarm' designates a leitmotif of metaphors, while 'form' stands for an object inhering in a leitmotif secured to the story line" (180). In terms of chess, *form (stroi)* would mean a combinational style, for it is concerned with plot development. Analogously, *swarm (roi)* alludes to the positional style, with its comparatively vague intent and gradual development. Obviously, some types of artists are inclined towards a detailed, "slow" method of narration. For them, the plot frequently appears in the capacity of a general frame that allows them to develop their endless lyrical digressions, numerous descriptions, and details. Fundamental research on the positional style in Tolstoy's *War and Peace* has been done by Gary Saul Morson. Morson finds 150 episodes that do not relate to the plot line. In applying Katsenelinboigen's predispositioning theory to the analysis of Tolstoy's style, Morson reveals the role of the unnecessary and the insignificant in the literary work. He shows that from the point of view of predispositioning, "the unnecessary is necessary, the radically insignificant is radically significant" (*Hidden* 147). Indeed, for the combinational reader, the pragmatic value of details and descriptions, which do not link directly to the development of the plot, is zero and is therefore redundant. For the positional one, on the other hand, this type of detail and description enriches the artistic structure, adding new meanings that cannot be derived directly from the plot. According to Katsenelinboigen, the positional style is a basis for the aesthetic method of creation.

> Predispositioning requires a special explanation. The aesthetic method is relevant to situations where at least the direction of the system's development has been selected but where the path from the present state of the system to some future desired one cannot be fully and consistently described. In this case creation of the system's predisposition is needed. (*Concept of Indeterminism* 62)

9. In O. Henry's works, predispositioning is combined with unexpected outcomes, creating a sparkling effect. O. Henry's descriptions are, besides, short and capacious, and the plot development is dynamic enough to keep the reader interested. Needless to say, the majority would prefer reading such works with an engrossing plot rather than wondering what all those boring descriptions are about. The comparison of literature to the game of chess was initially introduced by Vladimir Volkenstein, a chess player who in his book on aesthetics elevates the combinational style in the chess game to the level of drama, with sharp collisions, peripeteias, and adventures (42–47). On the other hand, he describes the positional style as boring, dull, and inert. Volkenstein writes:

> Beauty in chess springs forth from expediency of moves involving peripeteia, from the unexpected and paradoxical (at least, at first glance) handling of a difficult situation. These are the moments when sacrifices take place. Victorious

play conducted by means of gradual accumulation of tiny advantages without enchanting combinations could be called solid, well composed, perhaps even instructive and fine, but there is no way it could be called beautiful. (45–46)

The combinational style in chess alludes to the type of literary work that is occupied with plot development and is focused on intrigues and clashes. As a rule, such works minimize the number of literary digressions and descriptions that do not directly link to the clash. Another type is characterized by a descriptive manner with a highly schematic, additional role of plot. In literature, the two styles are always combined in varying proportions (depending on the types of works and writers' goals).

10. The most confusing part of defining an object or a phenomenon concerns the perspective from which the system is observed. As a rule, a single perspective becomes the basis for one's definition of a system. As Katsenelinboigen states, such neglect of the multidimensional perspective causes "unnecessary arguments among scholars in the same field" (*Selected Topics* 13). Indeed, if the system is distinguished by (1) having a certain structure, (2) fulfilling a certain function, (3) performing a certain process of transformation of its elements into a final "product," as well as (4) possessing an operator who manages all elements, and (5) the genesis, why should one impoverish one's view of the system by narrowing the angle from which it is approached? While observing a system from a single perspective, scholars generally determine all characteristics from that viewpoint. Thus, structuralists determine function, process, and the like, from structure; functionalists determine everything from function; operationalists determine all aspects from the operational analysis of the system, and so on. In literary criticism, the genetic approach is often the basis for interpreting structure, function, process, and the role of the operator in the literary work. Scholars refer to diaries, letters, and other documents, assuming that this is the only way to be "scientific" in confirming their statements. Admittedly, it is sometimes possible to determine all aspects from a single perspective, but in most cases, different perspectives reveal multiple sides from which the system can be approached. They *do not determine* but merely *complement* each other; the multidimensional perspective is concerned with a complete description of the system, whose various aspects can be viewed independently. Independence thus denotes a certain degree of freedom inherent in all other aspects while one of them is fixed.

11. Let us compare two different translations of Nikolai Gogol's *Dead Souls* in order to see the difference between the positional and combinational styles of thinking in literature. An episode from Gogol's *Dead Souls* has the main protagonist, Chichikov, coming to a party to meet the governor. In the original Russian text, an extended description of various things precedes the narration of the important meeting. As is typical for Gogol's style, this description has nothing to do with plot development, nor does it give any new information about other characters or Chichikov himself. Constance Black Garnett's translation is very close to the original. All details are thoroughly kept, and their descriptions are in agreement with those of Gogol. Another translation, however, is far from the original, in the sense that the descriptive part is omitted by the translator, who presumably considered it redundant:

> Chichikov was almost forced to close his eyes on his entrance into the drawing-room, for the glare of the candles, the lamps, and the ladies' dresses was terrific. Everything was flooded with light. Black dress-coats, moreover, fluttered hither and thither, and Chichikov had not succeeded in looking about him when his arm was seized by the governor, who at once presented him to his wife. (Graham 17)

As one can see, the two translators have very differently evaluated the importance of the descriptive part of the episode. True, no one would defend such a cut; nevertheless, it presents interest from the point of view of positional and combinational thinking. If the first translator follows the original in order to show the beauty and richness of Gogol's artistic universe, the second one is exclusively concerned with plot development—a typically combinational approach to the text. In terms of a combinational game, the event of Chichikov's meeting with the governor becomes the main objective of the second translator, who "sacrifices" the digression in favor of the dynamics of the narrative. At the same time, he neglects the fact that the position formed as a result of his reductions is weakened—it does not relate in full measure the diverse relationships between the universe and the protagonists.

12. For example, the name Arkadina may suggest an allusion to Arcadia, a mythic country that is not explicitly determined by the artist. However, if the artist writes a novel about mythic Arcadia, this would belong to the space of action and not to the implied space. The transition from space of action to implied space occurs through one's associative net of allusions, generated by one's subjective evaluation of material and relational parameters forming the space of action.

13. For example, a more general representation of the space of action in *Romeo and Juliet* would be the struggle between love and hate inherent in humankind. In the implied space, one can talk about the interaction between inner and outer forces as an abstract representation of fate and chance.

14. A detailed discussion on text, context, and subtext is provided in the appendix 3.

15. About my definition of myth, see chapter 8.

16. For a detailed discourse on the space of action and the implied space, see chapter 8.

17. The question of the degree of balance is vital for the development of systems. In my book, *About Angels: A Treatise* (1995), I refer to a dialogue between Katsenelinboigen and me concerning this matter. Katsenelinboigen notes:

> [T]he basic problem of the economists was the question of how to bring a system to a stage of equilibrium. Economists believed that if technical advances appeared, then it was necessary to bring everything immediately back into balance. They dreamed that everything would be planned out and balanced, including technological progress. However, technological progress is precisely that factor, which creates imbalances, "splashes," in the system, unavoidable for any development in the system. But imbalance is just as dangerous as a tranquil equilibrium, in as much as both contain in themselves the concealed threat of the destruction of the system. These factors were undoubtedly understood by Joseph Shumpeter, who put the emphasis on a different role of economists. Their problem should be the creation in economics of such imbalances in the system, which would not destroy the system, and, furthermore, would bring the possibility of the beginning of new "splashes." That is, the complexity consists in finding that measure of the control by which the system would be able to develop without being rigidly determined or, on the other hand, without allowing it to take its own course. (qtd. in Zubarev, *About Angels* 22)

18. These stages of creating a holistic vision, with the subsequent integration of particular structures into a whole, becomes an essential part of systems thinking. As Russell Ackoff states, systems thinking requires analysis and the synthesis of all elements:

> [T]he difference between Systems-Age and Machine-Age thinking derives not from the fact that one synthesizes and the other analyses, but from the fact that systems thinking combines the two in a new way. . . . In the systems approach there are also three steps: 1. Identify a containing whole (system) of which the thing to be explained is a part. 2. Explain the behavior or properties of the containing whole. 3. Then explain the behavior or properties of the thing to be explained in terms of its *role(s)* or *function(s)* within its containing whole. (16)

2. The Dramatic as an Independent Category:
Chess, Economics, and Literature

1. This is a definition provided by Katsenelinboigen during our conversations.
2. As an example, I would like to refer to the Torah, particularly the first chapter of Genesis in which the creation of the world is discussed. The most enigmatic question that arises while reading the first chapter of Genesis is, why was light created in the beginning, while the celestial bodies appeared only on the fourth day? In terms of logistics, this problem can be formulated as a gradual establishment of the degree and magnitude of the initial and dual parameters of light during the first days of Creation. In general, a mature creator, whether an artist or a scientist, tends to avoid extremes in developing artistic or scientific models. The extremes would most likely appear at the beginning of creation as global dabs, allowing the creator to move further into the subject and to introduce subtler degrees and magnitude in later stages of development. Thus, in the beginning, God creates extremes: the light appears as the opposite of darkness. There is no scale created that can measure the degree and magnitude of the initial parameter of light. With regard to its dual parameter, the word *good* appears as God's positive evaluation of the initial parameter of light, though a degree and magnitude of the dual parameter remains implicit. As Katsenelinboigen notices, only later, after the entire diversity is created, does God introduce the degree and magnitude of the dual parameter, evaluating the entire creation as very good. As God continues in his creation, he moves onto more concrete objects; this helps him to integrate the abstract and the concrete, the global and the local, that are inherent in his intention. He now needs to elaborate a degree and to introduce magnitude in order to develop his universe. Therefore, the creation of celestial bodies may be interpreted as God's introduction of a degree of light that can be measured in special units and whose magnitude is linked to the quantity of celestial bodies. Since this moment, the dichotomy of "light and darkness" has been exchanged for a spectrum; while stars and planets regulate the degree of illumination of the world at night, the sun is responsible for the same variation during the day as it moves across the sky. Thus, from that day on, there was no dazzling light and no absolute darkness. To me, the fourth day of Creation is crucial in terms of God's shift from dichotomy to an elaborated spectrum inherent in his creation. In creating the world, God worked like most indeterministic creators, who develop works gradually and move from one stage of development to another (*Selected Topics* 206–327). The example from the Torah pertains to systems thinking; the stages of the system's development are linked to the gradual elaboration of the degree and magnitude of the system's initial and dual parameters. In an economic system, the product itself is the initial parameter, whose magnitude is established in items or pounds/kilograms. The evaluation of the product is its price, whose unit of measure is established in currency (dollars/cents) and whose magnitude is the number (five dollars, etc.).
3. The empirical approach to comedy is very common in literary criticism. For example, G. Beiner writes: "The proof of validity would be found in the results, not in the genetics or ideology of the method, though the choice of genre and strategies within a genre is not arbitrary or eccentric, and aims at constitutive patterns, not at superimposed imported abstractions" (10).
4. As Katsenelinboigen states, finding isomorphisms is the first step in approaching a system. The next step must be directed towards finding its peculiarities in order to see specific turns in its development, which may then enrich one's general view of the process of development.
5. These characteristics were elaborated during my course, "The Art of Decision-Making," taught with Katsenelinboigen at the Wharton School.

6. *Predisposition* is a measurement of any state, potential or position of a system in unconditional values.
7. See Altmann and Koch.
8. The background of much of the systems approach employed in my book is radical constructivism, a mostly European school of thought. See Alex Riegler's web site regarding radical constructivism: http://www.univie.ac.at/constructivism/.
9. Steven Tötösy de Zepetnek writes:

> In order to offer a more detailed taxonomy of the notion "literature as system," definitions by the originator of the polysystem theory, Itamar Even-Zohar, are relevant. But first, I would like to draw attention to the notion that Even-Zohar's and similar definitions are clearly located within an *a priori* notion of literature while they are applicable to culture in general as well. Even-Zohar writes that "if by 'system' one is prepared to understand both the idea of a closed set-of-relations, in which the members receive their values through their respective oppositions, and the idea of an open structure consisting of several such concurrent nets-of-relations, then the term 'system' is appropriate and quite adequate." This definition is, then, consolidated by Even-Zohar to "the network of relations that is hypothesized to obtain between a number of activities called 'literary,' and consequently these activities themselves observed via that network," and "the complex of activities, or any section thereof, for which systemic relations can be hypothesized to support the option of considering them literary." (28)

Tötösy de Zepetnek also writes:

> Also Russell L. Ackoff's definition of systems thinking—although not specifically in relation to literature and culture—is helpful to illustrate how systems theory can be applied in the study of literature and culture. (25–26)

10. Hegel writes:

> People only too often in this respect confound the merely *ridiculous* with the true comic. Every contrast between what is essential and its appearance, the object and its instrument, may be ridiculous, the contradiction by virtue of which the appearance is absolutely cancelled, and the end is stultified in the comic. (351)

11. Schopenhauer writes:

> The case of laughter in every case is simply the sudden perception of the incongruity between a concept and the real objects which have been thought through it in some relation, and laughter itself is just the expression of this incongruity. It often occurs in this way: two or more real objects are thought through one concept, and the identity of the concept is transferred to the objects; it then becomes strikingly apparent from the entire difference of the objects in other respects, that the concept was only applicable to them from a one-sided point of view. It occurs just as often, however, that the incongruity between a single real object and the concept under which, from one point of view, it has rightly been subsumed, is suddenly felt . . . All laughter then is occasioned by a paradox, and therefore by unexpected subsumption, whether this is expressed in words or in actions. This, briefly stated, is the true explanation of the ludicrous. (355–56)

12. About a new structure of emotions, see Katsenelinboigen, *Selected Topics* 229–59.
13. For a detailed analysis on the scientific discourse on laughter, see Simon 178–211.
14. For my definition of *traditional comedy*, see note 1 for chapter 1.
15. For my definition of the term *comical* versus *comic*, see chapter 3.

3. Protagonists of the Same Strata and Status in Different Types of Dramatic Genre

1. Katsenelinboigen writes:

    A contract between an all-powerful God and Man could turn into a useless formality used exclusively for demagogic purposes. It seems two basic preconditions are necessary in order for the covenant between God and Man to have any meaning: God must admit to his own imperfectness, on the one hand, and to the greatness of Man, on the other. In other words, the latter must be able to act independently and even more importantly have the capacity to create independently. Under these circumstances, it may be prove more expedient for God-Creator to grant Man basic autonomy while imposing only some conditions of development upon him. In other words, authors of the Torah judged parity between God and Man to be a more perfect system of operation of the world. God increases his overall power over the universe by delegating control over parts of it to the people. A more straightforward scheme of managing the world would be based on the assumption that God possesses absolute power and so has no need to share this power with anyone. Parity between God and Man in concluding the covenant would be further reinforced if some representatives of both sides were comparable in power, both physical and intellectual. Indeed, authors of the Torah provide examples of parity between God and Man. First of all, the legend of the clash between Jacob and God (Genesis, 32:24–32) testifies to the notion of the *physical power* of Man being comparable to that of God. In this struggle God was unable to overcome Jacob, merely "touched the hollow of his thigh; and the hollow of Jacob's thigh was out of joint, as he wrestled with him" (Genesis, 32:25). And God spoke to Jacob, "Thy name shall be no more Jacob, but Israel: for as prince hast thou power with God and with men, and hast prevailed" (Genesis, 32:28). "And Jacob called the name of the place Peniel: for I have seen God face to face, and my life is preserved" (Genesis, 32:30). Whatever the interpretation of this contest between God and Man may be (an angel, not God doing the battle) Man turned out to be comparable in his physical strength to a force greater than himself. Comparability of the *intellectual powers* of God and Man is in general affirmed by the authors of the Torah in their description of Adam after he tasted the fruit from the tree of knowledge: Adam becomes intellectually equal to God. The sole difference between them is that Adam is mortal. And God expelled Adam from the Garden of Eden so that he could not taste from the tree of life and become immortal. "And the Lord God said, Behold, the man is become as one of us, to know good and evil: and now, lest he put forth his hand, and take also of the tree of life, and live for ever: Therefore the Lord God sent him forth from the Garden of Eden . . ." (Genesis, 3:22–23) (*Selected Topics* 268–70)

2. For an analysis of Petruchio's potential as a lover, see Charlton 108.

6. Chekhov and Balzac as the Pioneers of the CNT

1. For melodrama, see Kirk; for drama, see Lucas; and for tragicomedy, see Fadeeva.
2. See Senelick and see Ermilov.
3. I will provide a detailed analysis of the comic nature of *Three Sisters* in chapter 8. In this chapter, I will only discuss some biographical evidences with regard to Chekhov's intent.
4. Such adherence to traditional interpretations and the denial of new approaches can be explained by the same lack of understanding of the analytical method that, as I have shown earlier, cannot be limited to programming. This means that in

interpreting facts, whether they are details in artistic works or in documentary evidences, scholars may face a serious problem, namely, the lack of a complete and consistent link throughout the analyzed material. What does one do in such cases? How does one overcome uncertainty and establish wholeness? These questions are related to the analysis of a predisposition because there is no other way to fill the gaps and to establish the whole. As Katsenelinboigen explained in one of our discussions with regard to the criticism of Viktor Suvorov's books on Stalin, critics of Suvorov's theory (that Stalin prepared a third world war) accused him of lacking documents that *directly* reveal Stalin's intention. (See Suvorov, *Icebreaker* and *Den'-M*) It is true that no documents still exist that can shed light on Stalin's genuine plans; it is therefore necessary to use indirect methods of investigation. Suvorov's goal, therefore, was to show the very high *predisposition* of such preparations, and all of the documents he analyzed should have served to show that his concept was credible. This approach was not understood by conservatively thinking colleagues, who were unable to accept the necessity of referring to the indeterministic methods required in indeterministic situations. My task with regard to Chekhov's *Three Sisters* is similar; I have no particular documents that directly suggest that Chekhov's subtitle of this play was changed without his permission. Moreover, I do not even try to affirm that the subtitle was changed by someone else, thus leaving open the possibility that Chekhov may have succumbed to others' persistent requests. I only attempt to show that my evidence reveals a *very high predisposition* that the play was intended, written, and completed as a comedy, and that only because of its innovative nature has it not been understood and accepted as belonging to the comedic genre.

5. In detail, see Zubarev, *Systems Approach* 102–20.
6. About the fates of Kozyrev, Prozorov, and Kulygin, see Zubarev, *Systems Approach* 108–9.
7. About the symbolism of birds in the play, see Zubarev, *Systems Approach* 106–7.
8. About the symbolism of the Russian fair in the play, see Zubarev, *Systems Approach* 145–59.
9. About the symbolism of the date of the auction, see Zubarev, *Systems Approach* 157–58.
10. This interpretation was made by Dasha Shushkovsky in my class "Mystery and Mastery of Chekhov's Comedy," which I taught at the University of Pennsylvania in spring 2000.
11. For example, see Rayfield 49.
12. About Pishchik's daughter, Dashen'ka, in regard to the symbolism of the fair market, see Zubarev, *Systems Approach* 157.
13. I agreed with Katsenelinboigen to introduce the term *segment* in order to differentiate between the part and the whole with regard to the entity's potential.
14. About the notion of textual and contextual analysis, see chapter 8.
15. Katsenelinboigen's concept of values is discussed in detail in chapter 7.

7. Quasi-Dramatic Effects in the CNT

1. In analyzing the relation between unconditional and semiunconditional values with regard to the taking of life, Katsenelinboigen refers to the Torah's various translations, which represent different approaches to one's extermination:

    The difference between these two approaches is clearly manifested in the various translations of the Torah. For instance, The Holy Scriptures (1955), a new translation based on the masoretic text (a vast body of the textual criticism of the Hebrew Bible), translates the commandment as "Thou shalt not commit murder." In The Holy Bible, commonly known as the authorized (King James) version (The Gideons International, 1983), this commandment is translated as "Thou shalt not kill."

Jeffrey Tigay (1996) examines this difference and sternly notes that such a translation of the commandment is too broad. Indeed, *ratsah*, the Hebrew word for *murder* is distinct from *killing*, for which there are other terms, such as *harag* and *hemit*. Kill obviously has the widest range of meanings and involves any taking of a human life. If interpreted widely, it may be applied to all living creatures. Not attempting a specific definition of murder, I will only note that the concept demands, at the very least, that the taking of life be a willful act aimed at improving one's own situation or that of another party. In literature, condemnation of murder goes far beyond the disapproval of selfish motives. In *The Queen of Spades*, Alexander Pushkin condemns Hermann, the leading protagonist, for murdering an old woman whose secret he wanted to use to ennoble his family. Impressed with Pushkin's concept, Dostoevsky develops it further in *Crime and Punishment*. Dostoevsky denounces the idea of murdering a dirty old woman who is a pawnbroker for the sake of giving her money to hundreds of widows with starving children. *The Brothers Karamazov* takes this idea even further. It condemns the possibility of sacrificing a newborn child, that its body might be used as the foundation of a crystal palace whose inhabitants would be happy for all eternity. Still, Dostoevsky believed it was necessary to help Serbs kill Turkish soldiers in the Slavs' struggle for independence from the Muslims. It seems that the argument between Dostoevsky and Tolstoy is largely over the interpretation of the commandment in question. Tolstoy was opposed to killing of any kind. It is not by chance that he was close to Gandhi and they even carried on a correspondence. It would be hard to imagine Dostoevsky in the same role! The difference between unconditional and semi-unconditional evaluations will become more prominent if we use the same example of "Thou shalt not kill" and "Thou shalt not murder" to illustrate the conduct of man in accordance with his precepts. In an extreme case, one who follows "Thou shalt not kill" will allow himself to be killed before he kills another. These views are held by one of the Hindu sects in Sri Lanka (the former Ceylon). To the best of my knowledge, the former prime minister of Ceylon, Solomon Bandaranaike (1899–1959), belonged to this sect. He did not allow himself to kill an attacker and was murdered. As he lay bleeding to death, he did crawl over to the murderer and knock the pistol from his hand before it could be used against his wife, Sirimavo Bandaranaike. She later became the prime minister of Ceylon-Sri Lanka. (*Concept of Indeterminism* 135–36)

2. This definition is a paraphrase of Katsenelinboigen's definition of beauty, which he understands as "complete incompleteness."
3. For the interpretation of names in "The Grasshopper," see Adamantova and Williamson.

8. Myth and Symbol in the CNT: The *Space of Action and the Implied Space*

1. About another symbolism of the lake in *The Seagull*, see Zubarev, *Systems Approach* 59–60.
2. For example, the reviewers of my article on myth in *Uncle Vanya* excitedly accepted all the associations regarding nanny Marina, Greek Moiras, and Slavic Marena, but they angrily rejected my associations of Astrov with Apollo, Serebryakov with Paris, and Vanya with Achilles because the latter were based on a selective style and the establishment of semiefficient linkages typical of indeterministic systems.

3. See Zubarev, Systems Approach 61–63.
4. About the relation of this couple to the myth of Arcadia, see Zubarev, *Systems Approach* 53–55.
5. See in detail Zubarev, *Systems Approach* 16–21.
6. For those who are concerned with the genetic aspect, references to mythology can be found in Chekhov's diaries, his personal correspondence, and his early stories. Among a number of brilliant studies of myth in Chekhov's short stories, one should mention those by Savely Senderovich, *Chekhov-S glazu*; Svetlana Evdokimova; Thomas Winner; and Daria A. Kirjanov. The analysis of these materials reveals that the early references to mythology are sources of Chekhov's humor. Chekhov plays skillfully with mythological names and characters, making his first attempts to combine mythological and literary structures. See, for instance, Chekhov, "Sovremennyje molitvy," "Sbornik dlya detey" in *Sochineniia* 2: 39, 283. However, not only Chekhov's early works but also his personal letters, which are replete with mythological names, attest to Chekhov's organic perception of daily life through mythology. Whether he describes a strike at St. Petersburg Academy or depicts his acquaintances, he does it through the humorous prism of mythological references, which only intensify the jocular nature of his speculations. For instance, Chekhov compares Russian policemen to "the heavily armed Hectors and Achilles, on horseback holding lances" (*Pisma* 4: 33). In an 1886 letter to an actress, Sakharova, Chekhov describes a meeting with the husband of one of his acquaintances in terms of Helen-Menelaus: "Ludmilochka sang. I met Menelaus—the general" (*Pisma* 1: 253). Numerous allusions to Greek and Slavic mythology are generously scattered throughout Chekhov's letters, breathing of his wit and subtle sense of humor. Noticeably, no matter what topic is brought to discussion by his addressee, the parallel to mythology is often present in Chekhov's replies. Thus, in his letter to Suvorin of December 11, 1891, Chekhov compares Tolstoy to Jupiter: "Look at Tolstoy, look at him! He is, in accordance with our times, not simply a man but a man-giant, Jupiter" (*Pisma* 4: 322). In another letter, he draws a parallel between his contemporaries and Biblical heroes: "I swear, this is not a particularly nervous century at all. People live now as they lived before, and my contemporaries' nerves are no worse than Abraham's, Isaac's and Jacob's, not at all" (*Pisma* 4: 323).
7. In detail, see Zubarev, *Systems Approach* 32–40.
8. I introduce the notion of a *mytholiterary continuum*, which I define as an "interaction between literary and mythological structures that initiates the creation of a new 'body' of the artistic text" (Zubarev, *Systems Approach* 25). The literary and mythological structures conflate in the text and form a new structure, an uninterrupted unity that can be dissected only in one's analysis. At this point, one can see that numerous deviations of mythological paradigms appeared in the literary work, deviations that in some cases prevent one from recognizing the primary pattern.
9. About the ironic notion of this symbol, read Chances.
10. See Kirjanov 31–37, for a discussion of the symbolism of spring and Easter in regard to the theme of renewal.
11. About the myth of the eternal return in Greece, see Eliade 109 10.
12. About the network of associations to Rome in *Three Sisters*, see Zubarev, *Systems Approach* 101–20.

Conclusion

1. See Katsenelinboigen, *Concept of Indeterminism* 110–18.

Works Cited

Ackoff, Russell L. *Creating the Corporate Future.* New York: Wiley, 1981.
Adamantova, Vera, and Rodney Williamson. "Chekhovian Irony and Satire and the Translator's Art: Visions and Versions of Personal Worlds" *Chekhov Then and Now: The Reception of Chekhov in World Culture.* Ed. J. Douglas Clayton. New York: Lang, 1997. 211–25.
Altmann, Gabriel, and Walter A. Koch, ed. *Systems: New Paradigms for the Human Sciences.* Berlin: de Gruyter, 1998.
Aristophanes. *The Frogs.* "The Bacchae"/Euripedes. "The Frogs"/Aristophanes. Trans. and ed. Francis Blessington. Arlington Heights: Harlan, 1993. 49–113.
Aristotle. *The Basic Works of Aristotle.* Ed. Richard McKeon. New York: Random, 1941.
———. *Poetics I; with, the Tractatus Coislinianus; A Hypothetical Reconstruction of Poetics II; The Fragments of the "On Poets."* Trans. Richard Janko. Indianapolis: Hackett, 1987.
Balzac, Honoré de. *The Works of Honoré de Balzac.* 18 vols. Freeport: Books for Libraries, 1971.
Barber, C. L. *Shakespeare's Festive Comedy: A Study of Dramatic Form and Its Relation to Social Custom.* Princeton: Princeton UP, 1959.
Beaumarchais. "The Barber of Seville." Trans. Albert Bermel Frederick. *Three Popular French Comedies.* New York: Ungar, 1975.
Beiner, G. *Shakespeare's Agonistic Comedy: Poetics, Analysis, Criticism.* Rutherford: Fairleigh Dickinson UP, 1993.
Beizer, Janet L. *Family Plots: Balzac's Narrative Generations.* New Haven: Yale UP, 1986.
Bergson, Henri. "Laughter." *Comedy.* Ed. Wylie Sypher. Garden City: Doubleday, 1956. 61–193.
Bertalanffy, Ludwig von. *General System Theory: Foundations, Development, Applications.* New York: George Braziller, 1968.
Blistein, Elmer M. *Comedy in Action.* Durham, NC: Duke UP, 1964.
Bol'shaia sovetskaia entsiklopediia. Vol. 19. Moscow: Sovetskaia entsiklopediia, 1975.
Bowie, A. M. *Aristophanes: Myth, Ritual, and Comedy.* New York: Cambridge UP, 1993.

Works Cited

Brooks, Peter. *The Melodramatic Imagination: Balzac, Henry James, Melodrama, and the Mode of Excess.* New York: Columbia UP, 1985.

Champion, Larry S. *The Evolution of Shakespear's Comedy: A Study in Dramatic Perspective.* Cambridge: Harvard UP, 1970.

Chances, Elen. "Chekhov's Seagull: Ethereal Creature or Stuffed Bird?" *Chekhov's Art of Writing. A Collection of Critical Essays.* Ed. Thomas Eekman. Columbus: Slavica, 1977. 27–34.

Charlton, H. B. *Shakespearian Comedy.* London: Methuen, 1961.

Chekhov, Anton P. *Chekhov: Four Plays.* Trans. Carol Rocamora. Lyme: Smith, 1996.

———. *The Essential Tales of Chekhov.* Ed. Richard Ford. Trans. Constance Garnett. Hopewell, NJ: Ecco, 1998.

———. *Pisma.* 12 vols. *Polnoe sobranie sochinenii i pisem.* Moscow: Nauka, 1974–1983.

———. *Sochineniia.* 18 vols. *Polnoye sobranie sochinenii i pisem.* Moscow: Nauka, 1974–1983.

———. *Three Sisters.* Trans. Lanford Wilson. Lyme: Smith, 1994.

Cox, Roger L. *Shakespeare's Comic Changes: The Time-Lapse Metaphor as Plot Device.* Athens: U of Georgia P, 1991.

Dargan, E. Preston. "Introduction: Balzac's Method of Revision." *The Evolution of Balzac's "Comédie Humaine."* Ed. E. Preston Dargan and Bernard Weinberg. New York: Cooper Square, 1973. I–22.

Derman, A. B. *Tvorcheskiy portret Chekhova.* Moscow: Mir, 1929.

Donatus, Aelius. "A Fragment on Comedy and Tragedy." Trans. George Miltz. Lauter 27–33.

Eliade, Mircea. *The Sacred and the Profane. The Nature of Religion.* New York: Harvest, 1959.

Emerson, Caryl. "Bakhtin's Carnival Idea." Paper presented at Harvard U, May 1999.

Evdokimova, Svetlana. "The Darling: Femininity Scorned and Desired." *Reading Chekhov's Text.* Ed. Robert Louis Jackson. Evanston: Northwestern UP, 1993. 189–201.

Fadeeva, N. I. *Novatorstvo dramaturgii A. P. Chekhova.* Tver': Tverskoy gosudarstvenny universitet, 1991.

Frye, Northrop. *Anatomy of Criticism: Four Essays.* Princeton: Princeton UP, 1957.

Garnett, Constance Black, trans. *Dead Souls* By N. V. Gogol. New York: Modern Library, 1936.

Goldoni, Carlo. *The Servant of Two Masters.* Trans. Frederick H. Davies. London: Heinamann, 1974.

Gottlieb, Vera. *Chekhov and the Vaudeville: A Study of Chekhov's One-Act Plays.* New York: Cambridge UP, 1982.

Gozzi, Carlo. *"The Love for Three Oranges," "Turandot," and "The Snake Lady."* Trans. John Louis DiGaetani. Westport, CT: Greenwood, 1988.

Graham, Stephen, trans. *Dead Souls.* By N. V. Gogol. New York: Stokes, 1915.

Grawe, Paul H. *Comedy in Space, Time, and the Imagination.* Chicago: Nelson-Hall, 1983.

Hegel, Georg Wilhelm Friedrich. "The Philosophy of Fine Art." *Theories of Comedy.* Lauter 350–53.

Henry, O. *The Complete Works*. Garden City: Doubleday, 1937.

Herrick, Marvin T. *Tragicomedy: Its Origin and Development in Italy, France, and England*. Urbana: U of Illinois P, 1962.

Hirst, David L. *Tragicomedy*. London: Methuen, 1984.

Hobbes, Thomas. *Leviathan*. Ed. Richard Tuck. Cambridge: Cambridge UP, 1991.

Hunt, Herbert James. *Balzac's "Comédie Humaine."* London: Athlone, 1964.

Jensen, Ejner J. *Shakespeare and the Ends of Comedy*. Bloomington: Indiana UP, 1991.

Katsenelinboigen, Aron. *The Concept of Indeterminism and Its Applications: Economics, Social Systems, Ethics, Artificial Intelligence, and Aesthetics*. Westport, CT: Praeger, 1997.

———. *Indeterministic Economics*. New York: Praeger, 1992.

———. *Selected Topics in Indeterministic Systems*. Intersystems, 1989.

Kelly, Michael, ed. *Encyclopedia of Aesthetics*. Vol. 1. New York: Oxford UP, 1998.

Kirjanov, Daria A. *Chekhov and the Poetics of Memory*. Studies on Themes and Motifs in Literature. Vol. 52. New York: Lang, 2000.

Kirk, Irina. *Anton Chekhov*. Boston: Twayne, 1981.

Kleist, Heinrich von. *Amphitryon*. Trans. Charles E. Passage. Mantinband and Passage, *"Amphitryon": Three Plays* 209–83.

Kostrova, E. "K istorii teksta 'triokh sestior.'" *Literaturnaia gazeta* 6 July 1954, 80 ed.

Kovalevsky, M. M. "O A. P. Chekhove." *A. P. Chekhov v vospominaniiakh sovremennikov*. Ed. N. Gitovich. Moscow: Khudozhestvennaia literatura, 1986. 361–67.

Lauter, Paul, ed. *Theories of Comedy*. Garden City: Doubleday, 1964.

Leibenstein, H. "A Branch of Economics Is Missing: Micro-Micro Theory." *Journal of Economic Literature* 15 (June 1979): 447–502.

Limon, Jerzy. "Rehabilitating Tybalt." *Shakespeare's "Romeo and Juliet": Text, Context, and Interpretation*. Ed. Jay L. Halio. Newark: U of Delaware P, 1995. 97–107.

Lucas, Frank. *The Drama of Chekhov*. London: Cassell, 1963.

Mantinband, James H., and Charles E. Passage, trans. *"Amphitryon": Three Plays in New Verse Translations. Plautus: "Amphitruo," translated by James H. Mantinband. Moli_re: "Amphitryon," translated by James H. Mantinband. Kleist: "Amphitryon," translated by Charles E. Passage*. Chapel Hill: U of North Carolina P, 1974.

———. "From Molière to Kleist." Mantinband and Passage, *"Amphitryon": Three Plays* 193–208.

———. "From Plautus to Molière." Mantinband and Passage, *"Amphitryon": Three Plays* 109–30.

Meerhold, V. *Statii. pisma. rechi. besedi*. Moscow: Iskusstvo, 1968.

Merriam-Webster, Inc. *Merriam-Webster's Encyclopedia of Literature*. Springfield, MA: Merriam-Webster, 1995.

Molière. *Amphitryon*. Trans. James H. Mantinband. Mantinband and Passage, *"Amphitryon": Three Plays* 131–93.

———. *"Don Juan" and Other Plays*. Trans. George Graveley and Ian Maclean. New York: Oxford UP, 1989.

Morson, Gary Saul. *Hidden in Plain View: Narrative and Creative Potentials in "War and Peace."* Stanford: Stanford UP, 1987.

———. "'Sonya's Wisdom,' in a Plot of Her Own." *The Female Protagonist in Russian Literature.* Ed. Sonya Stephan Hoisington. Evanston: Northwestern UP, 1995. 58–71.

Nemirovich-Danchenko, Vasilii. *Iz proshlogo.* Moscow: Academia, 1936.

Olson, Elder. *The Theory of Comedy.* Bloomington: Indiana UP, 1968.

Pasco, Allan H. *Balzacian Montage: Configuring "La Comédie Humaine."* U of Toronto Romance Series, 65. Toronto: U of Toronto P, 1991.

Pitcher, Harvey J. *The Chekhov Play: A New Interpretation.* London: Chatto, 1973.

Plautus. *Amphitruo.* Trans. James H. Mantinband. Mantinband and Passage, *"Amphitryon": Three Plays* 39–109.

Prendergast, Christopher. *Balzac: Fiction and Melodrama.* London: Arnold, 1978.

Pushkin, Alexander. *Selected Works in Two Volumes.* Moscow: Progress Publishers, 1974.

Rayfield, Donald. *"The Cherry Orchard": Catastrophe and Comedy.* New York: Twayne, 1994.

Reckford, Kenneth J. *Aristophanes' Old-and-New Comedy: Six Essays in Perspective.* Chapel Hill: U of North Carolina P, 1987.

Riegler, Alex. *Radical Constructivism.* 30 Mar. 2001 <http://www.univie.ac.at/constructivism/>.

Schopenhauer, Arthur. "The World as Will and Idea." Trans. R. B. Haldane and J. Kemp. Lauter 355–78.

Senderovich, Savely. *Chekhov-S glazu na glaz. Istoriya odnoy oderzhimosti Chekhova. Opyt fenomenologii tvorchestva.* St. Petersburg: Bulanin, 1994.

———. "*The Cherry Orchard:* Chekhov's Last Testament." 35 *Russian Literature* (North-Holland) (1994): 223–42.

———. "Chudo Georgiya o zmiye: Istoriya oderzhimosti Chekhova odnim obrazom." 139 *Russian Language Journal* (1985): 135–225.

Senelick, Laurence. *Anton Chekhov.* New York: Grove P, 1985.

Shakespeare, William. *The Riverside Shakespeare.* 2nd. ed. Gen. and textual ed. G. Blakemore Evans and J. J. M. Tobin. Boston: Houghton, 1997.

Shklovsky, Victor. *Theory of Prose.* Trans. Benjamin Sher. Elmwood Park, IL: Dalkey Archive P, 1990.

Simon, Richard Keller. *The Labyrinth of the Comic: Theory and Practice from Fielding to Freud.* Tallahassee: UP of Florida, 1985.

Sophocles. *Three Theban Plays.* Trans. Robert Fagles. New York: Viking, 1982.

Stanislavsky, K. S. "A. P. Chekhov v khudozhestvennom teatre." *A. P. Chekhov v vospominaniiakh sovremennikov.* Ed. N. Gitovich. Moscow: Khudozhestvennaia literatura, 1986. 373–417.

———. *Sobranie sochinenii.* 8 vols. Moscow: Ikusstvo, 1954–1961.

Steiner, George. *The Death of Tragedy.* Vol. 7. New Haven: Yale UP, 1961.

Sukhikh, I. N. "'Smert' geroya' v mire Chekhova." *Chekhoviana. Statii, publikatsii, essay.* Ed. V. Lakshin. Moscow: Nauka, 1990. 65–77.

Suvorov, Viktor. *Den'-M: Kogda Nachalas' Vtoraia mirovaia voina?: Prodolzhenie knigi "Ledokol."* Moscow: AO "Vse dlia vas," 1994.

———. *Icebreaker.* London: Grafton Books, 1992.

Tötösy de Zepetnek, Steven. *Comparative Literature: Theory, Method, Application.* Studies in Comparative Literature. Amsterdam: Rodopi, 1998.

Turner, C. J. G. *Time and Temporal Structure in Chekhov.* Birmingham Slavonic Monographs, No. 22. Birmingham: Dept. of Russian Language and Literature, U of Birmingham, 1994.
Volkenstein, V. *Experience of Contemporary Aesthetics.* Moscow: Academia, 1931.
Waller, Gary, ed. *Shakespeare's Comedies.* London: Longman, 1991.
Winner, Thomas. *Chekhov and His Prose.* New York: Holt, 1966.
Winnington Ingram, R. P. *Sophocles: An Interpretation.* Cambridge: Cambridge UP, 1980.
Zubarev, Vera. *About Angels: A Treatise.* Odessa: Russian Book, 1995.
———. *A Systems Approach to Literature: Mythopoetics of Chekhov's Four Major Plays.* Westport, CT: Greenwood, 1997.

Index

Adamantova, Vera, 185
Amphitryon (Kleist), 6, 11, 56, 57, 63, 71, 72, 73, 74, 75
Aristophanes, 15, 43, 53, 71
Aristotle, 11, 12, 13, 31, 39, 47, 91, 93, 165
"At the Cemetery" (Chekhov), 144

Balzac, Honoré de, 19, 42, 43, 79, 111, 112, 118, 123–25, 127, 130, 134, 137, 138, 140, 142, 183
Barber of Seville, The (Beaumarchais), 65, 67, 68
basic type, 3, 4, 167
Beaumarchais, 65, 67, 68, 69
Beiner, G., 181
Beizer, Janet L., 140
Bergson, Henri, 41, 47, 48
Bertalanffy, Ludwig von, 33
Blistein, Elmer M., 15
Bowie, A. M., 31

chance, 13, 34, 49, 56, 60, 82, 91, 92, 93, 95, 96, 97, 100–103, 106, 108, 117, 119, 120, 122, 137, 155, 164, 180, 185
Chances, Elen, 186
Chekhov, Anton, 37, 46, 89, 109, 111–19, 122–29, 131, 134, 135, 139, 143, 144, 147, 148, 151–53, 155, 158–62, 183, 184, 186
Cherry Orchard, The (Chekhov), 4, 46, 47, 89, 112–14, 118, 119, 120, 121, 153

CNT, 16, 89, 109, 111–13, 118, 123, 127, 128, 130, 131, 133, 135, 139, 142, 143, 150, 151, 163, 167, 177, 183, 184, 185
combinational style, 17, 18, 19, 26, 127, 129, 178, 179
comedic genre, 42, 68, 111, 113, 177, 184
comedy, 4, 5, 7, 9, 10, 11, 12, 15, 16, 26, 28, 30, 31, 32, 33, 34, 35, 38, 40–43, 46, 47, 49, 51, 52, 57, 58, 60, 61, 63, 67–71, 73, 74, 78, 79, 81, 85, 86, 87, 88, 89, 90, 91, 92, 93, 102, 105, 108, 111–14, 117, 119, 127, 130, 131, 142, 143, 147, 151, 165–68, 173, 174, 177, 181, 182, 184
comic, the, 10, 11, 16, 28, 31, 32, 35, 38, 40, 42, 46, 47, 48, 58, 89, 111, 118, 164, 165, 166, 167, 168, 182, 183
comical, 10, 26, 42, 54, 63, 65, 68, 103, 105, 117, 142, 168, 182
conditional values, 144, 145, 146
context, 31, 51, 98, 104, 124, 151, 158, 175, 176, 180
contextual subtext, 175, 176
Covetous Knight (Pushkin), 75
Cox, Roger L., 89

Dargan, E. Preston, 142
Dead Souls (Gogol), 23, 179
Derman, A. B., 119

development, 1, 4, 8, 12–15, 17–19, 23, 24, 26–29, 33, 34, 42, 44–49, 51, 52, 60, 62, 67, 68, 83, 92, 93, 99, 100, 106, 108, 111, 122, 124, 126, 127, 128, 132, 135, 141, 143, 146–48, 150, 153, 154, 160, 161, 164, 165, 177–81, 183
disjointed vision, 65, 127, 129, 130, 139, 158
Donatus, Aelius, 32
Don Juan (Molière), 78, 81, 82, 83, 84, 88, 174
drama, 4, 5, 7, 9, 10, 15, 16, 26, 28, 32, 42, 46, 49, 57, 58, 67, 74, 85, 86, 87, 89, 90, 92, 102, 111, 112, 113, 114, 117, 119, 128, 165, 166, 167, 173, 178, 183
dramatic, the, 1, 3, 12, 32, 33, 35, 42, 45, 48, 49, 86, 92, 117, 132, 139, 150
dramatic genre, 1, 3, 4, 5, 9, 11, 14, 15, 16, 26, 28, 30, 32, 33, 42, 43, 46, 48, 49, 56, 74, 85, 113, 164, 165, 167, 174, 177
dramaturgy, 33, 48, 117
dramedy, 5, 6, 9, 15, 26, 49, 57, 60, 61, 63, 73, 75, 79, 84, 85, 86, 87, 89, 90, 92, 102, 128, 142, 164, 165, 166, 167, 173
dual parameters, 29, 30, 181

Eliade, Mircea, 186
Emerson, Caryl, 38
evaluative process, 1, 36, 39
Evdokimova, Svetlana, 186

Fadeeva, N. I., 183
fate, 14, 25, 34, 49, 56, 71, 91, 93, 95, 97, 99, 101, 102, 108, 112, 120, 148, 164, 180
feelings, 4, 29, 38, 57, 59, 60, 61, 62, 63, 73, 74, 76, 79, 80, 82, 84, 87, 89, 104, 121, 122, 124, 128, 137, 140–43, 154, 166, 168
free will, 92, 93, 94, 95, 97, 98, 99, 108
Frogs, The (Aristophanes), 15, 43, 53, 56, 71
funny drama, 9, 10, 11, 57, 58, 60, 67, 69, 73, 102

general systems theory, 33, 43
global goal, 19, 128, 129, 130, 131, 132
Gobseck (Balzac), 79, 80, 81, 130
gods in comedy, 51, 52, 149
Gogol, Nikolay Vasilyevich, 23, 151, 179, 180
Goldoni, Carlo, 65, 66, 87
Gottlieb, Vera, 121
Gozzi, Carlo, 63, 64
Grasshopper, The (Chekhov), 123, 125, 147, 185
Grawe, Paul H., 30–32, 42
growth, 45

happy comedy, 9
Hegel, Georg Wilhelm Friedrich, 14, 38, 182
Henry, O., 19, 20, 21, 22, 44, 146, 178
Herrick, Marvin T., 11, 32
Hirst, David L., 11
Hobbes, Thomas, 38
holistic conclusion, 176
holistic design, 158
holistic vision, 127, 130, 141, 152, 158, 165, 175, 176, 180
Human Comedy, The (Balzac), 42, 43, 112
Hunt, Herbert James, 142

implied space, 3, 23–26, 109, 151, 154, 155, 157–59, 161–63, 175, 180
indeterministic system, 1, 23, 36, 45, 159, 185
initial and dual parameters, 29, 30, 33, 40, 99, 167, 181
inner force, 95, 108
Ivanov (Chekhov), 124

Jensen, Ejner J., 58

Katsenelinboigen, Aron, 17, 18, 20, 21, 22, 29, 34, 36, 37, 40, 45, 49, 52, 85, 86, 94, 128, 130, 144–46, 152, 165, 166, 177–86
Kirjanov, Daria A., 186
Kirk, Irina, 183
Kleist, Heinrich von, 6, 74, 75
Kostrova, E., 115
Kovalevsky, M. M., 114

Index 195

"Last Leaf, The" (O. Henry), 20, 146
laughable, the, 9, 11, 26, 30, 31, 32, 38,
  42, 47, 48, 60, 73, 111, 167, 168,
  174, 177
laughter, 3, 9, 11, 28, 30, 31, 36, 38, 39,
  40, 41, 47, 48, 57, 72, 74, 165, 167,
  168, 182
Leibenstein, H., 177
Limon, Jerzy, 100
local goal, 129, 131
Lost Illusions (Balzac), 118, 127, 130,
  137, 138, 139
Lucas, Frank, 183

material parameters, 17, 18, 34, 37, 54,
  145
Meerhold, V., 153
Merry Wives of Windsor (Shakespeare),
  4, 60, 61
Midsummer Night's Dream, A (Shakespeare), 6, 9, 16, 44, 61, 62, 86, 105,
  106
Miser, The (Molière), 75, 87, 88, 89
Molière, 15, 56, 57, 74, 75, 78, 81, 83,
  84, 88, 174
Morson, Gary Saul, 134, 178
multidimensional perspective, 1, 23, 33,
  48, 156, 164, 179
mytholiterary continuum, 3, 109, 154,
  156, 161, 162, 163, 186
myths, 151, 157, 159–62

natural relationships, 85–87, 89, 90
Nemirovich-Danchenko, Vasilii, 113,
  114, 115, 116, 117

Old Goriot (Balzac), 123
Olson, Elder, 31, 34, 38, 39, 40, 41
open comedy, 5, 26
open drama, 5, 26
open dramedy, 26
open-ended systems, 18
outcome, 5–7, 14, 18, 32, 38, 42–44,
  47, 48, 63, 74, 75, 91, 92, 95, 100,
  102, 103, 145, 147, 174
outer force, 93–95, 102, 108, 180

Pasco, Allan H., 142

Pitcher, Harvey J., 134
Plautus, 11, 15, 56, 57, 71, 74, 75
positional sacrifice, 45, 76, 141
positional style, 17, 18, 26, 127, 145, 178
potential, 1, 3–15, 16, 19, 23, 26, 28, 32,
  33, 35, 45, 47–49, 51–53, 56–67,
  69–75, 81–90, 94, 95, 103, 105–9,
  111, 112, 118, 119, 122–25, 127,
  131–34, 138, 142–44, 146, 147,
  149–53, 159, 161, 163–68, 171,
  173, 174, 177, 182–84
predisposition, 6, 12, 14, 17–20, 26, 27,
  37, 42, 44–48, 52, 56, 58–60, 63,
  68, 75, 78–80, 83, 92, 93, 95–98,
  100–108, 111, 114, 121, 122, 127,
  130, 132–35, 137, 139, 144, 146,
  147, 150, 151, 154, 159, 161, 163,
  164, 178, 184
predispositioning, 11, 14, 16, 19, 21, 26,
  34, 35, 47, 49, 51, 95, 108, 137,
  154, 155, 178
Prendergast, Christopher, 91
probabilistic approach, 21
programming, 16, 20, 26, 34, 38, 95,
  108, 154, 176, 183
Pushkin, Alexander, 4, 75, 76, 81, 83,
  84, 137, 139, 185

quasi-strong potential, 8, 111, 127, 131,
  143, 163, 167, 177

randomness, 16, 26, 34
Rayfield, Donald, 184
Reckford, Kenneth, 51
relational parameters, 22, 24, 26, 45,
  54, 55, 76, 83, 85, 101, 145, 149,
  151, 152, 180
Riegler, Alex, 182
Romeo and Juliet (Shakespeare), 6, 23,
  43, 44, 47, 58, 59, 86, 91, 92, 95,
  98, 100, 102, 103, 107, 180

satire, 4, 11, 54, 113, 171, 174
Schopenhauer, Arthur, 14, 38, 98, 134,
  182
Seagull, The (Chekhov), 6, 23, 89, 112,
  128, 134, 137, 151–53, 155, 162,
  185

selective method, 19
semiefficient linkages, 23, 24, 34, 154, 159, 185
semiunconditional values, 144–46, 160, 184
Senderovich, Savely, 113, 186
Senelick, Laurence, 183
Servant of Two Masters, The (Goldoni), 65, 67, 86, 87, 102
Shakespeare, 30, 57, 61, 88, 92, 98, 100, 148
Shklovsky, Victor, 178
societal relationships, 86
Sophocles, 100
space of action, 23, 24, 25, 109, 151, 154, 156, 161–63, 175, 180
spontaneity, 93, 95, 108, 124
Stanislavsky, K. S., 113, 114, 116–18
Steiner, George, 14
Stone Guest, The (Pushkin), 81, 83
subjectivity, 1, 36, 37, 38, 118, 154
subtext, 23, 180
succedy, 6, 9, 12, 26, 30, 58, 62, 63, 69, 75, 102, 105, 106, 167
Sukhikh, I. N., 143
survival, 1, 18, 28, 42–48, 56, 111
Suvorov, Viktor, 184
symbol, 24, 25, 47, 78, 84, 104, 140, 151, 155, 162, 186

Taming of the Shrew, The (Shakespeare), 60, 62
text, 23, 35, 37, 74, 107, 115–17, 133, 140, 156, 161, 164, 175, 176, 179, 180, 184, 186
textual subtext, 175
Three Sisters (Chekhov), 46, 112–20, 133, 162, 183, 184, 186
Tötösy de Zepetnek, Steven, 35, 182
Turandot (Gozzi), 63, 64, 65
Turner, C. J. G., 143
types of dramatic genre, 3, 10, 12, 33, 48, 67, 85, 86, 89, 166, 167
types of goals, 34, 127, 131, 132

unconditional values, 18, 19, 87, 144, 145, 160, 177, 182
unexpected outcome, 19, 21, 101, 178
unhappy comedy, 174
unhappy drama, 102

values, 7, 17, 22, 27, 29, 35, 40, 42, 45, 51, 53, 81, 82, 83, 94, 95, 97, 125, 127, 130, 133, 144–46, 149, 160, 161, 164, 177, 182, 184
Volkenstein, V., 178

Williamson, Rodney, 185
Winner, Thomas, 143, 186
Winnington-Ingram, R. P., 94, 99

V. Ulea (Vera Zubarev) is a literary critic, a writer, and a film director. She has a Ph.D. in Russian literature and literary theory from the University of Pennsylvania, where she is a lecturer. She is the author of eleven books of prose, poetry, and literary criticism.